Gangster

By: International Bestselling Author
Sapphire Knight

Melissa ♡
enjoy!
xoxo
Sapphire
Knight

Gangster
Copyright © 2017 by Sapphire Knight
Cover Design by CT Cover Creations
Editing by Mitzi Carroll
Formatting by

Uplifting DESIGNS

Acknowledgements

My husband - I love you more than words can express. Thank you for the support you've shown me.

My boys - You are my whole world. I love you both. This never changes, and you better not be reading these books until you're thirty and tell yourself your momma did not write them!

My Beta Babes - Sarah Rogers, Lindsay Lupher, Wendi Stacilaucki-Hunsicker, Patti Novia West, Kelly Emery, Tamra Simons, and Jamey Weber. Thank you for all the love you've shown me. You've all helped me grow tremendously in my writing, and I'm forever grateful. I was seriously freaking out over this book and y'all gave me the reassurance and confidence that I needed to keep trucking on. This wouldn't be possible without your input and suggestions.

Editor Mitzi Carroll – Your hard work makes mine stand out, and I'm so grateful! Thank you for pouring tons of hours into my passion and being so wonderful to me. One day I'll meet you and one day I'll squishy hug you!

Cover Designer- CT Cover Creations, thank you sooo much! I feel like this cover was made specifically for me and I couldn't be happier. Thank you tons for your continued support and friendship.

Formatter Alyssa Garcia – Thank you for making my work look professional and beautiful. I truly appreciate it.

Sapphire's Naughty Princesses – You ladies are brilliant; thank you for everything that you do to help promote my work and for all your support and encouragement. Some days it's one of you that keeps me writing my next book, excited to bring you a small escape in this world. Thank you for giving me a piece of your heart—I adore you!

My Blogger Friends –YOU ARE AMAZING! I LOVE YOU!

No really, I do!!! You take a new chance on me with each book and in return share my passion with the world. You never truly get enough credit, and I'm forever grateful!

My Readers – I love you. You make my life possible, thank you.

Dedication

To everyone out there who's working their asses off, every single day to become a better person.
Not all of our pasts are perfect; some of us are tainted and strive every day to overcome our personal obstacles.
Look in the mirror and repeat after me; You Fucking Rock.

WARNING

This novel includes graphic language and adult situations. It may be offensive to some readers and includes situations that may be hotspots for certain individuals. This book is intended for ages 18 and older due to some steamy spots. This work is fictional. The story is meant to entertain the reader and may not always be completely accurate. Any reproduction of these works without Author Sapphire Knight's written consent is pirating and will be punished to the fullest extent of the law.

Chapter 1

A fish with his mouth closed,
never gets caught.
- Tony Accardo

Grace

I snort a little watching Kaleigh cough after she downs her shot of tequila. She doesn't drink much, especially at lunchtime, but I dared her and she went for it. Exactly why she's my best friend; she lets me corrupt her just a smidge to keep me entertained, and in return, she lives a life that's slightly more exciting than one without me in it.

"That was gross." Her nose scrunches, making my mouth turn up in an amused grin.

We're in our usual lunch spot—*Moricio's Italian Cuisine*. It's not too fancy and small, but they make food quick enough to eat for a lunch break and it tastes fantastic.

"It's not bad after you have three or so."

"No way. You said one."

"I know. You have to work and I'm not going to carry you back to your cubicle."

"Gee thanks, you're so thoughtful."

"Hey, the burn from the tequila will keep you warm on the walk back. You'll be thanking me later."

"If I'm not puking," she mumbles, sipping her Coke to chase

the tingle the tequila left behind.

My lips part, about to reply something snarky about her being too tame, when the small 'ding' from the bell above the door announces the arrival of a new customer. We both glance over, my eyes growing wide at the eye candy that just entered.

"Yum," slips free and I swear Kaleigh makes a choking sound.

"Ho-ly *fuck*." The swear word comes out as barely a whisper. If I weren't sitting directly across from her, I'd had never heard it. "Shhh!"

"Oh please, look at him," I reply, gesturing my hand towards the man. He commands attention, mine included.

Everyone in the restaurant grows quiet, staring at him standing in the doorway. Four men with his stature and larger enter next, coming to stand behind him. Their presence radiates power, bringing naughty thoughts to mind. I'm not sure of how much work I'd get done at the office if I had to work around men looking like that.

I bet they're lawyers with enough money to purchase the decent suits they're sporting with lonely, unmarried lives so they hit up the gym every morning to sculpt those impressive bodies. They've most likely won a few cases, forming that cocky, dominant attitude they wear on their faces. I'd do them. Well not all of them, but the first one I saw. His demeanor portrays him as the alpha of the group and that's just plain sexy.

Whispering again, Kaleigh leans in closer, "Do you have any idea who that is? And stay quiet, be respectful."

"No clue, and I'm always respectful; it's not like he's the Godfather." My eyes roll at her dramatics, waving her off. I'm a little put off that she feels the need to scold me in the first place. Like my comments are so bad; men are ten times worse when they see an attractive woman.

A strangled noise comes from her throat, making me wonder if maybe she shouldn't have had that tequila after all. I think I'll order one for myself before heading back to work. I'd ask hot stuff up at the front to throw one back with me, but I doubt he'd take the stick out of his ass long enough to have some fun. He shouts all work and no play, hence the money to pay for that suit, no doubt.

"That," she whispers intensely, cocking her head toward the man in question, "is Thaddaeus Morelli."

"Okay." I nod. I still have no idea why she's acting like a fruit loop. So, the last name's Italian; half of the damn city's Italian.

"That's the *Joker* Grace—in the flesh! He's a freaking *gangster*; a very, very bad *gangster*."

I snort again, laughing. I can't help it. She's crazy. There's no way that man is a gangster. There's nothing 'thuggish' about him. If anything, I'd be more likely to believe that he's a prominent, rich businessman in that custom-tailored suit. I wouldn't think twice about him stealing my purse if I was walking down the street.

He has medium brown hair, slicked back—trimmed short, but not too short—with enough to wind your fingers in. I don't see any tattoos on him, but if he has any they're most likely covered by the suit he's wearing. I doubt they'd be covered though, if he *was* a gangster. I've watched The History Channel and their specials on organized crime before; he looks nothing like any of them. It's safe to say that if I saw him getting into an expensive car, I'd believe it was his—not that he was stealing it. That is, after all, what the gangsters on The History Channel do. They steal, cheat, bribe, and sell drugs. This man clearly is not a drug addict and has enough money in his pocket to pay for his lunch.

My disbelieving snort must be louder than normal with everyone being quiet, because suddenly I'm in an intense eye lock with the man himself; only he's not as amused as I am. His gaze is dark and stormy with unmeasured anger. He could probably blow someone up with that lethal look. I don't know if he wants to skin me alive or yank my skirt off and go to pound town.

Swallowing, my throat grows dry at the glower. And so help me, my dumb ass wants to roll my eyes to push his buttons, curious to discover what he'll do and see if I can make that scowl become even darker. I'm not normally so self-destructive, but Ka-leigh's proclamations have my stubborn side rearing its head.

I can make out my best friend in the background, still murmuring details as I have a stare down with one of the finest men I've ever seen. "Everyone calls him the *Joker*, but it's not because of his love of laughs; it's the opposite. He *never* jokes with anyone. He's not even nice and he doesn't speak to regular people."

That gets me. I blink, breaking the stare off and meet her gaze, "Um ... regular people? You mean like you and me?" She nods her head just a touch, not wanting to move and call attention to herself. "What a dick," I grumble and she gasps at my blunt but truthful reply. Shortly after, my arm warms.

You know how you get the prickly feeling when you can tell someone is watching you and sometimes your cheeks heat? I have that, but also the uncanny suspicion that he's not simply staring at me anymore, but like his body's physically near me. I can *feel* his presence as if he's sucked all the air and energy out of the room.

Inhaling a deep breath, I turn to my left and damned if I wasn't right. I knew I felt someone approaching us when I questioned her about being 'a regular person.' Sure as fuck, I glance up, and it's him—right beside me.

He glowers down at me with golden irises blazing, full of intimidation. He's a broody one, I can already tell, and for some odd reason I find it incredibly sexy in a man.

When I get nervous or irritated, I tend to get a bit sarcastic, so before I think about my words, I let a little snark come out. "I'll take a refill. To go, please. Oh, and the check. Thanks." Turning my head away quickly, I push my glass closer to the edge of the table and bite the inside of my cheek so I don't babble, concentrating on pushing my food around my plate.

I can't believe I just let that come out of my mouth. So much for the shot idea. I have a feeling he may lose it and get us kicked out before I can reunite with my old friend, Jose Cuervo. Or else Kaleigh may pass out from hyperventilating and make me tote her ass back to my office.

The restaurant's so silent, you can hear the refrigerator kick on behind the waitress area.

I swallow again, trying not to exhale to loudly.

A throat clears, but I keep my head still and count to myself.

Three.

Four.

Five.

Six.

Seven.

Holy shit.

Seven.

Holy shit.

What number was I on?

Five of the longest seconds I've ever experienced. My self-coping method of counting out random numbers comes to a smashing halt when warm fingertips brush my chin. They're soft and careful as they gently turn my face toward him again—the movements commanding, but not forceful.

His voice is low, almost gravelly, like he's not used to speaking or perhaps he's used to yelling a lot. He is Italian, after all. "Your bill is taken care of, *Bella*." He licks his bottom lip. "I will send someone with your drink."

Pure sex. That's what comes to mind when he speaks. I would climb him like a goddamn jungle gym right now if the circumstances were different. I could fucking die. Legit, just keel over after hearing the sexy rasp that no doubt matches his beautiful face. I bet his body's insane under that suit, no flaw about him. And that accent, *definitely* Italian.

My hands clench into fists as I stop myself from doing the sign of the cross, thanking God for creating a man so divine to look at and listen to.

I'm too embarrassed at my rude behavior—at the entire scene and knowing that everyone is staring—to meet his gaze. Barely nodding, mimicking Kaleigh from earlier, I keep my eyes trained on the rich texture of his deep blue tie. It's nearly black, but there's a hint of color that I can make out with the hanging light over our table. It's one of my favorite colors, but that's irrelevant right now.

"Th-thank you." My reply comes out quietly, damn near sounding like a choke, all too aware of everyone's attention. I'll probably never be able to have lunch here again after this. That means a farther walk and less time to eat, thanks to me not listening to my friend and not keeping my thoughts and noises to myself.

His fingers slip away, his demeanor radiating disappointment from me not looking at him. He wanted me to challenge him. I know it. I also know when to tuck my tail and shut up. He didn't deserve my bitchiness.

Kaleigh said to be respectful. That should mean me not meeting his stare, right? It's hard to think at all—about anything—with him so near, the only thing on my mind is his smell and how fast my heart is beating. I'm surprised you can't hear the rapid thrum as the organ thunders away under my breast.

Men don't just randomly come up and touch me, and in that spot? It was a more of a caress. That alone says so much about him. My friend's right; *he's different.*

Most guys would touch your shoulder or place their hand a little too close to your breast or even your ass. However, he chose two fingers, right under my chin. He wanted me to meet his gaze like earlier, but I just couldn't bring myself to do it. Having him near, snuffed out my bravado and scattered my thoughts, not an easy feat when it comes to me.

God, he smells so fucking good too, like rain mixed with alpha male. Pheromones such as those should be bottled up and sold. I'd dump that shit all over my pillow at night. How can you possibly think when a man smells like that?

He's remains standing beside me for a moment longer, almost as if he wants to say something else, but refrains. I wish he wouldn't have held back. I wanted him to speak some more, even if it was merely to tell me to fuck off. I want to hear that voice again so I can commit it to memory, along with those furious golden irises.

The door chimes, and this time when I look up, he and the other men have left.

The restaurant buzzes with excited chatter in the aftermath, as if they can't stand to remain quiet a moment more. Kaleigh just stares at me like I'm a glitter-covered unicorn giving out free donuts that she's never seen before or something.

A Styrofoam cup with a lid secured and a new straw is placed down in front of me. "Ma-ma'am," the server interrupts nervously. "Anything else? A piece of Tiramisu or a cappuccino, maybe?"

She wasn't so friendly before. Not that we minded anyhow; we're used to her since we eat here a few times a week. You'd think she'd know us by name by now, but like I said, she's not that kind to us usually.

"No thanks. Just our bills please, separate if you don't mind."

"It's been taken care of, along with anything else you'd like."

"So, if I wanted to stay all afternoon, sitting around, drinking your most expensive liquor, I wouldn't get a bill?"

She shakes her head, black hair secured in a tight ponytail. "No. You wouldn't get a tab for the rest of the week either."

"Whoa, what do you mean, exactly?"

"I was instructed that your bill is paid, and that if you returned again this week, then it would be taken care of as well."

"You're kidding?"

"No ma'am, not even a little."

"Wow—" I should get a bottle of wine or something to take with me.

Kaleigh interrupts, "Well, thank you. We should go then."

"Right, I have to get back too." I agree with her and the server walks off without another word.

Collecting our things, we head out the door. I don't know what to say. I have a million questions running through my mind now, and it's all a bit overwhelming, rendering me speechless.

"Maybe we should get you a cab back to your office," my friend suggests, making me pause.

"It's gorgeous out here; I'll save the fare and walk. You should too."

"Look Grace, I'll be frank. Those aren't the type of people whose radar you want to be on. You need to be careful. My God," she mutters quietly, closing her eyes for a moment, her hand going to her forehead as if she still can't believe it. "He *spoke* to you."

"And? He's just another guy. A gorgeous one at that, but he was in the flesh, you said so yourself. You act like you've seen a freaking ghost or something. He wasn't rude and just bought us lunch. Maybe he's not so evil."

"No, you don't get it. He doesn't do that sort of thing. The Joker doesn't pay for people's meals or act like they even exist, but today he calls you beautiful and then pays for your food for an entire week. I'm scared just from being at the same table with you."

"You've never had a man buy you a meal before? And how do you know so much about him?"

"Of course I've been taken out to dinner, but never by some-one like that. I don't know too much, honestly. But there are sto-ries and I've heard my fair share of them. Please listen to me, Grace, just this once, and be careful—at least for a while."

"I love you, Kayleigh, but I have to get back. We can talk more about him later, okay?"

"You're not going to listen to me, are you?"

Shaking my head, I'm honest with her. I always am. "Probably not." My mouth turns up in a grin, as I squeeze her shoulder affectionately. "I just don't see what the big deal is. But, I'll talk to you later and you can try to convince me some more, okay?"

She nods, worry in her gaze as I turn away. She clearly doesn't care for my response, but she knows me. If she tells me not to do something, I'm going to want to know why and in some cases figure it out for myself. It's like that Jelly Bean game, Bean Boozled. After playing it with her nieces, she warned me never to try it. So naturally I did, wanting to see what the fuss was about. It was all fun and games until I got the puke flavored one.

The walk back to my job is pleasantly quick and I hate to admit it, but I do check over my shoulder a few times. I feel like an ass by the time I get to my building though. I learned a long time ago that rumors are just that—rumors and nothing more. Well, usually anyhow. In this case I think everyone was being a little melodramatic. People love a good story to get worked up over. The guy was a businessman, maybe not completely straightlaced, but I highly doubt it's what Kaleigh was saying.

Why would she lie about it, though? She would never do it on purpose, but she does buy into that shit the realtors she works for feed her. That's probably where it all came from.

"Hey, Grace, have a good lunch?" Keisha, the receptionist asks as I step out of the elevator. She's worked for the same marketing company as I have for nearly ten years. She's a curvy, mocha-skinned, vivacious woman with one of the biggest hearts around.

"It was interesting, that's for sure."

Her full lips pull up into a curious grin, as she catches me off guard, "Well, maybe it'll get more interesting then. You had a delivery about five minutes ago."

"Really? From who?" I rarely get surprises. I wonder if my mom sent me something. It's not my birthday or anything though.

Her smile grows more until she's beaming, full of excitement for me. "Wouldn't leave a name and said his boss wanted you to have something beautiful."

"No way!" She has to be teasing me. I haven't been seeing anyone in a while for a man to be sending me something. It must be my mom.

"Go look on your desk." She wags her eyebrows and I damn near skip to my door with curiosity.

Sure enough, there's a large bouquet sitting right in the middle of my desk. The flowers are encased in a thick crystal vase, swirls and hearts expertly carved into the base. It's not something you'd find in a regular florist; it had to have cost a fortune and been made specially to order. There must be fifty lilies, all a deep violet color—the exact same shade as the shirt I have on.

Whoever sent them knows how to pay attention to detail, or else this is a strange coincidence.

The small, light gray piece of cardstock tucked into the arrangement draws my eyes away from the stark color. Carefully, I work it out of the prong holder, bringing it closer. In small Modern number twenty font—I know this because of my experience in design—there's one word printed, black and bold. It's enough for a cold chill to crawl up my spine, heeding my friend's warning from earlier.

Bella

Holy shit. There's no possible way, they're from him. None. He knows nothing about me.

"So?" Keisha asks, causing me to jump at her voice. "You okay, girl?" Her eyes light up in amusement.

"Yes, um, they don't have a name. Are you sure they were for me and not Rose? Wasn't it her anniversary or something?" As beautiful as they are, I'd feel better right now discovering that they were delivered to me by mistake. Naïve, I know, but it doesn't hurt to ask.

"Yeah, it was last week. Besides, the guy that delivered them gave me your name specifically, so those gorgeous flowers are all yours."

"Oh. Great," I mumble sarcastically. If only Keisha knew why it was so disturbing, but I'll keep what happened to myself. No need to freak her out. Kaleigh would fall over, too, if she were here right now.

"You don't seem too thrilled. If it were me, I'd be thinking of a special way to thank the man who spent a grip on them—maybe with my mouth." She winks.

They are beautiful and a thoughtful gift from whomever they came. Not to mention they smell fantastic. But thanking him with my mouth is most likely the last thing he wants at the moment. I can't believe I was rude earlier and then he sent flowers. Who the hell is this guy?

"Or did he fuck up? Do I need to hurt someone for you? I will, if he cheated. I'll dick punch him for you."

Laughing nervously, I shake my head, "No, nothing like that. But thank you, it's nice to know that you have my back."

"Always girl, you just say the word."

"Thank you, Keisha, it means a lot. If I figure out who they're from, I'll be sure to thank him."

"Oh my God! You don't know who they're from? Shit! You have a secret admirer, this is so cool."

Nodding, I send her a brief, shaky smile. She has no clue that it could be from a certain 'supposed' *gangster*, according to Kaleigh. Hopefully he's just a rich guy with a good secretary to be able to find me like that. I should send him a quick email at least to thank him for the blooms and the lunch.

The phone starts ringing so Keisha hurries back to her desk, leaving me with my thoughts.

First thing I'm doing is moving these damn flowers from the middle of my desk. Picking up the heavy vase, I start to put them on my small side table against the wall, but can't push myself to move them that far away. Instead, I place them on the right corner of my desk.

They're too lovely to not enjoy having them close by. There's a small leather couch pushed against the wall next to my door, my two matching leather office chairs, my desk, and my own chair. Not really a good spot for them in here, although they sure do make it feel more welcoming. Maybe I should get a plant or something to keep in here regularly to liven things up a bit.

So, he wanted me to have something beautiful and chose the same color as my shirt. How ironic that it's also one of my favorite colors. I love violet, fuchsia, and really dark blue, just like the deep blue color of his tie earlier. I'm a woman, and I'm allowed to have twenty favorite colors if I want and when these choices are paired together, the colors look even more vibrant.

First, he buys me lunch and now flowers? I can't be one hundred percent sure that they're from him since he didn't sign the card, but I'm not dense. I know inside that he sent them. Most women would be creeped out by it or head over heels already, but not me. I don't know what to think about it all or what he wants and I hate the uneasy feeling that comes along with it.

If he's as notorious a Kaleigh seems to believe, then I'm a little apprehensive garnering his attention. But if he's not … well, then, he's just another boring rich guy throwing money at me. Why do I have to be so hard to please when it comes to men? I want some excitement, but I also don't want to get hurt. I suppose that's most women though; however, they eventually end up settling on someone mediocre and I refuse to.

I had a nice boyfriend a while back. He had a good job and was pleasant. He also had a receding hairline, judged people based on their net worth, and thought that doing 'the helicopter' in bed was the way to satisfy me. *Ugh.* He didn't last long and I'm happier being single than sharing time with someone like that. My B.O.B has more of a personality.

I'm twenty-nine, unmarried with zero children. I know I'm not 'the norm,' but I wanted a career and the right man never came along, so here I am. Only getting older. By my mother's reaction to my nonexistent love life, you'd think I was on my deathbed or something. She wants grandbabies and with the amazing life she's always worked hard to give me, she deserves some grandchildren. Hopefully, one day I can make that wish come true for her, but until then, I'm pretty happy with my life. I don't need a man to make things better, but it would be nice to have someone to share some free time with.

Once I'm home and settled, I try calling Kaleigh before I jump into bed, but she doesn't answer. I chalk it up to her sleeping already, but part of me wonders if she's too scared to talk to me on the phone now too? No use in worrying; she'll come around. We don't ever go without talking for more than a few days, so I'm sure she's fine.

Chapter 2

I love gangsta rap. I like to think I'm
still from the hood that I never lived in.
Just keepin' it real.
-Funny Meme

Grace

Hurrying into work the next day, I flash Keisha a quick smile as I rush to my office. I sneezed while putting on my mascara this morning and I had to completely redo half of my face. Probably gave the neighbors an earful with my colorful language; I'm sure they hate me by now. I'll most likely be the blame for their two small children learning curse words, but that mascara pissed me off.

I hate being late, almost to the point of me calling in. The last time I came in wearing no makeup, two people asked me if I was feeling sick. *Jerks*.

Instead of flaking out, I'll eat the disgruntled look my boss will give me if he notices. Hopefully, I can slide in without anyone paying attention though.

Plopping into my plush leather office chair, I'm surprised to see something else resting on the middle of my desk. I still have the gorgeous flower arrangement. I left them here instead of taking them home with me. I'm not a generally a paranoid type of person, but Kaleigh had me thinking. Naturally 'tracking device' came to mind when pondering over how he found out where I work so quick and easily, so they stayed here.

"Keisha?" I call loud enough so she can hear me from my office.

A few seconds later she appears in my doorway, "Yeah, babe?"

"Hey, did you put this on my desk today? And if so, who's it from?"

"What is it?" she asks, coming closer. I point down at the box, wrapped in lovely dark blue paper.

"Nope, I haven't had any deliveries yet."

"Hm. Okay, I'll ask around the office and see if it's from or for one of them."

"You're the first one in today, so you might want to wait until a little later. Why don't you just open it? There could be a card or something inside."

That means a free pass with my boss then. No one's here and I know Keisha won't say anything. Nobody will have any idea about me being late and my makeup's on point. Double win. *Thank you mascara gods.*

"Yeah but I'd hate to open it if it's not really intended for me."

"Could be from him." She nods toward the flowers and I have a strong suspicion that she's probably right. But how did it get on my desk if Keisha or another coworker didn't put it in here? The only other person with office access is an old man that does the cleaning at night. "Just open it and if it's not yours then I'm sure whoever it belongs to will understand since it's in your office and doesn't have a name tag on it."

"You're right, but I'm going to wait until later I think, just in case anyone mentions something about it."

"Suit yourself, Grace." She shrugs and leaves my office. Keisha's always busy with a million tasks, so I know she's probably too preoccupied to talk me into opening it now. She's nosey like me, so I know she'll be back later.

Powering up my computer, I dig out my favorite quote covered notebook that I keep my random notes in. I don't have any new clients this week, so I get to touch base with all of my current jobs I've worked on recently. I try to call them occasionally in case we need to update or add anything to their accounts.

Marketing isn't my favorite thing in the world, but it pays the bills and allows me to have a small apartment in the city. Another benefit is that I'm usually always off on the weekends and evenings, so I can't complain much. Too bad I don't have much of a life outside of work to actually use the free time.

Scrolling through my contacts on the spreadsheet in front of me, the blue box on my desk is practically taunting, daring me to open it. It's medium sized and could be absolutely anything. I think that's why it has me so intrigued, plus the fact that it could be from the *Joker*, the man himself, from the restaurant.

What kind of nickname is that anyhow? I think of Joker and it instantly brings Batman to mind. Now that is another fine specimen to think of.

Why would he send me something two days in a row, though? We'd barely spoken to each other and I could've been a bit friendlier instead of pretending he was the waitstaff. There's no way in hell you could mistake him for one of the servers anyhow. He was in an expensive suit, probably worth my monthly salary, and everyone who works at the restaurant wears a plain white button-up shirt and black slacks. And he called me beautiful, in another language, no less.

Screw it. I'm not waiting any longer. I'm going to open the gift. If it's not for me, I'll just apologize like Keisha suggested. I'm hoping it is for me but from my mother or something. We know how that played out yesterday when I thought the last delivery was from my mom though. And since when do I wish a present was from my mom and *not* from a man?

Since now. I think and roll my eyes at myself.

Peeling the delicate paper away, I'm left with a plain white garment box. The pounding in my chest grows stronger as my heart starts to race. I'm excited and curious. It's like Christmas; I wasn't expecting anything at all and I'm surprised. I just want to rip through the box and remaining paper because I can't wait to see what's inside, but I don't. Instead, I take my time to truly appreciate the thoughtfulness just like my mother taught me as a girl.

Lifting the top away, I carefully push aside the tissue paper, a soft gasp escaping as I peer inside. It's one of my absolute favorite things—a Chanel bag that's bigger than any I've ever seen before at the mall. It had to come from a specialty shop. It had to cost a small fortune and there's no way on earth my mother could've afforded to send it to me.

Delicately, I open the purse to look inside and find another gray cardstock. It's the same color and font as yesterday, only it has a set of initials this time. It's him.

T.M.

T.M. - meaning Thaddaeus Morelli. Be still my heart. I chant to myself as I close my eyes and remember his face from the day before. The way he consumed every ounce of air in the room, staring at me as if he couldn't get his fill.

Setting the soft leather bag in my lap, I run my fingers lightly over the smooth surface. It's exquisite, just like him. How on earth can he send me such extravagant gifts though? He doesn't know me. Even if he did, this is entirely too much. I'm not materialistic; at least, I don't think I am.

Did I come off that way to him? I hope he doesn't think I'm a snob and that's why he's doing this. I would gladly just talk to him, maybe get a drink to see if we even like each other's company. It's hard imagining not liking anything about that man though.

For Chanel, it's huge and a complete work of art. Any woman could appreciate the leatherwork and creativity that was so obviously put into the design. The creepy thing is that it's the exact shade as my earrings and necklace I had on yesterday and still have on—sapphire. They're my birthstone and I wear them often.

It's like he knows me without knowing me.

He had a few glances, five minutes at the most to really look at me and yet he remembers little details such as my shirt color and my jewelry that vividly? When's the last time I can remember a man ever paying that close of attention to me? Never, that's when.

Why's he doing this? First lunch, then flowers, and now a bag. I don't even have a way to reach him to thank him properly. I shouldn't keep the purse; a gift like this is way too expensive. Eventually he'll come to expect something in return—they always do, and I'm not one to be bought or blackmailed. I wish he'd left his number on the card, but I suppose this way I can't argue with him or try to send it back. Damn bossy businessmen so used to getting their way. I work with them here in the office and in my field.

You'd think he'd want to hear from me though, and that he'd want me to thank him. Surely, he expects me to be grateful and flattered. I mean, I am and a little shocked to be honest.

Screw it, I'm googling him.

Pulling up the handy search engine on my computer, I type in his name. Biting the inside of my lip, I watch as article after article and a few pictures pop up. They're candid shots, nearly all of him walking into the Chicago courthouse. One expensive suit after another, I swear the man dresses amazingly. Either he's showing up to court or he's a lawyer. I seriously doubt he's a lawyer though if I go by what Kaleigh says.

Like that doesn't scream scary criminal right there.

Scanning over the search page, I'm met with headlines such as: Murder in the Streets; Another Dead; Dangerous Crime Lord; Chicago's Modern Day Gangster; Missing Hands; No Evidence; Morelli Associates Found Dead; Let Off on a Technicality; Morelli Innocent but Police Force Disagrees; Highly Dangerous, and another that makes me cringe—Lock Your Doors Because He's Free.

He's really that horrible? *Fuck.* How can someone so gorgeous with such a commanding presence really be that corrupt? It shouldn't be allowed, but I guess that's the universe's way of screwing with you. Find someone you finally want to lick like an ice cream cone and he's a dud.

Moving my mouse to the top, I click the images tab even though I know I shouldn't. I don't need to be reminded of how good-looking he is. Plus, what if I find some with women? I can't imagine him with another female. Is that crazy? I know it is. I shouldn't be thinking that I have any sort of claim over him or who he associates with. Hell, I don't even know the man. He's sent me a few gifts—nothing more.

The pictures don't compare anywhere close to the real thing, that's for sure. There's one though where he caught whoever was behind the camera watching them and that fierce gaze is so potent it almost feels as if he's staring at me through the screen. There's another of him in a leather jacket. It seems sort of out of place with all the others of him dressed to the nines and then seeing him in a suit yesterday. It's like his body belongs in a suit, commanding attention and respect.

Right clicking the mouse, I hit 'print' on the leather jacket photo, shaking my head at myself for doing it. I want to see him up close dressed like that. He'd almost seem more human, maybe easier to approach. Would I have treated him differently at the restaurant had he been dressed like that instead? Possibly. He's got the whole James Dean bad boy vibe going on and it's beyond hot.

Once it's done printing, I fold the five-by-seven-sized photo and stuff it into my bag. I don't want anyone seeing it on my desk; they may put two and two together to realize who the gifts are from. Earning the eye of a criminal isn't exactly good for promotional possibilities at work. I like my position here, and I'm not one to turn down a potential raise in the future if it were offered.

I should call Kaleigh. No, I'll text her and see if she wants to meet for lunch. I may blab about the purse over the phone right now, so it's safer to hide behind a quick message. If she finds out about the bag or the flowers, she'll freak and most likely never leave her house again. I'd see her on an episode of Hoarders or something and I wouldn't be able to live with myself knowing I played a part in it.

Me: Hey, want to meet for lunch today?

Kaleigh: Yes, is the sandwich shop on 25th ok?

Me: Why so far away?

Kaleigh: I'm helping with a new listing.

Me: Okay, see you soon.

She's a secretary for a real estate agency and sometimes they drag her along if they think there'll be extra paperwork involved. I don't know how she does it. That job has more paperwork than mine does. I'd pull out my hair working over there.

Setting the box with the new purse on the floor beside my desk where no one can see it, I get to work on making my business calls. After touching base with eleven clients and taking a coffee break, it's time to catch a cab to lunch. To be honest, I'm kind of happy about not walking today. It's probably silly, but I'm paranoid now. I can't help but wonder if he'll show up at my office or somewhere else.

Climbing into the cab, I greet the older Indian man, "Hi. Vino's on twenty-fifth , please." He doesn't answer, just gives me a short nod and then we're on our way.

Being late this morning, I was so distracted that I hurried to work but after this other gift and the Google search, I'm somewhat anxious to be alone on the street. It's absurd, I know. He's buying me nice things, so I doubt he wants to hurt me, but it's still nerve-racking to know that at some point I'm going to have to speak to him.

I wonder if Thaddaeus is watching me or having someone else do it for him? That would be too crazy, too soon. I need to relax; I'm acting paranoid and that's not like me. Am I being ridiculous about all of this? Maybe just a bit, I need to reel it in.

Keisha's right. I should be coming up with a decent way to thank him. Perhaps offer to have dinner with him if I get the chance to? Pretty presumptuous to think he wants to eat with me. He most likely just wants to fuck and then disappear. Weird, but I didn't get that vibe from him. It seemed like something stronger, something a little more than just the sexual chemistry all piled up into five explosive minutes of me not even having the guts to meet his gaze. The tension was so dense in that brief time, we may combust the next time we come face-to-face.

Another thing riding in the back of my mind about him watching me is if he'll notice that I'm not using the bag he sent. Surely, he wouldn't expect me to carry something that expensive around on the street. But then what would he know about being safe? According to the articles, he's one of the criminals that I do my best to watch out for daily.

If I try and consult my mother for some advice, she'll end up figuring out a way to contact Thaddaeus. Knowing her, she'd send him a marriage proposal and make it seem like it came from me. I've already busted her in the past setting up an online dating profile for me. The crazy woman does it with love, but it drives me nuts.

I'm so screwed; I had to be snarky when I saw him. I should've just kept my mouth shut like Kaleigh had said. With that thought, the cab comes to a halt in front of the sandwich shop.

"Twelve-fifty," the tan Indian man says with a mild accent.

I give him $13.50 and smile as I climb out. It's a shitty tip, but I have to eat and catch a cab back. Hopefully one day I'll be able to tip better, but my budget doesn't allow it right now. That's one thing I hate about living in such a large city; everything is so damn expensive and you have to take a cab anywhere that's not close by. If not, then you risk getting stuck in traffic or not being able to find a parking spot. I bet Thaddaeus tips well, if his gifts are any indication.

Entering the restaurant, Kaleigh's easy to spot. She's waiting for me at a tiny table near the back so I send her a small wave and make my way over, weaving through the other patrons. The place is packed, and everyone's in a rush to eat quickly on their lunch breaks. It's loud as they all carry on, laughing and visiting. The air's filled with delicious scents of fresh-baked brownies, a staple at Vino's.

"Hey lady, how did everything go with the new property today?" I ask as I sit in the empty chair across from her.

She instantly appears guilty, glancing at her hands and picking at her manicure of white polished nails. "I wasn't exactly honest about that," she admits reluctantly.

"What do you mean?"

"I didn't really have work on this side of town. I um, didn't want to stay in the neighborhood for lunch after what happened with *you-know-who*."

Jesus Christ. See, episode of Hoarders in the making. "Please tell me that you're joking."

"No. I'm sorry, Grace; I'm not. I didn't want to run into them again. Those guys are scary."

"Who's to say we won't see them anywhere else? Especially here, you picked another Italian joint, crazy. And you owe me twelve bucks. No, make it twenty-five bucks for cab fare, both ways." I can't freaking believe this, I would kick those guys' asses if it came down to her safety. She should know this.

She cringes, expelling a breath. "I'll get your lunch today too. I'm a terrible friend."

"You're not a bad friend, you were just trying to keep us safe and I appreciate that. However, I would've liked to save my money, we could've ordered in to the office or something. I'm a little surprised you went this far away to avoid them too."

"This was the first place I thought of. But that's a good idea; maybe we can order in tomorrow or Friday."

Nodding, I take a sip of the ice water with lemon already waiting on the table for me. "Did something happen after we left to spook you more? Did anyone contact you or send you anything?"

I can't help but be curious. It never even crossed my mind that he could've sent her something too; it would make sense why she's still tripping about seeing them. That'd be an easy way to piss off a woman too, send a gift to two women at the same time. I wouldn't feel so bad about keeping that new purse if that's the case.

"Oh no, nothing happened. Everything's fine. It's all been pretty boring actually, but last night I started watching a crime show and then I had crazy dreams. I woke up four times because of it. Eventually I took a Benadryl so I could get some good sleep."

"Jesus, Kaleigh, you need to watch *Pitch Perfect* or something to get the scary stuff out of your head. You're lucky you didn't oversleep or anything today." I'm a hypocrite. I'm guilty of getting sucked into the crime shows too and now I'm freaking paranoid.

"I know, tonight I'm watching *Fifty Shades*. I figure if I have crazy dreams at least let them be of a man spanking me or something fun like that. Besides, everything's been okay for you too, right?"

Now that's a fantasy I can get on board with—Thaddaeus doling out sexual punishments on my body.

Pasting on my business smile, I wave her off, as if she's being overzealous. My teeth clamp down, biting back my urge to blab about the gifts that have been delivered to my office. Technically things have been great. No need to freak her out more and let her in on what's been going down with me.

"I figured I was being dumb about the whole thing. I'm sorry again for not being upfront with you."

"No worries. Let's get some food, I'm starving."

I'm going to Hell for being a terrible friend. I pride myself in always being honest with her, but if I tell Kaleigh about the gifts, I know she'll completely flip out on me. She's always the low-key, cautious one; me, not so much. Even after the Jelly Bean lesson.

It looks like I'm already lying for him and we haven't even officially met yet. At this rate, I'm going to earn that damn bag he sent.

Chapter 3

He who is not impatient
Is not in love.
-Italian Proverb

Grace

Day number three...

The moment I stepped into my office and saw the giant basket on the middle of my desk, I decided to start numbering either the days or the gifts in whichever order they show up. Today is gift number three from him and day number three, counting our run-in at the restaurant, so that's what I'm going with.

This time the gift is an enormous, honey colored wicker basket filled with strawberry, white chocolate chip muffins. They're not the cheap, plastic wrapped ones you find in the shitty coffee shops either. These muffins are supersized, nearly the same size as a softball with big chunks of white chocolate that melt in your mouth.

They're so fragrant too, like pure heaven in the edible sense. I could smell them in the hallway before I even got into my office. It's like the baker was in this exact room, making them and the delicious scent has filled up the entire building. I'm either going to eat them until I make myself puke or else get so sick of smelling them I never want to eat them again.

Today's cardstock had the same initials as yesterday, and again, nothing else. I even pulled out the decorative fabric the muffins were resting on. There was nothing but the beautifully woven basket, dark blue material, massive sized muffins and a gift card for the bakery, Beanery Bliss. I'm assuming maybe for coffee or more muffins and then the small note with Thaddaeus' initials.

Damn it, he has to tell me what he wants from me already. I *refuse* to sleep with him to pay him back, and I cannot financially afford to give him the money that all this stuff costs, so these gestures need to stop before he sends anything else. I don't use people and I don't like feeling as if he's attempting to buy me. I make my own money, granted it's not a lot, but I can purchase my own food and my stylish, much cheaper purses.

The lunch was unexpected. The flowers were nice. The purse was over-the-top, now these muffins and a gift card. I feel absolutely spoiled and giddy inside, but this must stop.

Getting on my computer again, I pull up the White Pages program that our company subscribes to. I seriously doubt he has a home or cell number publicly listed, but it's worth a shot. I wonder if I could call the courthouse and ask for it? That's terrible for me to think like that, but they may be able to reach him quicker than me attempting to hunt him down.

I type in his name *Thaddaeus Morelli* and click the 'search' button. Almost instantly a listing pops up with a number beside it.

No way.

He knows where I work already, so I may as well call from my business phone and hope that the company doesn't record any of the calls. They'd have to tell us if they were; I think anyhow. I should Google that as well and see what the Illinois laws are about listening devices. Pressing in the phone number, it starts to ring. And ring and ring and ring, and finally someone picks up.

"Uh … hello?" It's an old man; I'd guess seventy years old or so judging by the sound of his voice. He sounds like he'd be someone's grandpa.

"Hello, sir," I reply, respectfully. "Is there someone there named Thaddaeus Morelli?"

"This is he," he says in a huff as if he's been woken up from an afternoon nap.

"I see. Is there another, perhaps younger man living there with the same name as you?"

"No, it's just me and my Hilda here."

"Right. Okay, thank you."

"Uh … young lady?"

"Yes, sir?"

"Is that all you were calling for?"

"Yes, I was calling for someone else; I apologize if I disturbed you."

"I don't get many phone calls anymore so I don't mind. Good luck to you on your search for your fellow."

"Thank you, goodbye."

"Bye," he responds quietly and eventually hangs up.

Getting old sucks.

I hope my mom never sounds that lonely when someone calls her. I should start bugging her more than once a week. I'm alone when I'm at home, but I have people that I talk to at work and Kaleigh, so it's not that bad.

Well that number was a dead end. Eh, I cringe, bad term to use when it comes to Thaddaeus, according to the internet anyway.

I have no more leads so I do a quick Yellow Pages search and come up empty with that route as well. If he has a business, then it must be listed under another name. Can't say I'm too surprised at that tidbit of information.

Since I can't get ahold of him, I should probably eat these muffins. No sense in letting them go to waste, especially if I have to end up paying for these suckers down the road. There are enough muffins here to feed me for a week, maybe even Keisha as well.

"Keish!" I yell, grateful that the walls are thick that only she and Rose next door can hear me. "Want a muffin?"

"Hell yeah!" She appears in my doorway, smiling. "Another gift?" Her eyebrow rises as she comes to stand in front of my desk.

"Yes."

"Mmmm and they smell so dang good, too. Wanna tell me why you don't sound too happy about another present?"

"Because, I have no way of contacting the guy who sent it to tell him to stop sending me stuff."

"You want him to stop? No way girl; take all the gifts you can get. Most men wouldn't know how to spoil a woman if it hit them in the face. You've found a good one it looks like."

"I'm not so sure if I'd use the term 'good' for him exactly."

"Well, he can't be all that bad if he keeps taking the time out of his day to send you these things. Flowers, purse, muffins; most men aren't that creative or kind."

She has a valid point. Unless, I'm right about him having one hell of a secretary and she's doing all of the purchasing and sending for him. My head's still spinning about his color choices also, did he really pay that close of attention to me in those few brief moments that we had?

Her words sink in a bit further, "Wait...You know about the purse?"

"Ha! I know everything; just who do you think you're talking too?" She smirks and I giggle. Keisha's one of the smartest people around here, and if you ever want to hear any gossip, she has dirt on everyone it seems.

"Remind me to stay on your good side."

"Keep feeding me muffins like this and you have nothing to worry about." She laughs.

"Deal."

Day number four and there's a box about five inches by five inches, wrapped in light pink paper on my desk.

What the fuck.

I was expecting something to be here today and it isn't a good thing that I was right. This has to end… and it will. Soon, right? Maybe today there'll be a card or something with more than just initials on it. Something, anyway, let there be some kind of way to contact him.

Steaming inside over this new box, I leave the package on my desk and march back out to Keisha's.

"Dude, another freaking gift. Did you see anyone?"

"No. Mr. Marks came in, but he wasn't carrying anything besides his coffee."

He's our boss and usually the first one in to work each day besides Keisha and me. Some people think he meddles in everyone's work, but I believe he just has to know what's going on all the time. It is his business after all, and he's done well with it so far.

"Well, shit."

"Why, was it bad? Your admirer's done really good with the others, I thought."

"No, well, I don't know. I haven't opened it yet. I'm too pissed that he sent another."

"Mr. Admirer hasn't called or anything?"

"No, nothing."

"Not even a text?"

"Nope."

"It is getting kind of weird then that he hasn't contacted you yet. Hope he's not some psycho stalker or something. I'd hate to see you get tied up in somebody's basement. You're way too pale for that shit and bruises would show up on you in a heartbeat."

Jesus of all things, she has to put that thought into my head now too. "I'll be back," I huff and storm into the elevator. My fingers tap against my thighs with nervous energy on the way down. My office is on the fifth floor so the ride's fairly short.

The doors open and I rush outside, forgetting that it's chilly today and that I should've thought to grab my coat. You'd think spending a few years in Chicago, I'd have my jacket glued to my hip or something by now. If anything, my blood's thicker now and I don't get cold as easily as I used to.

The street out front's busy as usual with the hustle and bustle of cabs in a hurry to get people to work on time. I don't know what I expect to find by coming back outside, It's not like he'd be parked in a car, waiting at the curb in front of my job.

Ignoring the chill from the wind the best I can, I still shiver and get goose bumps as I scan the sidewalk and the street. I'm looking everywhere for something—anything that's amiss—but come back with nothing. No one appears suspicious and no one seems to pay any attention to me at all.

As much as the thought disturbs me, I was wondering if he'd have someone posted up, watching me. That's creepy to imagine, but at least I'd have someone to question about everything and perhaps weasel his number out of. The only possible lead that I have in finding him is that new package sitting on my desk.

I cross my fingers that it has his number or some sort of contact information on it. I'm also beginning to wonder if I should perhaps contact the authorities. At first the gesture was sort of sweet and romantic, but now, gifts keep showing up. It's starting to make me freak a little, especially after what Keisha just said about basements. Fuck, that's a super creepy thought.

Making the trek back up to my office, I hurry in and start to rip through the paper. Catching myself, I pause briefly when I think about the beautiful purse he sent. Could it be a matching wallet for it? The box is a bit heavier than the other one though, so that wouldn't make sense. Unless there's a few things tucked inside making it seem heavier, rather than only one item.

Taking a deep breath, I slow my pace, tearing the paper away much more carefully. Once it's ripped through and completely gone, I'm left with a plain cardboard box. Using my letter opener, I slice through the scotch tape that's holding the box closed still.

Inside is a lovely wooden box, painted a pale white, almost like a whitewash. According to the small information card that's included with it, the box plays music and the top is made of deep blue Murano glass. Set directly in the middle is a handmade, gold Venetian Filigree heart. The bottom of the music box has a tiny imprint of 'Venice, Italy' and something else in Italian; I'm guessing the place it was made. It's exquisite and reminds me of something you'd be more likely to see in a museum.

It rivals the purse. This seems so carefully thought out compared to the other gifts. Each was special in its own way, but this is so much more. It's different, just like I felt Thaddaeus was the other day. How can I ever yell at him for giving me something so beautiful like this? It doesn't seem like the sort of thing you'd give someone if all you wanted was a booty call. I can't stop wondering just who this guy is. I wish he'd show his face again so I could have a chance to be kind to him this time.

Opening the box, it begins to tinkle a sweet melody. There's a small satin pouch in one of the velvet covered sections. Opening the little bag, I tip it over and a pair of earrings falls out. They each have a matching heart and blue glass bead made from the same Murano glass as the box.

Again, it's my favorite color. I can't imagine a basement stalker sending me a gift quite like this. I should rule out that thought of him in my head.

I've never received something like this—from anyone—before. As the melody keeps playing, my eyes fill with tears like I'm a giant sap. I can't get past such a sweet gift. It'll stand out boldly on my dresser at home; I don't own pretty trinkets or boxes like this.

Sure, I'm a woman and I like lovely things, but I can't afford to just buy random stuff I see that I don't somehow actually need.

It's nice to get something that's purely to look at and listen to. I think the last time my mother bought me a jewelry box, I was twelve years old and I ended up painting the plain box in about ten different colors with my various nail polishes I had at the time.

I wish I had a way to tell him thank you for this. Maybe if I get a chance to speak to Thaddaeus, I can invite him over for dinner instead. I'm not the best cook around, but it'll be a much more personal way to thank him. I can make a mean homemade lasagna, thanks to helping my mom prepare hers many times when I was growing up.

I don't think I've heard this song before. Grabbing my cell, I hit the record button on my music app. After a few seconds, I tap the search feature. It brings up the artist Kehlani and a track titled *Gangsta*.

Now that's creepy.

Had he heard mine and Kaleigh's conversations? Does he know that she said he was a Gangster? Has he seen my search engine? God, I'm becoming so fucking paranoid over this man.

Maybe I won't invite him over for dinner. Keisha's warning blares loudly, taunting me that he's going to lock me in a basement or some other random tiny room and never let me out to see daylight again.

My phone gives me the option to play the song, so I turn the volume down and the catchy tune begins. Kehlani's trance-like voice sings about how she needs a gangsta to love her better, how she has secrets that nobody knows and to not let her down. Taking a deep breath, I turn the song off and add it to my favorite playlist. At this rate, it could become my theme song.

Grabbing my purse and digging through it until I find his picture, I pull it free. Unfolding the paper, I stare down at his jet black, leather-clad shoulders. He looks strong—really strong—like there are muscles hiding under his clothes, and he's tall.

Thaddaeus does have the whole bad boy vibe going on in this picture, and it's a huge turn-on if I'm being honest with myself.

His hair's slicked back so perfectly, I'd swear there wasn't a strand out of place. He has a sharp jawline and a clean-shaven face. I wonder what his teeth look like. Does he have a friendly smile or is it menacing? Does he even smile? According to Kaleigh he doesn't. He didn't at the restaurant, and he wasn't smiling in any of the photos I saw online. If I believed in supernatural things, I'd probably even question if he had fangs at this point. He's like an enigma; I know absolutely nothing relevant about him, yet he's consuming my thoughts daily.

The rest of my day goes by the same as all the others, quick and painless. Before I know it, I've said goodbye to Keisha and am out the door. I love my walks to and from work; it gives me time to clear my head and just be.

Except when it's cold and snowing two feet. That sucks ass. I usually just shiver along and try to walk as quickly as possible so I don't freeze to death or get frostbite. Kaleigh swears her toes have turned black and now hurt all the time because of it. I think she's full of it though.

I got lucky finding an apartment close to work. I'm able to save a ton of money on cab fare and don't have to ride on the sketchy public transportation. Sometimes I miss living in a small town with the ease of having your own vehicle and everything nearby. It was so much cheaper and convenient, but the city has some perks as well.

There's always a ton of people walking at the same times I am, so I've never really worried about it being dark outside before whenever I leave the office. But, I swear there's someone follow-ing me tonight. It's making me all edgy inside. Each glance back, I don't see anyone unusual but I can feel a watchful gaze on me.

Maybe it's the newest gift? I've learned to wear my purse un-derneath my big jacket so it's not visible, but I have the music box in a small gift bag I brought from my office. Is that what's making me so nervous and suddenly aware? It's not the value of the box itself, but the beauty of it that I'd hate for it to be stolen or get ruined somehow.

I can hear footsteps, but there are people bustling all around on each side of me. Surely it's not only coming from behind. Glancing back again, a strong hand lands on my right arm and jostles me yanking my body into a shallow, nearly pitch-black alleyway.

Immediately opening my mouth to scream, I'm shoved up against a rough brick building. A large palm is harshly clamped over my mouth, effectively quieting me. It all happens so fast, I barely have a chance to blink and realize what's happening to me.

The man's body forcibly pushes up against mine, pinning me alongside the solid surface, making it hard for me to squirm. I can't see him very well in this position. I'm able to make out the side of a dark hoodie or else stare straight ahead. If he wants to hurt me, he has the absolute perfect position and opportunity to do so.

Even with the warm hand over my mouth, I still attempt to scream. It's useless though, making him push into my body harder until I'm gasping against his hand for more air. It's enough to stun me but not actually do bodily harm.

Something soft strokes the side of my neck, his hot breath fluttering closely enough to make me believe it was his nose grazing my skin. My body begins to shake, my teeth chattering inside my mouth, in fear of what he plans to do to me. I never thought I'd be in this situation; I think that's what's shocked me the most. I'm strung too tightly now to realize what's happening, that I could be raped or even be murdered tonight.

He lowly murmurs against my throat so that I'm the only one able to hear him speak. "Careful. You don't know who's lurking in the shadows." His voice is gravelly and deep. when he moves his lips I can feel them along with stubble brush against my skin with each word.

The almost 'threat' in his supposed warning has my chest pounding so harshly, I wouldn't be surprised if I had a heart attack or fainted right here. That'd be me, just pass out and let my captor have at me without any type of a fight.

Moving as much as possible, I barely shake him, he's so strong. I'm able to jostle the guy just enough to make him chuckle darkly against my throat. It's the malicious type of sound that'll send chills up your spine—the kind that promises torment and suffering. No doubt in this moment he's a predator and I'm his prey. If I wasn't so goddamned freaked out inside, I'd think it was fucking sexy coming from such a powerful man.

It's not sexy though; in fact, his laugh brings tears to my eyes. It obviously amuses him that he can so easily subdue me, sick fuck. This shouldn't be happening here in the middle of my walk, surrounded by so many other people. I've taken self-defense classes before. Fighting off my attacker isn't supposed to go down like this. They aren't supposed to snatch you out in the open, only in abandoned parking lots, parks when you're alone, coming out of buildings late at night when no one's around, those sorts of times.

My captor shifts and the breeze catches his scent. I can smell him and surprisingly it's clean. I'd expect dirt and violence to come from him, but instead I get fresh linen and another flutter of his warm breath against my skin.

He mutters one more thing before violently shoving me out of the alley. "Careful, Bella."

It's a whisper off the tip of his tongue and it makes me quake inside. I know who it is. No matter how badly I want to ignore that Italian word, I can't. Only one person has *ever* called me Bella.

I don't stop. Once his hands are off me and I'm free, I run— as fast as my heels will carry me. With tears steadily streaming down my face, I run until I finally make it to my building. It feels like it takes forever to reach my door, even though it's only a few blocks away from my job. My feet throb from running in heels. My calves are burning with a scary reminder that I need to get into better shape, because the next time he may not let me go.

Frantically, I scan all around to see if anyone was coming after me, but I find no one. A few people walking by stare at me like

I'm nuts. Surprisingly, there are no men thundering down the side-walk chasing after me. My side aches from a running cramp as I pant, double checking behind me and then triple checking again to make sure.

I key in my code to get into the building, jumping when the door buzzes to signal it's unlocked. As soon as I'm safely inside, I yank the door closed behind me until I feel the locking mechanism click into place. Then I take off running up the stairs to my apart-ment, ignoring small stabs of pain from my ribs, calves, and feet.

Getting inside my actual apartment is pure relief, but still, I can't stop the tears from pouring out. You'd think I was brutally beaten or something, but I'm fine. I wasn't physically harmed at all, but my ego and my false sense of security has become severely tainted.

Be careful, he'd ordered.

I thought I was though. I'm so damn confused inside. Why on earth would he attack me like that, only to warn me about who could be watching? No, not watching. He used the phrase lurking in the shadows. Which is even scarier when it's put like that.

And he'd called me Bella of all names. Only one person has called me Bella before and that's Thaddaeus. It hit me in the alley-way as well, but it didn't fully register at the time that it could've been him back there; holding me so tightly, smelling me, touching me...

Fuck.

Is he toying with me? Is that what this is? A joke? Does he think it's amusing to send people gifts then go and scare the life out of them? I should've kept my fucking mouth shut that day at lunch when he came into the restaurant.

Thinking that the man who just had me in the alley back there is Thaddaeus has me sobbing for other reasons. I want to punch him, kick him, and hurt him for scaring me like that. After send-ing me something so thoughtful and beautiful today, how could he fuck with my head like this? What did I do to deserve this?

I have no way to protect myself from a man like him either. What am I going to do?

Chapter 4

I asked God for a bike, but I
know God doesn't work that way.
So I stole a bike and asked for forgiveness.
-Al Pacino

Thaddaeus

Day Number five...

"You're completely fucked in the head, Joker." My close friend Maximillian Macintosh smirks.

"Why? Because I'm teaching her a lesson? She needs to be more careful." She's careless and will end up getting hurt if she doesn't open her eyes. This life isn't for the weak. My enemies will have her strung up after I take her on one date at this rate.

"So, you're going to terrorize her? Did you see the poor yank? You completely spooked her. She was trembling like a terrified child for God's sake." His English accent's more prominent as he becomes increasingly entertained with our conversation.

"If I want any chance of spending time with her in the near future then she has to be prepared for the types of people we deal with. You know as well as I do, half the dirty fuckers would eat her alive, being so naïve. Even if her innocence is quite amusing, I don't want anyone else picking up on it."

"You're right there, but don't you want to keep the innocence in her, at least for a bit? You could slowly corrupt her; it could be a game of sorts." He snickers, excitedly. "Besides, she's not like us and you sending her things and then attacking her is going to have her filing a restraining order against you in no time. Unless you want her to, that is?"

"She can try. Half the cops would laugh if she were to say my name to them. Benny sent over her computer search history. She knows who I am. It looks like she tried finding out contact information on me and then read over other various articles." Benny, my tracker, is good. He finds anything and everything.

"If she saw the online shit, then no doubt she's already scared, especially after what you just pulled in the alley. Why don't you go after someone who's in the life? Right now, it's like you're playing with your dinner."

"Because I don't want a woman who knows the ropes; I want her." And after having Grace against me like that, smelling her, tasting her … I must have her.

Grace

Part of me thinks that I'm being stupid by standing here in the lobby of the police station, but I have to file a report. He said to be careful, well I'll show him just how careful I can be and he'll never be able to step foot around me again.

"Miss?" The young cop calls me back over to the front desk.

"Yes?"

"Officer Malcolm is busy I'm afraid, but I do have a gentleman wishing to speak with you. He may be able to help you with your issue." She nods over toward the door and my stomach drops as I turn and see who's standing there.

It's one of them—one of the guys that was with Thaddaeus at the restaurant. Seeing him standing there looking so imposing, has my stomach dropping and my heart speeding up. Does this mean that Thaddaeus is somewhere around here also? My fingers move on their own accord at my sides, nervous that he's so close to me, in the same building and in the same freaking room no less.

"Um...ma'am, please. I can just wait on the officer." Waiting around in the small, stuffy room for however long it takes is better than facing off with that man over there.

"It's okay, just talk to Mr. Macintosh, he'll get you sorted." She smiles kindly and I try not to hyperventilate at her words.

"I'd rather not. I prefer to see a police officer." Take the hint lady. No one can fix this but the law.

Shaking her head, she huffs, like I'm a pest giving her a rough time, "I'm afraid that won't be happening today. You need to speak to the gentleman over there about your issue."

I can't believe what I'm hearing right now. I can't talk to a cop? I thought that's how this worked. Granted I've never been at the police station before, but aren't they supposed to help you when you walk in? I'm supposed to just waltz on over to one of Thaddaeus' friends, and say what? Why the hell did your buddy attack me last night on my way home from work? I seriously doubt he'll be able to help me sort that out. For all I know, the man could be here to kidnap me or taunt me further.

However, I am in the middle of the police station. Maybe I'll talk to this other guy after all, if only for a moment and see what the hell he wants, why he's here. I'm basically surrounded by cops, in a sense, so surely, he won't hurt me without someone doing something. At least I hope not.

I'm decent at putting on a fake smile and pretending I have more bravado then I really do, so let's see what he has to say. Lifting my nose a bit higher, I trek on over to him, damn near dragging my feet to get them to approach the big man. He's freaking tall with wide shoulders, and did I mention imposing? He looks fucking evil, watching each step I take, while wearing that mischievous smirk. This is a man that I could believe would be plastered all over the internet from various crimes he's committed. Don't get me wrong, he looks extremely rich and well put together. It's the malevolent expression he wears that gives him away.

"Hello, Grace." That wicked smirk blooms into a smile as I approach and I instantly pick up on an accent in his voice. With the sandy blond hair and straight white teeth accompanied by the expensively tailored suit, he could be quite magnificent if he didn't have sinister intentions dancing around in his gaze.

"Hello. How do you know my name?" I ask once I'm about two feet away from him. I'm not actually brave enough to get any closer, screw that. Especially not after what happened with his buddy last night. Hell to the no. I may be a touch too trusting, but I'm not stupid.

His light gray irises sparkle with amusement. "Let's not be dense, little yobbo. You know exactly how and why I know your name."

So, he does remember me as well and I'm guessing Thaddaeus has spoken about me to him. He's a dick. I can tell just by his one reply. I usually either love or hate the type. I think I'm going to hate this one, but I hope I'm wrong. And what the hell did he just call me?

"Let's go somewhere more private so we can speak plainly."

Holding myself back from laughing, I shake my head, "I'm good right here. I'm not going anywhere with you." Does he think I'm an idiot? I was freaking attacked last night. I'm not that damn obtuse.

"Fine. Suit yourself then." A crack in his false sense of patience shows. "Why are you here, Grace?"

Not being able to resist, I throw his earlier words back at him. "Let's not be dense, you know why I'm here."

He chuckles and nods. "I'm starting to see why he's so taken with you, if you spoke to him like that. Tell me, did you give him a bit of tongue at the restaurant?" His eyebrow quirks up, thoroughly amused, using words with double meaning to be just on the edge of inappropriate.

"Look, all I said was to get me a to-go cup and to bring me my bill. Nothing else."

He makes a choking sound, his eyes growing wide. "Yo-you said those exact words to him?"

"Yes. I clammed up,'" I shrug, tossing my hands up, "I get nervous and sometimes I come out sarcastic or rude without meaning too." Shit, why am I even admitting this stuff about me to him? "You need to just tell your friend to leave me alone already. I'm sorry for treating him that way, okay? The gifts were nice, but if he ever touches me again, I'll …"

He moves so fast that I'm taken off guard and no one acts like he even skipped a beat. His hand is suddenly in my hair, cupping the entire back of my skull. They're fucking huge, just like the rest of him. He leans in quickly, talking quieter, being discreet so others around us won't overhear. "You watch what your about to say, twonk. It's in your best interest you sod off and don't come back here. We *own* the cops." His hand's strong as it palms my skull, applying just enough pressure to make me uneasy again with the underlying threat.

At his admission, I swallow down a large gulp of air.

"Now, I suggest you go to work. You're already late." He steps back with a new grin pulling at his mouth, his hand dropping away. He winks, like he just shared an intimate secret between the two of us and his intimidating touch was some kind of sweet lover's caress. The crazy thing is he doesn't even look like he's a criminal, more like some powerful lawyer just waltzing around the police station. "Oh, and it was nice to finally meet you," he finishes, putting his hand out for me to shake.

He's a fucking evil bastard.

On autopilot, I shake his hand, his grip dominating mine of course. God forbid he feel inferior to a woman. Once he drops my hand, I hurry out the door looking for the first available cab. If Thaddaeus and Maximillian own the cops, then I don't trust my safety being outside the police station because who knows what else they control.

Once I'm in the cab, I pull my cell free and dial my mom. She can't help me out of this situation, but I need to speak with someone who'll calm me down and get my thoughts away from the conversation that just took place. If I don't focus on something else at the moment, I may wig myself completely out. I'm like two steps away from losing my shit and crying in the back of the cab.

"Gracie-Lue?" My mom answers with my childhood nickname and my chest instantly calms down, just by hearing her voice.

"Hi, Mom."

"Oh honey! I miss you!"

"I miss you too Mom, so much."

God do I. No one else in the world is like my mom. If she were here she'd kick Maximillian Macintosh's handsome ass in a heartbeat. She's may be petite in size, but she's fierce, that's for sure.

"Aw kiddo, so how's things?"

"They're … confusing."

"Man trouble?"

"You could say that. There's a guy who's been sending me gifts."

"I knew it would happen sooner than later," she responds happily and puts her hand over the phone, shouting to my stepfather, "It's Gracie, honey, and she has a boyfriend!"

"Mom, I don't have a boyfriend. He's just this guy and there's drama already."

"There always is dear, just stick it out, it'll be worth it. Oh, I hope we get to meet him sometime soon."

Arguing with her is pointless. Once I say man, she won't hear anything else, and if I tell her about the rest, she'll freak out and want me to move back home. I wish I could talk to her about it all. I need to tell someone, but Kaleigh will run off to another country or something crazy and Keisha will go try and hunt Thaddaeus down.

Ignoring her suggestion, I change the subject, "Mom, I have to go, I just wanted to call and let you know that I love you. I'll give you a call again in a few days."

"Okay honey, thank you for thinking of me. Love you and hope you have a good day at work."

"Love you too, Mom, I'll talk to you later."

"Bye."

"Bye." I hang up as the cab stops in front of my office. I'm not completely better, but the call was enough to get me to take a few deep breaths and catch my wits. I'm glad she didn't sound lonely like the old man I spoke to the other day.

"Sixteen-fifty," the man says, eyeing me over his shoulder.

"Here's a twenty. Can you be outside, right here at five-thirty exactly?"

"Yes."

"Good, thank you. You may keep the change." No way in hell am I walking home tonight or tomorrow for that matter. The cab driver pockets the cash as I climb out and hurry into my work building. I won't need to work out at a gym at this rate if I continue to run and rush around everywhere I go. One interaction with a guy and he has me spooked and full of anxiety.

Keisha's at her desk when I make it to our floor. "Hey girl." She glances up and smiles at me softly.

"Hi, Keish. Anything for me today?"

"Nope, but I haven't been in your office either."

"Ugh. Okay, thanks." I'm so not in the mood for any gifts today. But I doubt he sent anything after yesterday evening.

"Hey, Grace, you okay girl?" Her face falls as she peers at me concerned.

"Yeah, I'll be fine, just a chilly morning." Flashing a fake grin, I head into my office, not looking forward to seeing my desk. If there's something on it from our neighborhood psycho, I'm probably going to lose my shit.

Surprisingly there's nothing on it. Glancing around, everything looks to be in order with nothing new. The pent-up breath I was holding, releases, my shoulders dropping as my body relaxes.

I wonder if his game is stopping now after what he pulled last night. I still don't get it. Did I do something wrong to deserve his crazy treatment? It's not like he left me anyway to find him or else I would've done the polite thing and thanked him for everything he sent. After the alley, though, I just want to cut ties and move on.

Hell, I would've even returned all the stuff immediately and been done with it, but who knows how he would've reacted to me doing something like that as well.

Why do I feel like I've opened an entire new shit storm by going to the police station? Well, at least I know now that I'm not losing my mind. I am being followed around after all. That means that they know where I live, that *he* knows where to find me outside of work.

For some odd reason that thought doesn't frighten me. I don't know if it's because he hasn't sent anything to my apartment or bothered me in any way at home, but it's the one place that he's kept off limits. Thank God for that too.

"Grace?" My boss pokes his head in my door with his plain brown hair brushed off to the side like he's still ten years old. His shirt's already wrinkly, telling me that he probably got here at six a.m. He must have no homelife for being here so much. The man eats, sleeps, and breathes his marketing firm.

"Yes, sir?"

"Give Mr. Anderson a call; he's looking at adding another account and he likes you."

"I will. Thank you." One good piece of news today anyway.

He nods, disappearing and I throw myself into work all morning, trying to forget the run-in at the police station and my stalker's knack for sending me gifts.

Thaddaeus

"We were right; she was going to the cops." Max fills me in as he sits on the chair across from me, signaling for my house staff to bring him a coffee.

"Good for her. But she needs to learn where her loyalty should lie." I'm glad she's not going to let someone push her around so easily. She needs to have a backbone in this life, especially if my plan works and she's at my side eventually. That little spark I saw in her at the restaurant was just enough to show me she may have what it takes to be with me. It takes a certain kind of woman to handle a man of my caliber.

"You've yet to speak to her, minus threatening her last night. You can't possibly expect her to be loyal to you already. The sprog was ready to hand you over to the plod just this morning."

"I haven't contacted her yet because you know as well as I do that when it finally happens, she'll become a target. Once I take her into the public, she's my number one weakness to all of my enemies and I need her prepared." I leave out the part that I may not be able to keep myself from touching her, possessing her if I see her so quickly. She needs time to warm up to me, because once I'm ready, I'll make sure she's mine and no one will be able to fulfill her once I give her a taste.

"Try telling her about it, perhaps. I'm sure she doesn't understand your gifts either. Woman's probably gone a bit potty by now."

"She's not a fucking imbecile. I'll explain the meanings when I'm done sending them if she wishes. I plan to send her a phone in a few days and she'll be able to contact me." Not that it's any of his business, but it'll get him off my case. Of course, he doesn't understand my notions; he's never found a woman that he's wanted to keep before or even be genuinely kind to.

"You'll get a bloody earful, of that I'm certain."

"I'm looking forward to it. She doesn't hold back, huh?"

I'm practically salivating to see that temper of hers and hear that smart mouth again. I fucking love it that she's not afraid to let me have it and that she's not fearful of me. I'm sure I could get her to submit if I wanted to, but where's the fun in that? Everyone around me does what they're told; I like it that she's different.

"Not a bit. I'm starting to see why she's caught your attention. I'd suspected it was the 'blow me' lips she's got, but apparently, she's got some wit in her as well."

"It's more than that; Grace is the type that could change things for me." And fuck, those lips. Can't wait to have her down on her knees and they're wrapped around my cock. I know she'll look even more beautiful then.

"I hope you don't mean that in a business sense. There's no place in this life if you're growing soft and a woman's the first thing to make you weak. You were just saying it yourself that your enemies will see her as a weakness. Why not take a mistress or two; you'll appear stronger."

Keeping my voice even is a struggle as his words ignite my temper. If he were anyone else, he'd pay for that little dig, but he gets some slack being my close friend. "Did you forget who you're speaking to? I remember finding you, abandoned by your familia because you liked to play with things a little too roughly. I took you in, remember that. I don't give a fuck if you're a rich bitch or not; never forget who put you in the spot you're in now. These streets are run by me, and it'll stay that way—woman or no woman."

"Of course. How can I forget, when you won't let me?" His face turns off to the side, angrily stewing inside by being put in his place. He doesn't run shit and he needs to keep that in mind when talking to me.

"Are you jealous? Is that what this is about? You're angry because I found someone who really interests me and now you're questioning my business sense? Rest assured, old friend, I will always take care of things whether a woman's around or not."

He nods, keeping his opinions to himself. "So what are you sending her today?" He changes the subject—a peace offering—and I can't wait to tell him about it.

Grace…

"Miss?" I'm interrupted by an unfamiliar voice.

Glancing up, I find a short, balding older man, snuggled up in a puffer jacket. "Yes? Hi, can I help you?"

"I have a delivery for you." He steps into my office and my stomach sinks at his words. I thought it was over with, that perhaps seeing me attempt to go to the police was enough to make the gifts stop appearing. Surely, he knows I was there today; Maximillian Macintosh would've said something for sure.

"Um, from who exactly?"

"Sorry, but I'm not sure on the details; I was just paid to deliver it to your office." He holds out a box about seven inches long by three inches wide, wrapped in plain black paper with a gold ribbon. It's shallow and light.

"Do you remember what he looked like?"

He glances at his feet for a second, then meets my eyes again. "He was a big fella." The old man shrugs, "Expensive suit, the same as most of the other guys coming in, asking me to do deliveries. Sorry lady, but I don't usually pay them much attention; they all look the same to me."

"No, I appreciate it, thank you."

Could it have been Maximillian after he saw me? That brings a shudder to my spine. There wasn't anything nice about him besides his looks. Could it have been Thaddaeus? For some reason, I don't think he runs many of his own errands. Maybe one of the other guys he had with him that first day.

I nod, quickly scribbling my signature on his clipboard and he sets the box on my desk. "Have a good one, Miss."

"Yeah, you too." He leaves and it's as if the box is glowing. I know I have to open it. No, I *need* to open it. It'll drive me mad and after everything that's happened, there's no telling what's in it.

Keisha appears in my doorway next. "Well? Is it anything good?" she asks.

"Shh! Come here."

She stands in front of my desk and suddenly I'm glad she's here to witness me opening the package. I didn't tell her anything about last night. Hell, I didn't tell anyone. She probably thinks I'm acting funny.

Tearing off the paper, she watches me, amused. I make light work of the wrapping and open the box. Inside, nestled upon black tissue paper, sits a pocket knife about six inches long.

"Wow, that's one fancy knife. What a strange gift." Her brow quirks and I couldn't agree with her more.

"I know, right? Who gives you a knife as a present?" A gangster, that's who.

"Apparently, Mr. Secret Admirer does." She shrugs. "Is there a card this time?" The phone up front starts to ring and she rolls her eyes. "I'll be back."

"K."

Once she's gone, I pull the knife out, palming the smooth silver surface. Underneath is the gray cardstock that's become a staple with Thaddaeus' gifts.

Bella,

To protect you from the shadows.

T.M.

Motherfucker. If I weren't in my office, I'd scream; I'm so confused, irritated, curious, and frustrated inside. What the fuck does he want from me? I knew it was him last night, bastard! The nerve of this man is absolutely astounding. I want to open the knife and drive it into his hand, after he grabbed me last night. I want to use the heavy weapon and chuck it at his face—he has me so upset. And that note, is he trying to give me flipping nightmares?

Feeling something on the other side of the knife against my palm, I flip it over. There's an inscription:

For in love and war comes strength. I'll be yours.

How in the hell can he say something like this after last night? Those words would've landed him a date with me in a heartbeat had he not scared me so badly last night. They're beautiful and seem so meaningful. I would love to have a man say them to me, but under different circumstances.

Am I being a wimp about the whole thing?

I don't think I'm being irrational. He pulled me into a dark alley for heaven's sake and wouldn't even let me speak, then he almost-kind-of threatened me. Sure, there was a warning in his words as well. Was he really trying to protect me? What do I have to be afraid of besides him? Is he so dangerous that he has to secretly warn me? I thought I was being fucking kidnapped, attacked, violated, and yet maybe I'm taking the whole thing wrong? And what about his guard dog, Maximillian, earlier at the police station? Surely, he told Thaddaeus he saw me there and about our conversation.

I feel like my head's going to explode if I don't get some answers soon. Wrapping my hand around the knife so no one can see it, I make my way outside. Once the cold air hits me, my skull falls back against the brick building and the tears flow freely. I hope whoever he has watching me can see how upset he's made me. I hope they tell him that right after his delivery that I was outside crying my eyes out. He sends me this … stuff without any real explanation. All I'd really like at this point is an apology.

Chapter 5

Fuck friends. I need more enemies.
At least they admit they don't like you.
-Wiz Khalifa

Grace

Day Number Six...

Every preconceived notion that I had of my place being off limits is thrown out the damn window when I arrive home to a package in front of my apartment door. One of the neighbors must've thought they were doing me a kindness by letting who-ever delivered the box into the building. I hope they didn't break into my apartment while they were here, but it wouldn't surprise me if they did. I don't have to look at the return info to know it's from *him*.

Taking a deep breath, I grab the gift and head inside. My door's still locked, so that's a good sign, not that it means any-thing. Glancing around, everything looks the same, but I doubt I'd know it if they'd been here if they didn't want me to. This man seriously needs to stop screwing with my head.

I don't know whether to be excited, scared, irritated, or what.

Setting my keys, the knife he sent me, and my purse on the entry table, I lock the dead bolt behind me and head to the table where my letter opener is. Taking a seat, I set out to open yet an-other box. This one's about ten inches long by ten inches wide and four inches deep.

I'm not going to even attempt at guessing what's inside. Thaddaeus has caught me off guard each day, so I doubt this'll be any different. On the plus side, he didn't yank me into a scary, dark alley to give it to me, so there's that.

Peeling the cardboard open, I nearly choke on my own spit when I see it's a cell phone. A brand new S7 too. These things cost a ton of money as I'm sure his other gifts have as well, but that's not the point. The thing is: It's a phone—finally! Could his number be listed in it? A way for me to reach him, finally?

Wasting no time, I power the phone on and let it load up. It's quick, being a new model with only the factory apps installed. The contacts tab is on the main page, so I tap it.

T.M. Is listed at the very top of the list, along with my own new number right below it.

You'd think that I'd won the lottery and I leap out of my chair. I jump up and down a few times, excited to finally have a cell number for him. I can't believe it. I can call him!

But what do I say? I've had so much building up inside, that now I have no idea what to bring up. I know for certain I want to let him know that shit he pulled yesterday is a no go for me. He needs to keep his hands off and not try to frighten the life out of me.

Is it insane that I'm excited to hear his voice again? I feel like we've been through so much this last week, yet we haven't even spoken. How can you start to form a relationship with someone when they haven't been around you, yet they've been present in a way every single day?

Part of me hates him already, while another piece wants to know everything there is to know about him.

Thaddaeus' gifts have said so much about him, but did he mean for them to or were they just simply presents to him? Either way, I need to tell him to take them back. I don't want him to think I'm ungrateful, but I have to put my foot down. After the alley, I'm scared to be alone with him, so dinner's out of the question now. Everything's out of the question with him. I want it all to just disappear and my life to return to normal and boring.

Oh hell, what do I have to lose by calling? I press the phone icon next to his name. It asks if I want to call or text, so I hit call.

"Bella?"

Shit, I wasn't expecting him to answer the phone. I was thinking this conversation would most likely be by voicemail where I could rant and not get a reply.

"Hi, my name's...umm...Grace."

"I know."

Of course, he knows; he's been sending me stuff every day for nearly a week. Shit. What did I want to say to him again?

"I got the phone you sent."

"So I hear." His reply sounds amused, and thankfully, he can't see my cheeks color with heat.

Fuck, I don't know what to bring up and I sound like I'm babbling already, making up random shit that means a whole lot of nothing to either one of us.

"The gifts have been unexpected, but I should return them to you."

"No you shouldn't." His reply is firm. *"They have meaning; just wait."*

"I get that, but..."

"No buts, once I'm finished sending them, if you want to know more, I'll explain them to you."

"There's more?"

"Of course. Patience, cara. On the tenth day, I'll call you."

"Okay."

I should say so much more, argue with him perhaps, but I just want to keep him talking. The low, rich, timbre of his voice has goose bumps covering my skin. It's not only my cheeks heating up, but my stomach as well. He sounds divine, like a creamy scoop of your favorite ice cream or something even better, like chocolate mousse. You know the kind, where you order it at a restaurant, and when it finally arrives, you can only take like five bites and then you're finished? You want to eat more, but the flavor's so potent that your taste buds can't handle it, so you suck the little remaining bits off the fork... Yeah, that's what he sounds like.

"Only call me if you're in danger." It's an order, not a suggestion. Fuck, he sounds even sexier when he demands shit.

"Why would I be in danger?"

"Oh, sweet Bella, I know you've looked me up online. Always watch the shadows and remember that you're on my mind."

There's that creepy reminder again. He had to bring it up. What can be so terrible that he has to warn me of repeatedly? Does he want me to be scared to death of him or just cautious in general? This type of stuff doesn't happen to me; my life's so blah, and now he's speaking of danger and me needing to be careful. This isn't some exciting James Bond movie; this is my life he's meddling in.

"Okay, I—"

"We'll speak soon. Goodnight."

Thaddaeus ends our conversation abruptly, interrupting me yet again. The man's infuriating. And bossy. And annoying. And fuck my life, so damn enticing. The sense of danger makes him even more alluring if that makes any sense.

"Night." I respond, completely enraptured by his voice.

How can he have this effect on me over the phone? The line's silent, telling me that he didn't even wait for me to respond to his order; he just hung up after speaking his last words. He's sort of a dick when I think about it. I bet he was spoiled growing up and used to getting his way in whatever. That'd make total sense with him being so damn domineering and assertive.

I think he may be ruder than I am. And I pretty much got nowhere with that phone call.

Me: This is my new number.

Kaleigh: Who is this?

Me: Grace.

Kaleigh: You got a new phone?

Me: Yep.

Kaleigh: What happened to your other one?

Me: I'll fill you in later, about to jump in the shower.

Kaleigh: Okay. XO

Me: XO

I'm such a horrible freaking friend. With that thought I make myself go take a shower; that way I'm not lying to Kaleigh. I'm just not divulging the whole truth.

Thaddaeus

"Cage, did you set up the delivery for tomorrow morning?" He's another friend of mine that's in our small group. There are four of us total, that are usually together—sometimes five. When it comes down to me needing something, they work for me. They've been around for years, all gravitating my way for various reasons.

"Yep. You going to tell us what you sent her this time?" His dark eyebrow rises as he sits down at my home bar.

They all live here with me. It keeps things much more convenient when I need to go somewhere. I learned the hard way by losing my younger brother to a hit from a rival, that it's always good to have backup with you. My brother didn't deserve to die, but he was unprepared. I refuse to make the same mistake.

In a way, these men are like my brothers now and they're enjoying themselves way too much over my gift giving to Grace. It's not normal for me and they think it's prime time to give me a rough go about it. They've never had anyone special like Grace come into their lives either, though. I know perfection when I see it, and she clearly stands out amongst the rest.

The minute I stepped into the restaurant and heard her carrying on to her friend, not cowering to my presence like the rest of the customers, I was intrigued. Then with her acting like I was nothing, like I didn't bother her one bit, presented a challenge that I was instantly obsessing over. I swear her skin was soft as silk. I had to touch her, if even for a moment. And that smart mouth of hers made my cock hard. I wanted to shove it in her mouth to teach her a lesson for speaking to me so rudely. I, of course, had to hold my breath, to control myself, but I gritted through it, while memorizing every detail of her that I could.

She was in violet and sapphires. So fucking beautiful too. Those sparkling eyes screamed mischief, and that little smirk she wore on her lips had me fantasizing about her mouth all week.

Grace is upset over the gifts, which can be expected. I get it that it's not her norm for men to be sending her random things each day which she doesn't know the full meanings to. I'll explain it all to her eventually, and hopefully, she'll stay after she hears me out. The fact that she wants to give me everything back tells me that she's not a gold digger. Not that I'd mind if she were; it'd probably make things easier.

She's never met a man like me and she'll soon find that out. I plan on showing her how I can be better for her and how she deserves to be treated. I may test her a bit at first, but it's only to see if she can handle it and handle me. I'm not a timid or boring man by any means. I'm headstrong, demanding, and used to getting my way. Things usually end up badly for others if I don't get what I want. Right now, that's Grace.

Sure, the alley incident was a bit crass, but she needed something to jolt her out of her everyday mundane routine. She was a target just waiting to happen. My methods are rough, but they work. They've kept my crew alive.

I've gotten reports that she's started taking a cab and watching her surroundings, something she needs to get accustomed to doing if she's going to be associated with me. Well, not the riding in a cab part, but the switching things up and being vigilant. She should've been doing those things all along anyhow.

Bad things happen to beautiful women when they get compla-cent. They need to protect themselves and be cautious. It'd be too easy to snatch her ass up and feed her to the sex industry or to the streets. They'd eat her up and spit her out, completely tarnished forever. She'll thank me one day, I know it.

Maximillian thought I'd be furious in finding out that she went to the police force, when in reality I was proud of her. The woman has a bigger backbone than I expected, and it made me want her even more. It'll take a strong woman to stand by my side in this life and I have to test the waters to see if she's really the one to do it. I want her to be already. It's only been a week, yet I want her in my bed every night and alongside of me in the future.

I'll continue my methods and hope for the best. My grand-father taught me what to do when you find 'the one.' He put my grandmother through it, and they lasted a good fifty years together.

"Well?" Cage presses.

"Fine." I relent and reply, "It was a coat and a pair of shoes." Taking a drink of my scotch, I wait for whatever teasing comment he can come up with about it.

"Yeah, but what kind? I know you T and you don't do things half-assed."

Of course I don't. What's the point of doing anything halfway, to just have to go back and fix it? Hell no. I'll do it once and get it right the first time. "They were Chanel and Louboutin's. She de-serves to wear the best." Especially if she's going to be at my side. I want her sexy ass drenched in the best my money can buy or that I can steal. I'm not picky.

"Fuck, Joker. You're going to completely spoil her and turn her into one of those prissy bitches."

"No I won't. Each item has a meaning. Well not the shoes; those were just to make her smile, but the coat has its purpose. You should know that I'll break her before she acts like an entitled fucking bitch."

"The purpose of the jacket being to hide a nine millimeter and help protect your ass?"

"If she wants a Glock, I'll get her one of those too. But no, it's to keep her warm."

"No offense man, but you have some weird ideas."

Shrugging, I finish off the expensive liquor. "The city's cold. She needs something to keep her warm until it's me doing the job."

"I'd fuck her friend, if you needed me to."

"She'd pass out before you got to touch her. Did you see her clam up when we walked into the restaurant?"

He laughs loudly. "I love when that happens."

"So do I … so do I." My smirk's cruel as I think back to the frightened faces of all the patrons. I should've shot someone just for the fuck of it. Showed them what true panic's all about, because they have absolutely no clue what it's like on these streets.

They all fear me, but they have no idea it's me and my crew helping keep most of those fuckwads alive. If it weren't for us, the two-one-five crew would've come through and cleaned this part of the city out. Yeah, I'm fucking evil, but I keep the devils at bay. They just don't realize it.

Grace

Day number seven which happens to be my day off, has begun with me opening my front door to find another large box. Never in my life has a man bought me a coat or shoes before and after seeing the tags belonging to Chanel and Louboutin, I felt completely spoiled. I sent him a quick text, briefly thanking him for the gifts and left it at that. I didn't hear back from him and the day dragged by at home. I got some cleaning and reading done and ended my day with Chinese delivery.

Monday morning and day number eight rolls around with me wearing my new coat and shoes. Thaddaeus said I had to keep the items he's sending, so I'm doing what he wants. I may regret it in the future, but for now, I'm going to enjoy the few surprises he's been sending especially after the shit that went down in the alley. He can grovel a while; Lord knows he needs to figure out how to be apologetic.

I went ahead and got a cab to give me a lift to work. I was not about to walk down the sidewalk alone, dressed in such a gorgeous coat and shoes. He wants me to be more careful, so I'm doing that too. I'm not so sure I'd have been much good out walking anyhow; I stayed up half the night playing on the new phone he sent me. There's so much memory on it, I could download all my favorite apps and sync my books onto it.

"Hey girl." Keisha perks up as I step out of the elevator. She does a double take, smiling widely, "Wowee, you look hot! Did you go shopping on your day off?"

"Not exactly," I reply, not being able to hold my grin back.

"Noooooo! He sent those as well?"

Nodding, I beam a wide smile. "Yesterday, they kind of showed up at my door."

"Are you kidding me? They're gorgeous! He definitely has good taste. Do you know who it is yet?"

My excitement falls. "Yes. I figured it out."

"Anyone good?"

"It depends on your definition of the word." I already told her before that I wouldn't use that word when it comes to him, and I definitely wouldn't now knowing what I do about him.

"Oh lord, I need to see this one, if that's your answer. He's gotta be hot, if you're looking like that. Or wait, is he a creepy basement lurker?"

Chuckling, I shake my head and walk into my office. She doesn't need to see him. No one around the office does by the sounds of his reputation. I wouldn't so much as call him a basement lurker—maybe an alley or shadow stalker. Like that's any better.

I need to move past what happened. He didn't hurt me, and he's clearly sorry if the knife and quote was any indication.

These shoes are gorgeous. I've never known what the big deal was about them though; what exactly made them so great? Well, now I know and it's official; I'm addicted. They're the most comfortable, sexy pair of heels ever. And the coat is soft as silk inside. Not only does it feel luxurious, but it kept me completely warm walking into work today.

I'm not one hundred percent comfortable knowing that they were gifts, but I am grateful for the nice things. However, that's just what they are—things. It gives me no idea about the man behind them, besides the assumption that he has a bank account large enough to afford them. Thaddaeus has my complete attention now. I only hope that when I do finally get to talk to him in person, that he's not as terrifying and corrupt as the internet portrays him to be.

As I work throughout the morning, flutters fill my stomach, tumbling over and over. It's the eighth day since this all began, which means there's only two more days away from number ten. He said that would be the last day, so now I'm super eager to see what he has in store, but also a touch sad the surprises will be over with.

They don't have to be grand gestures or anything like they've been, but a note or flower, a candy; that sort of thing every once in a while makes the day a little better. Part of me feels ridiculously selfish for not wanting our little countdown to end. It's like he's turned me into a young girl again, anticipating the next surprise coming my way.

In a week's time he's completely spun me around in my head; I can only imagine what he'd be able to do in a month. I'd be smitten in no time flat.

Keisha comes into my office—eyes huge; as she swallows.

Her normal happy demeanor is nonexistent, which is strange. Our customers enjoy her savvy personality and usually look forward to seeing her when they come for an office appointment. "Grace, you have a visitor," she shares quietly, glancing backward.

"Um, okay, sure. Is it a walk in or an existing client?" I don't normally see clients without an appointment, but I'm not busy now so no big deal.

She nods shortly, not replying and hurrying out of my office— not the usual Keisha reaction I'm used to. I glimpse down at my calendar to see if I had anything scheduled. *Nope, my day is all clear just like I thought. That was weird of her.*

As my visitor walks through my doorway, it's like a mist fills the room along with him. I see Thaddaeus standing in front of me, those tawny-colored irises scorching toward me with so many unspoken words as he peers down at me. I feel as if I'm staring through a distorted glass, not truly seeing him, just knowing he's there.

My throat grows tight and my belly warms as chills overtake the skin on my arms. How can he have this sort of effect over my body? He's here in my office and all I can do is gawk. His mere existence steals my voice every time he's near, as if nothing could possibly be important enough to say out loud, but rather, just *be* in his presence.

"Bella, you still refuse to greet me?" His glare is angry, believing that I'm purposefully being rude to him once again.

"No, I choke out, attempting to refrain from stuttering like a silly schoolgirl meeting her first crush. "I mean, I was taken off guard. I apologize if it came off as rude; that's the last thing I want you to associate me with."

He clicks his tongue, his momentarily irritation dissolving, "You were surprised by me? Didn't we have a lesson over expecting the unexpected?"

"If that's what you'd like to call it, then yes," I retort smartly, not fond in the slightest of being reminded of his unsettling ways to 'teach' me something. His gaze flairs with my smartass retort, but what did he expect after the last so-called lesson that he gave me? Maybe I should dress up as a nun and smack his ass with a ruler—see how much he likes being reprimanded.

No … I have an inkling that he'd enjoy that too much.

Thaddaeus leans over my desk, and his fingertips graze my jaw. His thumb slightly passes over my bottom lip before his hand drops away. "Always so flawless, Bella—even stuffed behind this desk for most of the day."

"Um…thank you. I sent you a message about the coat; it's beautiful. The shoes, they're unbelievable, nothing like I've ever worn before. I appreciate your thoughtfulness."

He nods, his gold gaze twinkling, full of approval at my gratitude. He enjoys it that I'm pleased with his offering.

"Have you never been courted before, Grace?"

"Courted? No-no, I haven't."

So, he is courting me! I had wondered, but now to hear it come directly from his mouth, it sounds like I should've been expecting his gifts. They don't seem so out of place, now that I know it's his intention. My answer brings a brief smirk to his face, clearly content with what he hears, knowing that he's the first one to do this for me.

Each time he speaks, that amazing voice of his, has me conjuring up images of him between my thighs, moaning with enjoyment. *Fuck. I can't think like that with him here. I know my cheeks must be red. No doubt that he'll notice it; he catches every little detail when it comes to me.*

"That natural blush makes you remarkably stunning Grace. Did you know that?"

I shake my head, unable to form a decent reply. The only thing coming to mind is me wondering if he'll keep talking if I beg him to. I just want to listen to that delicious baritone of his, over and over.

"Shame. I'm assuming you won't share those thoughts you have rolling around in that mind of yours, huh? Nevertheless, I've come to deliver todays surprise in person."

If only he'd done this from the beginning, maybe I'd be better at speaking to him by this point. It's close to lunch, so maybe he's brought food again. I am getting hungry and a chance to eat with him in a neutral place is a step in the right direction.

"That's very thoughtful of you. Are we having lunch or something?"

He draws in a quick breath, and I think I'm the one who's caught him off guard this time. His tongue pokes out just enough to wet his bottom lip as his eyes run over me and then my desk again. I'd almost swear that he's picturing me on top of it, *being* his lunch. The thought has me shifting in my chair, chanting silently to hold still so he can't tell that his regard alone has me squirming.

"I hadn't planned on it or I'd have brought something with me. I'd enjoy that in the future though, if you wouldn't mind?"

"No, not at all. I like getting eaten here; it's convenient." I don't even realize how I've screwed up that sentence until it's too late and it's out in the open. My cheeks are so hot from that little slip, if you saw me, you'd swear that I had a sunburn.

"Noted." He growls, his jaw flexing as he clenches his teeth and inhales deeply. Obviously catching on to what I'd said on accident and am thinking to myself while I sit, nearly salivating for him. "You like Italian, cara?"

"Yes." Staring at him makes me realize that I like everything Italian, not just my food.

After a moment, he swallows and pulls out an envelope from the inside pocket of his jacket. It's a plain, long white nondescript business envelope. He lays it on my desk and pushes it toward me with the exact same two fingers he used to touch me with earlier and in the restaurant.

"A letter?"

I can't fathom what on earth he'd write in one or remember the last time anyone wrote me an actual letter. I'm excited to find out what it says, especially after hearing that he's courting me. Hopefully it's romantic or makes me laugh.

"No, my dear, but perhaps I'll do that for you in the future as well."

I would love that. Simple gestures like that aren't utilized enough, especially when you care for someone. "It sounds like you're making a lot of plans past our ten days." I'm not exactly sure of how I feel about it either. Part of me is thrilled with the prospect while the other part is apprehensive.

"Indeed I am. I hope you'll start thinking about it as well."

Shifting in my seat again, I consider him losing the custom-tailored, formfitting jacket he's got on, and loosening that slim, black tie, he's knotted so perfectly around his neck. I bet his shoulders and arms are superbly cut and corded with hard muscles under all those clothes. His height's probably intimidating to many, but I'd bet underneath all that material the extra length showcases his body perfectly. My thoughts from before return full force; looking like that, how on earth can he possibly be so bad and do I really care at this point if he is?

He speaks so proper compared to everyone else. Is it his wealth? I'd expect slang or something to come out of his mouth instead with him being a supposed criminal. His words remind me more of a gentleman, someone you'd read about or watch in a movie. Could he be the modern-day version? I doubt I'd ever be so lucky to meet him, if so. Clearly, I've had one too many dates alone on my couch watching *Gone With The Wind*, if I'm busily searching for a hidden Rhett Butler amongst this man in front of me.

He'd give Rhett a run for his money.

"Can I open it now?" Either the envelope or his shirt, but somethings gotta happen before I explode inside with all this excitement welling up that I've felt since he walked through my office door.

Is this how it'll always be around him? Ten minutes in his presence, and all I can think about is the two of us—naked. I feel like a sex maniac with pent-up desires whose itch needs to be scratched. I need a booty call, evidently. It's been too damn long since the last time I had a guy in the sack.

"I'd love nothing more than to see your face when you do, but I'd prefer it if you waited until I've left."

"Why? Will it hurt me?" I can't help but ask, the fear creeping up in my mind from the night walking home.

"Oh Grace," He clicks his tongue. "Part of you is so naïve and then you'll show me a brief glance at the passion brewing inside, and it makes me wonder which one you really are. No, it will not hurt you. On the contrary, I'm hoping this will make you extremely happy. However, if you try to object or return it, I'll be offended. So, rather than have our first face-to-face argument before I've had the chance to take you to dinner, I'd prefer to leave, rather than bend you over and spank you. I'll let you worry it over in your head, before you realize the best route is to simply say thank you and use it."

Wow.

I don't know if I should be offended or not. He clearly thinks he has me pegged on what my reaction will be, and maybe he's right. But to come out and say it like that is somewhat pompous. And the threat to spank me in retaliation to me arguing has my core clenching at all the possibilities with him.

There's a small probability that he's a mind reader and can play me like a fiddle, but he seems to be intrigued, so hopefully that's not really the case. I love it that he's observant, but I don't like being too predictable to him so easily and so soon.

I can't stop picturing him spanking me now. Thanks for that, Thaddaeus.

Ugh, he makes me turn into this wanton shell of myself. I'm not normally sitting here, stewing over sex, imagining me taking it, whichever way he'd give it to me. It's him, being here, it has me all twisted up. He needs to leave so I can think clearly again.

"Or maybe you're a coward and you're afraid I won't like it? Are you always too scared to stick around?" I'm nervous and yet again my snark comes out to play. Him threatening me along with so much damn tension in the air has me almost begging for a fight with him. I need to be fucked by this man and badly, preferably on my desk and right now.

I swear he emits a low moan under his breath, and his hands close into fists. Obviously, I've pushed some buttons, either he's pissed or my attitude makes him hard.

"Open it," he demands while staring at my mouth. I'd swear the man wants me to open my mouth and not the envelope with the way he orders it, making a burst of air leave me in a rush.

"No, I'll wait." I wave him off. "Go ahead and leave."

"I said, *open it*." It's not a request and with the command, his jaw flexes again as he grinds his teeth.

Hastily grabbing my letter opener, I slit through the crisp paper at the top. My irritated gaze stares at him nearly the entire time while he watches my hands. I want him to meet my eyes, but he's waiting for the moment that I discover what's inside. He's way too sure of himself, a touch too cocky for my liking. I enjoy a confident man, but this one's head is held a bit too high.

There's a printout of some sort, kind of like a bill or something. Pulling it free, I check it over and notice all my information listed, along with a destination and confirmation number. Freaky that he knows so much about me when I've shared basically nothing with him or Maximillian.

Scanning over each detail, I come to find that it's a plane ticket to visit my mother. There's no date of flight or return; it's for whenever I'm able to get off work. I didn't know tickets like this were even possible. They always ask for dates.

This is the most meaningful thing anyone could do for me—truly. I don't know how he possibly knew, but he did. Now I understand why he appeared so smug; he earned that look.

Tears fill my eyes with his thoughtfulness. I don't know how he could've figured it out or who he could've spoken to, but I've wanted to visit my mom for so long. I couldn't afford it with my regular bills and expenses. I've been too proud to ask my mother to help me pay for it. I'm twenty-nine years old. Financially, I should have my shit together by now. For the most part I do, but Chicago is expensive.

A few tears cascade over my cheeks and when I look back up, Thaddaeus no longer appears irritated at my rude remark. His eyes are gentler as they take me in, watching their fill. I don't have a clue as to what to say to him.

He was completely right about me wanting to run it through my mind over and over, until I ultimately decide it's a gift that I don't want to give up. He's undoubtedly forgiven for the alley incident and he knows it. I don't know if it bothers me that he could figure out a way to frighten me and then turn around with a way to basically wipe it out. A man shouldn't be able to be that quick and cunning to pull something like that off, but he is. No wonder why the courts could never put him away if this is the type of man they're dealing with. He doesn't play fair.

"Do you love it?" he finally whispers, saying the last thing I would've imagined coming out of his mouth.

"I do."

"Then it's served its purpose. I must go, but I'll see you soon," he says, turning to leave.

I nod as another tear rolls down my cheek. "Um, Thaddaeus?"

He halts instantly at me speaking his name out loud to him for the first time. He remains turned away from me, his shoulders stiff, the muscles strung tight as he waits for me to finish. No doubt expecting to let him have it with one of my smartass retorts.

"Th-thank you," I breathe, drawing in another breath. "This is incredibly thoughtful and has made me so, so happy."

His ember irises meet my gaze over his shoulder, his back relaxing with my words. "You're very welcome, Bella," he mutters softly and exits my office.

I wish he'd stay. I want to hug him tightly for this and perhaps kiss him; he deserves a meaningful token of affection for a gesture like this. Nothing I can say will convey what this gift means to me, and the fact that he thought of it speaks volumes. He pays attention and eventually someday I want a man who notices the little things. I think in the end, it'll make a huge difference in our lives.

Staring down at the ticket again, all I can think of is that the other day in the alley is forgiven and forgotten. There's no argument about it; the anger has completely vanished. I've never believed that I could be bought, but he hit me straight in my heart. In the end, I'll either love him or hate him, because I have a feeling this is merely the beginning for us.

Chapter 6

Be careful who you call your friends.
I'd rather have four quarters
Than one hundred pennies.
-Al Capone

Grace

Day Number Nine...

"Hey, Keisha," I greet the next morning as I come into the office.

"Oh, Grace, I wanted to talk to you yesterday before you left, but everyone had me reconfirming weekly appointments and updating their calendars. I got distracted, but it's important, if you don't mind."

"You juggle us all well," I respond and chuckle. She's one hell of a secretary/receptionist to us all. "You know I always have time for you; what's up?"

"Thanks. So, about yesterday—" she starts and I interrupt.

"No worries, I knew who he was and I wasn't busy. It's fine, really."

"Good, but—"

I cut her off again, not to be rude, but because I'm excited. "He sent a car for me today. It was the ninth surprise. It wasn't just any car either; it was a beautiful BMW. I've never ridden in such a nice car, even my mom's Lincoln doesn't compare to it."

"That's great, but do you really know who he is?"

"Yes, I know him. Why, are you familiar with who he is?"

She nods with the same worried look Kaleigh first gave me at the restaurant when Thaddaeus showed up. I'm not in the mood for more lectures from people who have no clue what he's really like. He's been kind to me—spoiling me and showing me he cares in all types of ways. I find it hard to believe that he's as evil as everyone claims he is.

"Are you going to warn me off him? Because trust me, Kaleigh's already done that." I refrain from rolling my eyes, but the urge is strong.

"No, not necessarily. I was just curious if you knew him and what he's all about, is all."

"I mean, I know 'of him.' I've heard rumors and then I saw online where he was in the papers and at court a lot." No use sugarcoating it.

"And none of it bothered you? Not even a little bit?"

"Well, of course, it's disturbing to read and to hear that stuff, but surely it can't all be true or he'd be in jail. Plus, he's been nothing but kind to me."

She draws in a breath, chewing on her bottom lip for a moment before continuing. "It's absolutely all true and for your well-being, it's in your best interest to believe everything you hear. Trust me, please. I'm not trying to step on your toes, but he's not a good man, Grace. However, for some reason he seems to be taken with you. I don't know if that's a bad thing or if it's incredible that he's letting someone new in his group."

"Do you have proof of any of it? How is it that everyone has these horrible opinions of him, yet I've not seen it? He seems a little dangerous, definitely, but that isn't always a bad thing."

"As a matter a fact I do; I actually know all about him. I'm going to share something with you—between us—since we're friends, okay?"

I nod, not sure if I'm ready to hear this or not.

"Okay, so, I dated a guy back in high school who got mixed up in Joker's business." Her eyebrows rise. "That's his name, if you didn't know, and it suits him." She visibly shivers a little.

"Yeah, I know that's what some call him." He's smirked and grinned at me, so the rumor that he never smiles isn't true.

"Well, you know his boys that are always with him?"

"I've seen them."

"They run everything for him pretty much and Joker oversees it all. He's related to half of the Italian Mafia in Chicago. He's, I guess you'd call him their 'street guy' in a sense. Any issues that Joker can't take care of, the Mafia Boss steps in and handles it. But as I'm sure you've seen with the papers and articles published online about him, he does a decent job of running the streets. This way it looks like the gangs are doing all the damage, when, in reality, it's the Mafia behind everything—money laundering, sex trade, drugs, stolen cars, you name it."

"And this guy that worked for him, you're not with him anymore?"

"No, he's gone. Joker's buddy—Maximillian Macintosh—is in charge of drug distribution. He's the one that had my boyfriend killed. They'd never admit to it, but I know that's what happened. There's no way that Denzel would've up and left me out of the blue, he wasn't like that. He was pretty open to me about everything they were having him do, so I'd put my money on them killing him any day."

"Did you ever ask any of them about it or if they knew where your boyfriend was?"

"Hell no! You cross Joker in this city and it's not pretty. He may not kill you but he'll make sure that life isn't easy for you. He'll take your job, your car, your home, and anything else you might need or care for. I've heard of men missing their hands and tongues for messing with him. I grieved at home and minded my own business. If you get serious with him, you'll learn that's what a girlfriend or wife does in that lifestyle."

"What did your boyfriend do for them, exactly?"

"I'll be honest, I don't tell people about any of this stuff, but you need to know what you're getting into. Denzel was a drug runner for Maximillian. He'd fly all over the world and smuggle drugs back into the city for them to cut and distribute. How do you think they can afford to be dressed like that and drive around in exotic vehicles? Joker's got his hands in everything in this city."

I don't want to upset Keisha, but that right there is most likely what got her boyfriend killed. He could've been murdered in another country and she'd have never known. Am I really justifying things so Thaddaeus doesn't seem so immoral? It looks like it, but I've seen a different side of him than what everyone else has, and I don't like to judge someone without seeing it with my own eyes.

But that would explain how at his young age he has a ton of money. I'd guess him to be mid-thirties. That's plenty of time for him to have built a decent career or to have become a big-time criminal, I suppose. Too bad he chose the latter.

"I'm sorry you went through that, Keisha." And I am. It had to be heartbreaking and scary to experience that, but I'm not planning on going through anything like she did. I'm also not planning on cutting Thaddaeus off dry. I'm already invested in this weird nonrelationship.

"Hey, don't you worry about me; that was many years ago. I've moved forward and grown. If you want to date him, I'm not one to try to stand in your way. The heart wants what the heart wants, just please be careful. That's all I'm saying."

"Thanks, I will. I'm glad Kaleigh wasn't here for lunch when he stopped by or she would've freaked out. Oh, do you mind keeping this between us? I don't want the office to know and then me end up losing my job or anything. Not that it would happen, but just in case. I'd rather keep my personal life out of their sights if you know what I mean."

"Yeah, I get it. You have my silence girl, don't worry."

"Thank you." I send her a grateful smile and head to my office.

Am I crazy for not believing all the evidence? *Probably.* Do I care? *Not at this point.* Seeing him yesterday was like a nail in the coffin.

I want him, even if he's not so sweet to everyone else. Guess that makes me selfish and stubborn. So be it.

Thaddaeus

"You're not concerned that someone saw you go into her work yesterday?" Max asks.

Cage and another friend of mine, Dillion, sit with us around a table in a quaint restaurant. It's one that a distant cousin of mine owns, so we like to give them our business during their slow hours.

Shrugging, I slice my steak up some more, into bite-sized pieces. "No one has any idea who she is. That's another reason why I'm interested in her. If anybody saw me, then they'd think I was heading into the marketing business to most likely speak with the owner not an employee." I've thought about it a hundred times, before walking into that building and then afterwards as well. I don't want anything coming back on her because of my associates or me. Benny watched the building, looking for any threats and he didn't notice anyone. He's good at catching people so I'm not too concerned.

"Right," Maximillian replies, ogling one of the young waitresses busily cleaning her section.

Dillion pipes up, "So, guess we'll know if her Boss turns up dead then, huh?"

That's one way to think of it, but he's right. As long as it's not her, that's all I care about.

"Can we trust her?" Cage probes.

"We'll find out soon enough. I'm taking her to dinner this week."

At least I hope I am. I damn sure have been planning on it the past few days, especially after the little run-in we had in her office. Christ, she had my cock so fucking hard. Her cheeks flushed and the stuttering—getting her words tangled up whenever she'd try to respond. I've never wanted to clear a desk off so badly and fuck on top of it before, like I did watching her squirm in her seat.

That draws Max's attention from the waitress, "Wait, you asked her to dinner, already?"

"No, I was going to wait but she brought up us having lunch together yesterday when I stopped by her office. She knows some of my intentions."

Dillion mumbles, "Bet she doesn't know that you're planning long-term though."

"Let me worry about Grace. You take care of business and everything else will run like it's supposed to."

Day Number Ten

Bella: Diamonds?!

Gazing down at the text she sent me from this morning, I still haven't replied. What should I say? Yes, I sent her diamonds. She's lucky I'm a patient man or those diamonds would be on her left ring finger already. I could've had her kidnapped and gotten a priest to marry us in no time flat if I wanted to do it my way. I haven't even kissed this woman yet and I want her to belong to me. I've gotten what I've wanted for so long now, it's driving me crazy inside to wait and have her come around to the idea.

According to my grandfather, when I find the woman that I think may be the one—really the one—then I have to court her before anything else can happen. I don't think that's how it should be done, all this wasting time when she could be mine already. She may not like my way, but at least she'd have my last name already.

Today's the tenth day of my grandfather's courting period. It's the tenth day of me watching her, the tenth day of me wanting her, and the tenth day of me waiting—not so patiently.

I'm done.

Tonight I'm taking her to dinner if she'll agree and if she doesn't, I may just fucking burst.

Me: Dinner, tonight?

Bella: Thought you'd never ask.

Me: Is that a yes?

Bella: That's definitely a yes. Thank you for the bracelet.

Me: You're very welcome. Wear it tonight. I'll pick you up.

Bella: Okay. What time?

Me: Seven p.m.

That went over way easier than I'd expected. I figured she give me a glimpse of that fire inside, making me work for it. The ticket must've shown her that I'm serious. I'm not wasting my time with her and I won't be put off that easily.

Now what the hell do I keep busy with for the next three hours? If she wasn't at work, I would've said sooner but I'm sure she'll want time to go home and freshen up. Hopefully she has on those sexy-ass heels I sent her. I want to see her in them and nothing else—just her flesh and stilettos. Her stunning body laid out on my white silk sheets, completely bared and waiting for me.

"Hey, Joker, we found the guy who's been tagging up the fight pit." Cage comes into my office, not bothering to knock. I clear my throat, pushing the thoughts of Grace to the back of my mind.

We have a pit under one of the old buildings downtown that we use to host illegal fights. It's a risk having so many people stuffed into a building that's been long closed down, but it brings in a lot of cash and in this business, money talks. Lately someone's been spraying graffiti everywhere and I've been having Cage re-paint the place each week. It's a stupid expense and I've grown sick of messing with it. I knew once I put money on the culprit's head, that he'd magically show up.

"Oh yeah? Where is he then?"

"That's the surprising part. It's not a he, but a she. It's some young, tree hugger chick. She thought we were using the place to run drugs and build bombs so she was trying to protest. I explained to her that it's only used for fighting and she promises to stop."

"Tell me you're kidding. Did you at least bring me her hands as payment?"

"No, that's the truth; that's all that happened."

Evidently, he was thinking with his fucking cock.

"You told her we use it for illegal fighting and gambling and you just expect her to mosey on with her life, not spitting out a word about it to anyone? Are you a fucking idiot suddenly?"

"I know it sounds crazy, but for some reason I believe her."

"And you're fucking slow too? What in the hell am I hearing right now?" My voice rises slightly. "You know what? You go rough her up, if she talks; you let her know she'll get a bullet to the brain. I'm not fucking around with people destroying my shit."

"I know where she lives, works, everything; she won't say anything, I'm sure of it."

"You better be willing to put your own money on that, so help me, I'll kill her myself and you won't like the outcome if that happens. I didn't realize you'd turned so pathetic recently."

"Me, really? What about you? You've been pining after some uppity bitch for nearly two weeks. I don't see you going out and taking care of business like you preach."

"That 'uppity bitch' is going to be mine, just wait and see. And don't speak about her like that, she'll be sitting beside me before you know it and you'll damn sure show her the respect she deserves being my woman. You're my friend, but I won't hesitate to throw you out on your ass if need be. You can run in the streets like a fucking mangy rat. You forget how comfortable you've grown living the 'uppity' lifestyle."

"Right, some friendship we have here. She's been in your life for two minutes. Me—ten years—and this is how you treat me."

"Yeah ten years and you can be gone in five minutes. I plan to have her around for the rest of my life. Now get on board or find another place to live. I don't have time for people who only want to be halfway in this business. You know the deal, since day one it's all or nothing, loyalty and sacrifice."

It's the most respectful way I can threaten him, but Cage understands the underlying message. It means either get with the program or be cast out. He'd be away from a life he's grown very accustomed too. Cage's the last person I expected to hear a tantrum from anyhow.

With Max, I knew it would happen right away; he's jealous and always has been. He likes the bulk of my attention and it's taken years for him to not threaten anyone growing close to me.

The other guys? I figured they'd give me a little grief over Grace. After all, she is an outsider and isn't in this lifestyle, but this whiny shit that Cage is pulling—no fucking way. I won't tolerate it. They have to know it right away too, so they quit their shit. Sometimes I feel like I'm dealing with a group of twelve-year-olds going through puberty when it comes to them having a piece of my attention.

I work with some of the most notorious and ruthless criminals, and to have someone soft this close to me is a red flag. I've seen Cage beat a man to death with his fists. I would've more likely expected him to carry the graffiti chick's hands in here—bloody and all—before throwing his jealous fit over the woman who's quickly become my newfound obsession.

I don't know what it is about Grace either, but a piece inside me must have her. If she asked me to slit twenty men's throats, my friends included, I wouldn't hesitate to do it for her. That's what they should really fear. I don't hold all the power any longer, she does. In a matter of days, she's grown to consume most of my thoughts. It can't be healthy to think about someone so abundantly, but then there's nothing healthy about this lifestyle.

If I were a Boss, I'd sit at the head of the table and gladly let her sit on my lap, that's how much control she holds in the palm of her hand; she just doesn't know it yet. I hope she never realizes it, for it could easily be the death of me. I'm already taking a risk by bringing her into my circle, then to hand over so much influence to her as well. It could really fuck things up around here.

Luckily, I'm not a Boss, and according to the streets, I'm not a thug either. The rumors and papers paint me as being a gangster. Yes, there's a difference between that and a mobster in my world.

A piece of trash thug does as he's told, robbing small time and taking whatever handout he can get. A gangster takes care of his business and people know to fear him. I'm not the one to commit petty theft. I'm the one who'd take your entire familia outside into your yard and shoot them in the back of the head if I had to-to survive or keep them quiet. A mobster belongs to the Mafia; he does their bidding. I belong to no one and do my own.

I need a woman who can love and stand next to a man as hard as me. I need someone who isn't scared to pull that trigger to protect me if it came down to it. Grace showed me a fire deep inside her from the moment we first met, and it's given me hope that she could be the one for me—the Bonnie to my Clyde.

I'll find out soon enough if she can handle my life and if she can be my ride-or-die chick. If she shows me that she's the one, she'll have my loyalty for life. I'll love her with every breath that I have. I know it's soon, but I feel it in my soul each time I look at her, that she's meant to be mine, that she's the one. I'm not used to being wrong; it's one of the many reasons why I'm where I am today.

Are my feelings sudden? Yes. Do I give two shits about a lengthy enough timeline? Not in the slightest. I'll fuck her tonight at dinner if she lets me. I'd also gladly marry her ass tonight if she'd say 'I do.' I'm a bit traditional in the sense that I don't need to be in love with someone to make that commitment; I know our union could grow into it eventually. I'm more concerned on if she's a good fit. The men are right, I can't look weak so the right woman is imperative.

Chapter 7

Count your nights by stars,
not shadows; count your
life with smiles, not tears.
-Italian Proverb

Grace

Seven p.m. rolled around and Thaddaeus was at my apartment five minutes early. I love it that he was prompt, because I can't stand being late and that goes for other people as well. Going off Thaddaeus' usual attire of pristine business suits, I decided on a long, classy evening gown.

I'm glad I did, because I think it's more appropriate for the evening. It's not necessarily the place he takes me, but more of the fact that he's made sure we're the only guests in the entire restaurant.

The intimate dining area is dimly lit throughout with multiple sparkling chandeliers and small votive candles on each table casting a warm, welcoming glow throughout. There are ten square tables; each fully dressed in thick white linen tablecloths with black napkins, and one set with shiny silverware and crystal wineglasses. The place is set up for exclusive customers only to give them the ultimate dining experience.

I'm a little floored with how much thought he put into this, but then maybe I shouldn't be. He obviously knows what he's doing when it comes to wowing a woman. Makes me wonder how on earth he isn't already snatched up.

"So, what do you think?" Thaddaeus asks after helping me scoot in my chair and taking a seat in the chair directly across from me. He seems eager as he gazes at me expectantly. He wants my approval and it's adorable.

"Very romantic and I'm floored you've reserved the entire restaurant. The driver was cool, too, and your car is amazing." I could stammer on all night about how excited I am. The date's merely begun and it's already exceeded my expectations.

He shrugs. "I wanted to take you out, but also be alone with you as well. I'm selfish."

"Well, mission accomplished," I mutter, and then grin at my small outburst. He has this effect on me everywhere it seems, this habit of making me babble whatever's on my mind out loud or come off rudely from nerves.

"You wore your new shoes." His gold gaze regards me, observing every detail as he takes me in. He always notices small details about me and it's a bit flattering and unnerving all at the same time. I feel like I can't get anything past him, but do I want to? I enjoy him calling me out like he does; it keeps me on my toes.

"I did. They're my new favorites, I love them."

"I'll buy you a pair for each day then," he gushes, clearly loving the fact that he can spoil me. His comment has me blushing. He's never low-key, completely over-the-top with everything and I don't know how to react to it. I don't want to come off as ungrateful, but I also don't want him thinking the only reason why I'm here is so he'll buy me nice things.

"No."

"Really? You're telling me no?"

"I'm telling you no."

Delight lights his eyes as his lips turn up in a barely-there smirk. Others might not notice it, but I can't stop staring at him, so I see everything he does. He snaps his finger in the air and a server rushes over. He never takes his eyes away from me and it makes my stomach flutter excitedly.

"Sir?"

"Bring us the black forest cheesecake and the best red wine you have in house for my date. I'll have your top-shelf scotch."

"Very good, sir." The waiter scurries away.

"You surprise me." My cheeks will be sore by the end of the evening at this rate. His actions have me smiling nonstop. The evening's merely begun and I'm already happy that I decided to come out with him.

"I've only begun."

"If I knew we were having dessert and drinks, I'd have eaten a salad before you picked me up." I'd have preferred to eat a bowl of pasta but this dress shows everything and tonight I want to look perfect for him.

"Oh, Bella, we'll eat, but I wanted you to have a taste of what I'll be eating off of you later."

My throat grows tight and I have to swallow several times and take a sip of my water before I can reply. "You're quite confident that I'll agree." My body's already heating up just from hearing him say the words alone. My mind silently chants, *I agree, I agree, I agree*. I don't let it show on the outside, though; I must appear somewhat mysterious.

"You'll allow it; in fact, you'll be begging for it."

I love it when a man knows what he wants but can't help my eyes rolling at his over confidence. The waiter sets a generous serving of cheesecake between us, topped with cherries and chocolate cake crumbles. It looks divine. I'm starving, and when my stomach growls I go to swipe a little drop of cherry topping with my finger.

Thaddaeus' hand darts out, snatching mine before it makes it to the expertly decorated chocolate swirls on the plate. His grip's strong and controlling, but not punishing. He's the only man I've met that can be forceful but not hurt me. If anything, his movement makes the heat in my belly flare up another notch. I like this side of him. I enjoy pushing him.

Gasping quietly, my eyes fly to his stormy irises and hold his stare as he moves my hand until he can dip my finger into the dessert. Scooping up a chunk on my finger, he holds fast, leaning over and bringing the sweet treat to his mouth.

I'm pretty sure I'd fall out of my chair if he wasn't holding me so tightly. The man makes me freaking melt.

"Not so fast, my Bella. Manners." He tsks and places my finger inside his warm, wet mouth. His tongue swirls around my fingertip, my nipples hardening at the amazing sensations his tongue's inflicting. He sucks for a moment before drawing my hand away, pausing briefly to swipe his tongue up the side of it.

My throat's grown dry again, and at this rate, I'm going to be peeing every hour from having to chug copious amounts of water to keep up with him. Fuck me, he's hot. No, sinful is a better word for him.

As he licks my finger, my legs clamp closed, my core nearly vibrating as I deftly watch him kiss my finger. It's sexy as fuck. It's naughty and I want his tongue to lick me like that everywhere.

"Now that I've tested it, you may have a bite." He hands me a small dessert fork loaded with a generous sized bite and I count silently to ten so I don't attack the sugary piece of heaven, wanting to know what his mouth tastes like right now. I wish he'd just lean over and let me sample it from his tongue.

"Mmmmm." Moaning, the sweet decadence slides over my taste buds, nearly orgasmic in itself.

This is what he was just licking off me. This is what his mouth tastes like this very moment, and shit if I don't want that sinful set of lips on mine right now. Imagining his tongue tangling with mine has me groaning while my eyes stay tightly closed. I've never been so wanton and out of control of my sexuality before him, but Thaddaeus has complete control of everything tonight. I hope he doesn't realize that or I could be naked on this table before the evening's over.

Would that be such a bad thing, though?

"Grace, stop it."

"Hm?" My eyebrow shoots up as I chew slowly, swiping my tongue over my lips and enjoying each and every flavor of the cheesecake.

"You, moaning over that," he gestures to the plate between us, "has me wanting you right here. I'm not a man of self-control. I suggest you stop it before I smear it over you and eat it all myself."

Add mind reader to his list of qualities. He reads me so easily and it's unnerving. This is a man that I won't be able to fool with anything or push around. This man is alpha to the fullest power.

His threat shuts me up instantly. I want it, boy do I want it, but not in the middle of a restaurant and I have a feeling he's just crazy enough to hold up his warning.

He throws the scotch back in one large gulp and signals for the waiter again. His eyes have flames dancing in them as his nostrils flare, staring me down, hungry with his own need.

"Sir?"

"Another scotch and bring us whatever the chef's making this evening. Make sure it doesn't have onions."

"Yes, sir, right away."

"I thought we were having dessert for now?"

"We need to hurry up and eat so we can get out of here."

"Already? But we just got here."

His jaw clenches and flexes as he looks me over, taking a moment longer to gaze at my breasts. They're swollen from the pheromones churning between us, making me feel naked under his observation. "Yes, but after that little taste, I can't stop wanting you and I know you wouldn't be keen on me taking you over the table. Or would you, Bella? I can make that happen, you know; same with your office."

"You can't just say stuff like that!"

"Why not?"

"Because, you don't just come out and mention things like that on your first date with someone."

"I say whatever I want. And, I mean what I say. Would you prefer if I lied or held back?"

"Well no, but yes, I mean … shit. Most people fib or tone it down for a while in the beginning."

"I'm not most people, Grace; you haven't caught on to that yet?"

"I've noticed, believe me."

"Then it shouldn't surprise you in the least bit. This doesn't feel as if it were our first. We're already past that. I don't screw off when it comes to something that I want. And let me make myself very clear here; I want you. I'm not one to pussyfoot around."

I keep my thoughts to myself and sip the red wine. It's crisp and delicious, pairing wonderfully with the sweetness from the cheesecake. I was starving when we got here, but Thaddaeus' words have my heart racing and my stomach doing cartwheels. His proclamation makes sense though. After the last week and a half, I feel like we're past the first date jitters as well. At this point, he wants me to be his, and I want to be. It's strange, though How can you feel connected and want someone so badly when you hardly know them? It's almost on a primal level, our bodies seeking each other out. He's a headstrong male and I'm a woman in her prime. It's basic biology, our being drawn to one another.

Our food should be out soon and the only other thing on my mind besides him eating cake off my body is the conversation we'd had about him sharing the meanings of each gift with me. That was supposed to be the initial purpose of us having dinner anyhow. Should I bring it up?

The waiter sets a basket of fresh rolls on the table wrapped in a heavy towel to keep them warm and brings Thaddaeus a new scotch. "More wine, miss?"

"No, thank you."

"Is it not to your liking? I can bring another selection for you to sample."

"It's amazing, but I'd rather wait for dinner." It's probably the most delicious glass of red I've ever had. If I were at home, I'd be pouring a hefty serving, but around this domineering man, I need as many of my wits about me as possible. I can barely keep up with him while sober; I can only imagine it in a wine daze.

"Very good then, I'll get your entrees now."

The man's like a magician, appearing with food left and right. The perks no doubt of having a chef here who's only worry is to prepare our dishes and no one else's. No wonder this place gets booked out completely.

Mere moments later, it seems, and he's back with our plates. Medium-sized, white square dishes all understated so the focus is on the food itself. Strategically arranged in the middle is a small salad made up mostly of spinach and other vegetables cut into thin spirals and tossed in a light lemony dressing. For being a salad, it looks delightful and the lemon smell reminds me of sweet lemon cookies coated in powdered sugar. God, I could eat an entire box of those cookies.

Taking a few bites, I wash it down with my red and softly clear my throat.

"So, you had mentioned that the gifts you sent—which I loved, by the way—each had a particular meaning. Would you mind sharing them with me?"

He finishes his own bite, wiping his already clean mouth with his linen napkin and places it beside his dish before sitting back in his seat. "They do. I notice you wore your bracelet too." He glances to my wrist and I smile, nodding.

"Yes, it's exquisite."

His mouth quirks into a slight smirk, his eyes light at my appreciation. It happens each time I praise something that has to do with him. I'm beginning to believe that Kaleigh's wrong about him never smiling. If anything, I'd bet that Joker got his name from wearing a smirk frequently. He may not share it with the world, but he doesn't seem to mind showing it off to me.

"I'm glad you approve. The first gift was simply because I wanted you to have something beautiful. I'd seen you that day at the restaurant and your beauty was enrapturing. I couldn't get you out of my mind and I had to do something about it, had to figure out a way to show you even a hint of the stunning perfection I'd witnessed."

Holy shit! I was not expecting an answer like that. He's going to earn some serious brownie points already. "Wow, thank you! They were my favorite colors, too; did you know that?"

"No. I picked them because of what you were wearing; you made those colors stand out."

I made them stand out, not the other way around. Jesus Christ, this man. Finishing the small portion of salad remaining, I press on. "And the purse?"

"Ah, the sapphire Chanel bag. That one was easy too. I wanted to spoil you and show you that I plan to spoil you in the future as well."

"Call me spoiled, but not rotten, I promise." My smile's wide, but I can't help it; he just admitted to me that he thinks I'm stunning and he wants to spoil me. He must hide dead people in his walls or something to say such perfect things like that.

The server collects our empty plates and brings us fresh ice water.

Without skipping a beat, he continues. "And the third, the strawberry-cream cheese muffins. They're my favorite. An uncle of mine owns the bakery they're from and I wanted to send you a treat. The meaning behind them is that I wanted to feed you, to break bread and let you know that you will never go hungry on my watch."

Out of the past few compliments, this explanation starts to get me choked up. Promising to feed someone has nothing to do with being materialistic. It's about providing a basic need that another human being needs to survive. His words come out earnestly, and the fact that he wanted to break bread with me, shows that he wants a relationship, not some quick tussle. You break bread with friends, family, loved ones. He wants that with me?

I take a gulp of my wine, cause let's face it, a sip isn't going to do after that. "They were delicious and very thoughtful." I caught Keisha trying to sneak out with the basket at the end of the day too. She loved them as much as I did.

"I'm glad you enjoyed them." He copies me, taking a hefty gulp of his scotch.

Our next course is delivered, the aromas of rosemary and garlic with lobster and filet mignon making my mouth water as the dishes are set in front of us.

"This looks wonderful."

There's a generous sized lobster with six ounces of perfectly grilled meat. Off to the side is bright green broccoli and a few baby red potatoes. It's the last thing I'd expect to be served. I was thinking snails or something crazy. This is perfect. I love it all. "Wow," I can't help but mumble as I cut into the meat, and it's so tender I could probably use my fork alone. It was definitely marinated in something to make it that way and cooked to perfection.

"I love the food here."

"I can see why." I chew and swallow a bite, ready to hear more. "What about the music box?"

"Ah, the fourth gift," he replies, his gaze running over me as I smile, excited to hear about it.

"Its purpose was to enrich your life in some small way."

"The colors were so vibrant and it came from Italy?"

"This whole courting process is something that my grandfather insists on. I put a lot of thought into it all and I wanted you to have something authentic from the country that my family's from. It's also an Italian gift that's given frequently when courting a woman. I picked the blue because it reminded me of your sapphires. I had it hand made because you deserve the best."

At this rate my panties will be sliding down my legs on their own. How on earth did a man like this come into my life? I must've done something right in another life, that's for damn sure.

"And the song?"

"You know what I am."

"A very generous man?"

"A very dangerous one."

Hearing it come directly from his mouth has me swallowing a bit roughly, so I toss back a decent sized drink of my wine. I need something to dull the implications of his last statement. So, he's not perfect after all, but when it comes down to it, who is? I'm not; I'm far from it.

"Does that bother you? Knowing that people fear me?"

"In some ways, yes."

"I sense a 'but' with that statement."

"But I'm not frightened of you."

"No? Not even after I had you slammed up against a building in a dark alleyway? I remember hearing you cry and feeling your pulse go out of control when my nose grazed the skin over your artery."

Why's he being this way suddenly? Does he want me to fear him? He's going to ruin an amazing evening quickly talking about this.

"You weren't very kind that night. Had I known it was you—"

He interrupts, his eyes growing hard. "You would've what? Fought me? Please," he scoffs. "You couldn't move, I didn't allow it. You were careless."

"I was just walking home," I say defensively, not sure if I should be pissed off or sad with his sudden mood change, "What's your deal with it?"

"My deal? Shocking, but I'd like to have the actual chance to spend time with you, but as I stated prior, I'm not a very good man. There are plenty of people who want me dead or anything I care about taken from me."

"And you care about me?"

"It's soon, but yes. I find myself thinking about you daily and imagining what it's like to lay next to you at night. Your honesty is refreshing. Your fearlessness is sexy, but also a touch naïve. If I want you in my life, then I have to teach you to be more vigilant."

I don't know what to say. He's mean and then says sweet things, just like that night. He was so rough and cold, and then he sent me something to protect myself with the next day, the fifth day of our courtship.

"So, the knife?"

"It was for protection. I will always protect you. That I promise."

"What about yourself?"

He shrugs. "One day, I hope, if it ever came down to it, you'd decide to protect me, if necessary. Don't fret over it though; I have my boys if we need them. My driver you met, being one of them."

I don't want to think about anyone hurting him. It's so strange to grow attached to someone already and be worried for their safety. He has real threats. If he's indeed that bad, who knows the types of people he deals with. Maybe it's a good thing I've decided to carry the knife on me at all times now.

Would I protect him if it came down to it? I don't think I'd be much help, but I would do my best to not let someone hurt him. Would I put my life in front of his? Something inside says he'd do it for me, but I'm not quite there yet. That sounds horrible and shallow, but it's the truth, self-preservation and all that.

"I don't know if I'd be much help." And suddenly that thought has me wanting to change that. I want to be able to protect him if needed.

"Tell me, if someone were to try and kill me, and you had a gun in your hand … would you shoot them to save me?"

"Of course," I answer immediately, barely thinking of any repercussions that could come from it. I'd do the same for myself or any of my friends if their life was in danger. Just because I'm a woman doesn't mean that I'm weak. It just means I love a little more than some and have a few more curves. The need to protect and survive still fills my veins.

"That's all that I need to know then." He lifts my hand to his lips and presses a soft kiss to my palm. It tickles and ignites a new tirade of flutters in my stomach. His lips are soft, and the scruff from his five o'clock shadow scratches lightly against my skin. Thoughts of that feeling touching me everywhere fill my head.

We finish our filet and lobster, momentarily making small talk while the server clears away the empty plates and brings us fresh drinks. I know we've been here for at least an hour's time, but I couldn't care less. The romantic atmosphere from the low lighting, the cool, crisp wine, and delicious food has me wanting to stay longer. My body's content and with Thaddaeus as my date, my mind has stayed enraptured with him.

"We should go soon, unless you'd like more dessert?"

"The cheesecake was divine, but I'm too full right now."

"I'll get some to take with us then."

"That would be amazing."

Smiling, I finish off the new glass of wine and collect my things. Thaddaeus gets a full cheesecake to go, and when I laugh about it, he plays it off that his friends will eat whatever we don't. I was secretly hoping he'd hold true to his earlier promise and was getting the cake so he could eat more of it later—off me.

I loved the wine so much, the server sent me home with a

bottle of that as well. We never received a bill on our way out; they must really like my date or something …

Chapter 8

Live, Love, Laugh.
If that doesn't work,
Load, Aim, and Fire.
- @theclassypeople

Thaddaeus

We arrive at Grace's apartment, and I'm taken off guard when she invites me up. I was trying to keep dinner short so she wasn't too uncomfortable, it being our first official date and all. The scotch was going down slightly too smoothly around her. Generally, I find it hard to trust people, even familia, but she makes it easy. I don't know what it is about her that causes me to relax and feel as if I can tell her anything. It's dangerous and before she becomes mine completely, I need to watch what comes out of my mouth.

She sets the cheesecake in the fridge and the wine on the kitchen counter. Her place is neat and tidy, no clutter. I prefer my house be kept the same, I'm glad to see we have more than sex appeal in common.

"Would you care for a glass?"

Wine's not my thing normally, but for her, I'd probably drink bleach if she asked.

"I'd love one. Would you like some help with your coat?"

It's the one I purchased for her and I must admit it fits her well. She's ridiculously beautiful tonight, clad in such a striking gown. It's elegant and classy with its length and solid color, but her curves turn it into a thing that fantasies are made of.

"Oh, yes, please." She turns, giving me her back.

I can't refrain from running my hands up her biceps until they're resting on her shoulders. Her muscles stiffen slightly with the contact and I take it as a sign to concentrate on the coat and not on touching her. If I don't move my hands, I'll be trying to peel more than just that one item off.

She's so feminine compared to my build. She's all woman and I'm all man and fuck if it doesn't do things to me. I'm beginning to wonder if I'll always have a chub when I'm near her. I'm in a constant state of arousal when I'm around her and I need to figure out some way to stop being so affected by my cock when it comes to Grace.

"Where do I hang it?"

"Behind the entry door, please."

Doing as I'm told, I hang up the coat. I breeze over the few photos on her small sofa table she has up against the wall as an entry table where her coat now hangs. There's a photo of an older woman who resembles Grace, definitely her mother. Two other frames with her and a few women her age, most likely friends of hers. My guy did a background check and said she's an only child with a close relationship to her mom and only has a few friends.

Her apartment's tiny, probably the size of my sitting room and bar at my own home. It's cozy though and girlie—a lot like her.

"Wine?" Grace holds a glass out and I join her back in the miniscule kitchen. She peers up at me, waiting for me to grab it from her. Her face is tilted in just the right position, her lips nearly begging for me to take a sample. I could do so many things to her in this kitchen that'd make her never look at it the same way again.

One hand resting lightly on her hip, the other cupping her jaw, I chastely press my lips to hers, unable to hold myself back. If I go any deeper into the kiss, I'll end up fucking her right here on the kitchen floor and while that sounds rather enticing, she deserves someplace softer the first time I take her.

Pulling back, her eyes are closed tightly with her chest pushed out just a touch, and so help me, I want to brush against her breasts. I don't do it, but it takes hellacious self-restraint to refrain. Brushing my mouth against hers once more, the kiss is tender and needy, but once I feel her frame lean into me a bit more, I pull away. I must practice some self-control with her.

"Shall we sit?" she asks, and I feel like a putz, standing around while she waits on me.

"Yes, in here or?" I gesture toward the living room.

"The couch."

"Okay." Following her, she sits first and in doing so, I make sure to sit close enough that her thigh brushes my own when I turn a little so I can lean back and face her.

"So, my phone..." she trails off.

"Did you need to make a call?"

"Oh no, I was referring to the sixth day."

"Shit, right. The cell phone I sent; it was so you'd always be able to reach me if you ever need to."

She nods, pushing her shiny golden locks over her shoulder. *I love her hair.*

"The seventh day—the coat was to keep you warm when I'm not around."

Her cheeks tint, knowing I mean it literally and sexually.

"It's like silk inside and is definitely warm. I love it."

"Good." Two fingers on my left hand gently stroke the top of her shoulder. Her neck is so damn sexy and with her hair pushed to the side, it's on full display. "It's getting late, should I go?"

"No!" Grace practically shouts, making my mouth tilt up slightly. She wants me here. "Tell me why you sent a car on the eighth day ... please."

"It was a chilly morning and I wanted to take care of you."

"That was so thoughtful, thank you."

I nod. She has no idea just how much I want to take care of her though. Not only by giving her a ride to work each day, but in every other way as well.

"Not just then, I'll always take care of you. For as long as you're with me."

"Why?"

"Because, you mean something to me and I want to."

"But how, Thaddaeus? We don't really know each other. How can I mean anything to you, besides just being a woman who wasn't frightened when you came into the restaurant that day?"

"I don't have to know you for years on end. I gazed down at you, and I knew you needed to be mine."

"Yours?" she asks, taking a hefty gulp of her wine, and I nod, running my eyes over every curve of hers and they're plentiful. She's enticing with her thick thighs and plump lips.

She sets the goblet on the glass top of the coffee table and I follow suit. Once Grace sits back, I yank her to me, tired of holding off. She needs to be kissed something fierce. Maybe then she'll understand the strength of the chemistry I feel whenever I think of her or look at her.

With a gasp, she falls into me, exactly where she belongs and my mouth lands on hers, not giving her a second to think twice about it. One hand holds her wrist tightly while the other tangles into her gorgeous, sunshine-colored hair. It's so damn soft that I grip it firmly, holding her in place as my tongue curls around hers. Back and forth, my lips perform their own silent confession of sorts. Her mouth is hot and wet and so, so giving.

After thoroughly kissing her to the point I know she's going to be feeling tender from my scruffy face, I pull back. My motions are slow, not wanting to completely redden the delicate skin around her lips, just enough to leave a memory. Each time her lips or fingers feather over that spot, I want her to think of me, and remember who was kissing her tonight.

A soft moan escapes as I gently suck and nip at her bottom lip, wanting to be easy with her, but at the same time feeling the urge to ravage her entirely. She's exquisite, her tongue cool with just a touch of tartness from the wine.

"You keep making sweet sounds like that and I'll have your panties off in no time." It's whispered gruffly against her lips, her eyes flashing open in surprise.

"Tell me about you, about your life," she requests out of the blue, pushing back a bit, attempting for some distance.

"No. Not yet. We'll work our way to it." I'm enjoying the feeling of her in my arms entirely too much to want to dampen it by divulging in my daunting secrets about myself.

"You can't be that evil; I don't believe it."

She has no fucking clue just how immoral I am or can be. Her precious naïveté makes me want her more as her view of me isn't yet skewed. It's unfair how much I'll taint her eventually. She'll learn in the end; I just don't want it to be right this very minute.

"If you were smart, you would heed the warnings you hear. Those rumors you've heard are very true, cara."

She shakes her head, not wanting to listen to what I'm saying. I don't know if it's the time together or if it's the wine making her so honest and open with me right now.

"Fine. Tell me what that means then."

"Cara?"

"Yes, please."

There's a few words associated with the Italian meaning, so I give her the one off the top of my head, "In English it means 'dear.'" I leave out that it can also mean beloved.

Too soon.

"Your language is so beautiful. Especially when you say words like that." She peers down at her lap and then moves on. "Let's discuss day number nine."

I nod, letting her pull away a bit so we can talk, and I won't keep kissing her instead.

"Why did you do it? It's the best gift anyone could've ever given me. How did you know?"

Benny thoroughly checked her out. He discovered a lot. I saw her bank account, her bills, and learned about her relationship with her mother. I knew she'd wish she could visit her; it's been years from what we discovered. I'm not going to let her know that tidbit, though. It may spook her to find out that we dug up whatever we could on her.

"I did it for happiness, Bella. I wanted you to be happy and to show you that I'll do my best to make *you* happy in a life with me. It won't always be that way, but I'll do everything in my power to make it so." And also, to help make up for freaking her out in the alley. I didn't frighten her to be malicious but I still felt a bit of guilt for doing it. Imagine that, me feeling guilty over someone. That's a first.

At my answer, she bends forward, placing a few sweet kisses along my jaw line eliciting a rumble from my chest at her touch.

"People have no idea the type of man you really are inside, do they?"

"Don't be fooled by my gestures, Grace." It's a low grumble, my warning sincere. I have motives. Yes, I'm spoiling her, but I'm also not planning on letting her go either. I doubt she'd be so easy about this if she knew that much.

She seems blinded by a few gifts. Is this why my grandfather practically drilled it in that I had to court the woman first? So she wouldn't see me for the man that I truly am? Is this what he did to my grandmother that made her so stubborn and determined to stand with him, not behind him? She was as strong as he was, and I never understood how she could love a man like him so devotedly.

Grace shakes off my warning. "And my bracelet?" She holds her up wrist in front of us both, the light glimmering off the near flawless cut of the diamonds.

"Diamonds are for loyalty. They're supposed to last forever."

"I thought that was in a ring."

"Were you ready for a ring yesterday? Or even today?"

"No." She glances away, confirming my suspicions.

"Then the bracelet is perfect for right now."

She has no idea that I'd go out and buy her a fucking diamond ring right this minute if she'd agree to spend forever with me or that I have three sitting in my safe at home that'd work perfectly. She has no clue that I've been falling for her like some love-sick puppy since the moment I set my eyes on her.

I've never wanted to kiss a woman so badly and spank her all at once than in that moment when I set my eyes on her, snorting rudely and laughing when I'd entered that damn restaurant. She didn't cower when I faced her. She acted like I was nothing and from that moment on, I knew she was mine. That she was meant to stand beside me just as my grandmother had with my grandfather. I'm an idiot. I'm falling so hopelessly for her and yet she barely has an inkling. At this rate, I'll be the one getting hurt and it won't be from bullets and bloodshed.

The guys would most likely put a round or two in my head if they knew just how weak I've become when it comes to her, or worse, they'd put a few bullets in hers.

"And what about love, Thaddaeus? You didn't mention anything about 'love' at all this evening."

"I can tell you that I already love that sexy little mouth of yours. That I'd love the chance to take you out of that stunning gown so I can memorize every other body part of yours that I'm sure I'll love as well."

Do I come out and say the words directly to her? No. It's too soon for that, but fuck if I won't love every inch of that silky skin covering her body or the beautiful mounds on her chest that I so badly want to lick and touch and fuck. She's not only created like a goddess, but she's smart, witty, and driven. She's everything I could ever want in a woman.

Grace stands, facing me as she's directly in front of me, her knees brushing my own.

"This dress?" She fingers the hem over her breasts, eventually reaching around to the side to unzip the fitted gown. It loosens and pools at her feet making me want to say a prayer to whichever god created her and is allowing us this very moment.

She's left in a nude strapless bra and matching flesh colored lace panties that are completely see-through. Exquisite comes to mind when I gaze at her ivory skin, my fingers itching to rip them off and have my way with her. A barely-there peach tint covers her, as she obviously hasn't been outside in a bathing suit in quite some time, with winter in full swing, but I don't think she could possibly be anymore sexier than in this moment.

"Jesus Christ." The Louboutin's are making her calves flex, and showcasing all her best assets. Her thighs are lightly toned, no doubt from walking everywhere. They're perfect to wrap around my waist and help hold her up when I have her naked and writhing against a wall eventually. "You're fucking exquisite, Bella."

"Better than the dress?"

It's not even a real comparison; she far outshines anything I've seen. "Hell yes. Twirl around baby and let me see you." She obeys, carefully spinning in a three sixty as I run my hands lightly over her pert ass. She must do squats daily for that ass to be so damn impeccable, Christ almighty. She belongs in a magazine being photographed wearing top-of-the-line names, not stuffed up in some bland marketing office with a tart as a Boss.

"You're absolutely amazing."

She holds her hand out and when I wrap mine around hers, she lightly pulls me to my feet. I want to yank her down on top of me, force her to ride my cock, but I hold myself back. I'll save that for another day or maybe for a little later after I've worshiped every centimeter of her body.

Once I'm standing in front of her, towering over her with my height and gazing down upon her perky tits, transfixed on one of my favorite parts of her, she places her palms against my solid pecs. "You have too many clothes on." Grace's hands run up the front of my body to my shoulders, working the material over my biceps. She doesn't have to tell me twice. I'll happily walk around naked as much as she wants. I allow her to push my jacket down the remainder of my arms, freeing me from the constricting fabric.

Resting my hands on her hips, she deftly loosens my modern cut, slim, black tie, tossing it to the couch. Her skillful fingers work over my buttons, undoing them as quickly as possible, eager to see my naked torso. She's stunning and graceful as she frees me from each button.

I lean in, licking and sucking the delicate expansion of skin along her neck. She smells so good, cashmere mixed with something else like flowers and musk. The scent making me ponder if it's what heaven smells like.

She backs up slowly and I follow along like a love-sick fool, kissing all over her shoulders with each step.

"I should go." I don't really want to, but with each stride closer, my stomach churns with a bit of guilt. I haven't really given her much of a choice, just storming into her life and demanding she give me a chance. Who's to say I even deserve one? She's nothing like me, and I think that's why I'm so drawn to her. I'm going to ruin her life with mine, yet I can't stop myself from letting the train wreck take place. In many ways, I want to ruin her. I don't want anyone else to be able to have her—only me.

"I don't want you to leave. Please stay a while," she utters, crossing the threshold into her bedroom.

"I'm not going to do this and then have you wake up tomorrow morning regretting us being together. One night with you will never be enough for me and I'm selfish. I'll keep coming around until you accept the fact that I want you and I always get what I want, Grace. Once this happens, you can't turn back time." I'll tie her up in my house if I have too. There's no escaping me once I've had my taste.

"Then stay tonight and have me again tomorrow."

Does she hear the words leaving her mouth? It's the best damn thing she's said all night. I'm hoping this is her and not the wine doing the talking.

"All night, hm?" Muttering, I kneel before her, kissing across her stomach as her hands find the nape of my neck, playing with the short hairs, tugging and winding the strands around her slender fingers making me groan.

Grace

His lips are everywhere, fluttering over my skin, making me pant faster and faster as my body gets more worked up, my core growing wetter and wetter with each caress.

It's merely been eleven days and I'm already jumping into bed with a man that I hardly know. Part of me feels like I know him better than any man I've dated in the past, while the other part thinks I'm an idiot for giving in to him this quickly. I should be much more stubborn with him, but the truth is, I don't want to be, and I don't want to play any games. I want him and I'm not going to hold myself back.

The gifts and their meanings were so thoughtful and heartfelt. I'd believed they were nothing to him, but, apparently, I was completely mistaken. Letting him have my body already should be wrong in a sense, but it feels so right in my heart.

He doesn't want to hurt me; he wants to possess me. And after our time together tonight, that doesn't seem like such a bad thing. I can imagine myself happy with him and maybe even in love with him eventually. Thaddaeus speaking of how he won't be able to get enough of me has my heart thundering, but in a purely positive way.

The dinner was incredible—beyond what I was expecting. Every little detail was planned and taken care of. I've never been on a date anywhere near as lovely and the food was unbelievable. Thaddaeus has truly thought of everything and has said some very sweet things; he's made me feel like a princess.

"Lay back, Bella," he orders and I comply, resting on my plush, black and white bedspread. The light from the tiny hallway casts just enough of a glow so I can see every gorgeous inch of Thaddaeus. I knew his body had to be magnificent and imposing under those fancy suits of his, and I was completely right. He's extraordinary.

"I pictured you having tattoos." I reach behind, freeing my breasts from my favorite strapless bra.

I hope he realizes now that there's no way I'm only calling him in an emergency. I'll be dialing him every night to hear his sexy voice whisper sweet promises to me if this is how he's going to be treating me. I thought I was hooked on him before, thinking about him day in and day out. I had no idea.

"You thought of me naked?" he mutters, his gaze transfixed on my heaving chest, my breasts slightly bouncing with my excited breaths. "Fuck." It comes out on an exhale, full of awe.

"Yes, especially when you came to my office. Each time you clenched your teeth, my pussy throbbed."

"I wanted to toss everything from your desk and lay you over it," he admits, his tongue swiping over his lower lip.

"I was thinking of it too and having you touch and lick me in … places." The heat from his breath as he nips and sucks over my hip bone has my eyes rolling back. "Yes, right down there." His grip is nearly bruising as he anchors me in place, not allowing me to squirm away.

Sliding my panties over my thighs, he doesn't hesitate, putting his nose to my core and inhaling. My cheeks must be fire engine red from his forwardness, from him worshiping me.

"I've been dreaming of how you smell." His sigh of contentment flutters over my pussy lips, making my insides clench in desperation.

"Mmmm?" I'm not capable of much talking while his scruff rubs tantalizingly between my thighs, right where I've pictured him so many times. "Dreaming?"

"Yes, of you, Bella. How your pussy tastes and how I want to make you feel." His tongue swipes from the bottom to the top of my slit, making me gasp loudly. "Keep making noises like that, sweet Grace. You're like honey down here, sweet syrup that I could never get enough of."

"Please give me more." I'd get on my knees and beg right now if I had to. He knows what to do with that skillful tongue of his, flattening it to rub circles over my clit.

Pushing a finger inside, he does as I ask, making my world tilt and spin in the most fantastic ways. My orgasm builds, skyrocketing when he sucks and twirls his tongue. It's like he's French kissing my pussy and it's phenomenal.

"You smell like heaven and taste like candy, sugary and addicting." He stands, his cock, full and long, ready to have some attention.

"My turn to lick you?"

"That sounds so fucking good, but you lie down. I want to eat your pussy until my tongue's numb."

Climbing onto the bed, he stretches his long body out beside me, his cock full and proud, taunting me. I want to explore his body as he's been doing mine, but he's not having it. Pulling my hips toward him, he lifts me until my center is positioned over his face and he dives right in, making me scream in bliss as he thrashes deliciously up and down my slit.

"Good girl," he groans against me, "Just like a fucking peach, I swear."

Not one to hold back from touching him, my hands go directly for his own source of pleasure. I pump him a few times, his throaty rumbles feeling delicious against my thighs as he continues his blissful assault. He's heavy in all the right places. Cupping his balls, I track my nails along the smooth skin directly underneath and his hips jump in surprise as he emits a raspy moan.

"Fuck." It's nearly a gasp against my sensitive flesh. His hot breath does wonders, each puff sending glorious bursts of air against my clit.

I want to make him come—need to after everything he's already done for me. I want to bring him pleasure. And I want him to know that I can be giving as well. I may not be the type to be able to provide him with expensive gifts, but I can suck his cock so that's exactly what I do.

Like a woman possessed, I lean down, bringing his head to the back of my throat as far as I can. It's thick and has me chocking a bit, but I don't mind. He's French kissing and nibbling my pussy with so much fervor, I can think of nothing unpleasant at the moment.

Moans escape from me around his cock as he sucks and licks. I've been with a few men and none of them have ever dined on me like this. I don't think I could even call what they did 'eating out' anymore; clearly, they had no fucking clue as to what they were doing.

Long, skillful fingers enter my hole, pumping in and out, then plunging in and out again, stronger with each stroke and it has my mind spinning. Jesus Christ, the man can eat pussy. I should be the one baking him muffins for sure.

"Yes!" I groan, pulling his dick in between my lips, sucking and licking his precum clean, following along with Thaddaeus' own methods and it has his hips gyrating. I know if I were on my knees he'd have his hands tangled in my hair, while he fucked my mouth. He's not used to not being in control, but I can tell he wants to have me come too much to make me stop my onslaught on him.

That's fine, I'll happily come all over his mouth, but I'll make sure he does the same as well. Bobbing my head, I twist my free hand around his base. He's too long for me to fit him all into my mouth so I compensate. Twisting circles with my fist, lightly grazing my teeth and licking over his sensitive head, I use my other hand to graze my nails over his nuts, pulling and tickling them as I go. It doesn't take long before he's roaring out in satisfaction, his huge cock expanding as it throbs and pumps my mouth full of his warm, wet semen.

He tastes delicious. Like fucking peanut butter with just a hint of salty and sweet. I could suck him off every night if this is what I can expect.

His cock, thoroughly sated for the moment, lays spent, but still thick. I wouldn't doubt it if it's always this size. It appears swollen, but, in reality, it's just bigger than average. It's the type of cock you can't help but want to touch and have inside you all the time. He's big enough that he'll leave behind a sweet reminder after he has me.

My pussy pulses from all the attention he's given it. One more powerful pump with two of his fingers and a strong lick has me spiraling out of control, coming all over his lips and chin. The room grows darker, birds chirp somewhere and I swear the Milky Way clouds my gaze. The feeling's like being swept out into the undertow, and you can't stop it. You can fight, but it still overtakes your body—pulling, consuming, until you belong to the water.

That's what he does to me; he consumes me and my thoughts. Crazy thing, it's way too fucking incredible to put up a fight. So I don't. I let my body relax and ride the wave. Piece by piece he's slowly stealing bits of my soul.

Chapter 9

You're either at the table,
or on the menu.
- Al Capone

Thaddaeus

I enjoyed every moment I had with Grace on our first official date, so for the next two nights we do the same thing. I take her to dinner, learn a bit more about her, and then leave her sated in bed; her thighs are raw from my scruff between them and her fat little pussy so tender from me tasting my fill.

We haven't gotten further than that though and surprisingly I'm okay with it. I've never been one to hold back when I've wanted something, especially sex. But I've never really had to either. Grace is different from the rest. At this point, I need her to think straight. When I'm not near her, the stress of this life consumes me. When she's close, it's like I can take a step back and finally see things that I've been missing.

Crazy to think that rather than a woman making you weaker, she could indeed make you stronger.

I don't want to pressure Grace with being intimate. I've inserted myself damn near everywhere else in her life in the matter of two weeks. In this, I want her to come to me when she's completely ready. I'm just hoping that's sooner instead of later. Until then, though, I'll have my fill of her in other ways.

"Joker?" Maximillian seems surprised to find me on the top-level balcony, going over various spreadsheets. My home could be considered large to some. I think of it as comfortable and there's a lot of nooks to hide weapons and cash if we ever needed it.

"In the flesh."

His eyes light up as he takes the seat to my right, pleased, no doubt, to catch me alone. "Are those the shipment expenses?"

"Indeed, they are. Have any input as to why we're either A, missing a crate; or B, missing forty thousand dollars?"

"It's the latter. A small coast guard boat caught wind of the shipment. Luckily the two officers settled for twenty k each when the transporter made him believe he only had one shipping container of marijuana on board."

"Those two were dumb enough not to search the entire ship?"

He snickers, "Yep. The crew thinks that they spooked them so the officers wanted to get some quick cash and get out of there."

A chuckle breaks free. "Fucking idiots." That boat was loaded with drugs and cars getting sent overseas. I'll make a cool four-and-a-half-million dollars. Forty thousand is merely breadcrumbs to get out of a potential bust.

"I know, nothing like the Australia shipment." He makes everything sound much more proper with his English accent.

"Speaking of, have you heard from Tyson?"

He's an old friend of mine that I met back when I was a teenager. He's become a good business contact to have over the years. Seems like the guy knows everyone who's someone over in Australia.

"Nope, not a word in a month or so from the lad."

"I'll have to give him a call and touch base, see if they're ready for a new shipment of exotic vehicles. Appreciate you handling this mishap with the shipment."

"Of course, bloke; you know I won't fuck it up."

I hate losing money, but, if anything, this little mishap seems to have brought my friend back to me. Hopefully by him seeing that it's business as usual, he'll cool off toward my relationship with Grace. Eventually I want her here in my home and they'll have to be around each other. I'm optimistic that by then Max will have moved past his little grudge he seems to have against her.

Grace

The next week passes by with frequent texts from Thaddaeus checking in on me and admitting that he's been missing spending time together. I cherish each message, knowing he's been thinking of me and that he's not so open with everyone else.

Work's boring, and when Friday rolls around, I couldn't be happier, knowing that my week's officially over, and I'll have time to see Thaddaeus. I can't believe it's been a month since the man first stepped foot into my life. The more that I'm around him, the more I find myself letting him into my heart and my life.

We've gotten an influx of new clients at work that's had me staying late after my normal schedule to brainstorm and figure out marketing strategies for each of their businesses. Coming up with whatever a company is looking for is the most difficult part of the job. The client has to approve, you have to believe in it, and it has to be built toward the intended market where you need it to flourish. Once you figure that part out, then it's all about applying it in the right places to get it seen and utilized in the correct field. To sum it up, it's boring, and I could do it in my sleep.

My boss has been handing off a lot of new accounts to me lately, so I'm hoping it's a test or a sign that he's going to be looking at me for a promotion. I mean, more responsibility usually means a bigger paycheck and a new title beside my door, right?

At least I hope that's what it all means. If not, I'm going to be pretty upset knowing I've been swamped and have had to put in all this extra work for nothing. Salary's good, but I'm always thinking about the next step, career wise.

And then there's also the fact that I haven't gotten to see Thaddaeus much this past week with our conflicting schedules. I work all day and he does a lot of business at night, which I admitted to him that I don't want to know anything about. I figure the less I know the better. I've gotten used to having a man around in so little time, it's a bit scary.

"Grace?" My Boss peeks his head in my office.

"Hi, David. Another new account?"

"I thought I'd come see if you'd like to attend a business lunch with me."

Finally, this could be the break that I've been waiting for. I paste a grateful smile on my face. "Of course, when is it?"

"Today, if you're free, say in ten?"

"Um, ten minutes?"

"Yes, is that a problem?" His brow creases.

"Nope. Not at all."

"Great, meet you in the lobby in ten then."

"Okay, thanks."

He leaves my office and I gather my purse and coat, quickly typing out a text to Thaddaeus.

Me: I can't meet you for lunch today after all.

T.M.: Everything okay?

Me: Yeah, I have to go with my boss instead, for a business lunch.

Me: I was looking forward to seeing you in an hour, but I'll have to wait until tonight if you're free.

T.M.: For you Bella, always. Where are you and your boss going?

Me: I'm not sure yet, but we're leaving in a minute so I have to get going.

T.M.: Okay, text me when you get to the restaurant. I like knowing you're safe.

We've been over this all week, and I know he's protective, so it doesn't bother me. He worries and he has every reason to, with what he does to make a living.

Me: I will. xoxo

T.M: XXX

Of course, he sends all x's. The man's been turning me on all week long with him calling me at night before I drift off and talking all sexy to me. I've had to bite my tongue each night from begging him to come over to fuck me silly and then sleep next to me. But I knew if I asked that he'd come, and then he'd keep me up all night long, and I wouldn't be able to wake up for work each morning.

Taking my seat in the busy restaurant, I quickly type out a short text to Thaddaeus so he doesn't worry.

Me: We're at Café Blanco. I'll text you later. xoxo

He doesn't respond right away, so I silence my phone and put it away in my purse. It's a business meeting, so I want to be completely professional for my boss and whoever's meeting us.

David sits in the seat across from me, placing his napkin in his lap. "Thanks for joining me, Grace."

"Of course. So, which client were we here for today?" I ask as a server sets a glass of water in front of both of us.

"Well we aren't meeting them today, per se." He turns to the waiter. "I'll have a coffee black, please, and a club sandwich with chips."

"Yes, sir, and for you, miss?" the server asks me as I take a sip of my ice water.

"I'll just have the water and a club as well. Sandwich dry please, with fries and a side of ranch dressing."

"Sounds good, I'll have it right out." The guy nods and saunters toward the server's station to key in our order.

"As I was saying before," David adjusts his tie, loosening it a tad, not meeting my gaze. "There isn't a specific client today; I just wanted us to have a chance to touch base and have lunch."

"Well, that's nice of you." I smile. It's fake.

And it's odd of him. He never invites me out for lunch or engages in chitchat. I think he usually eats alone or with Bryan, one of the guys a few offices down from mine. Could this mean a possible promotion in my future like I was hoping for? I haven't heard of any positions opening, but maybe he knows something that I don't in that department. I'm excited that this could be the right step for me, but if I'm honest with myself, I'd rather be sitting across from Thaddaeus right now. It's been a long week, and I've been craving his touch.

"Do you like to go out a lot?"

"To lunch?"

"Yes, or to dinner, see a show; that sort of thing."

"Oh, um—" It's a bit out of character for my boss, and I don't know what to say really. I don't necessarily want to share any of my personal life with him.

I'm cut off as the chair next to me pulls out and a body takes its place.

"Occasionally, but she's picky," Thaddaeus answers for me, resting his hand on my shoulder protectively. It's large and warm and feels wonderful. I can't believe he showed up! Was that the real reason he asked where I was going for lunch? So he could surprise me and crash my lunch meeting?

David's eyes bug out when he sees the sturdy man standing next to me. "Excuse us, but we're having a private conversation here." He gestures between us with his forefinger making me cringe. He has no idea who he's speaking to like that. This conversation could get ugly—fast.

"Yep, and it's over," Thaddaeus says shortly. "Grace, baby, it's time to go," he orders, gripping my arm in his hand tightly, pulling until I stand up.

"What? No, I'm having lunch with my boss."

"You want to have a tantrum here in public or shall we discuss this in private?" He scolds as if I'm a child and it infuriates me. He may be powerful and scary to some, but now he's forgetting who he's talking to. I don't take orders.

We're so having this conversation somewhere else. He has no idea the storm he's stirring up by ordering me around like that. Glancing at my boss, I'm a bit fearful to say anything as I may get fired being mixed up with a criminal. "Please excuse me for a moment, sir."

He nods, staring at me as if he's never seen me before. That's fine, if he knew who was standing at my side, he'd be thanking me for taking care of this right now.

Spinning around, I stomp toward the bathrooms where there's a small alcove off to the side that we can use to argue in more privately.

"You've lost your mind if you think you can command me to do anything! I'm not one of your minions," I rush out as soon as no one's around us, my muscles tight with my irritation.

"I've lost mine? No. You've clearly lost yours!"

"That's my boss over there, and I want to get a promotion. You're not helping by being rude to him."

"That's a man over there taking my woman out to eat and wanting more."

"You're wrong; he doesn't see me like that. And besides, it's not the point, you don't own me; you don't get to dictate who I go out with."

Stepping closer, his lips nearly brush mine, his breath fluttering over them as he speaks. "Really? Don't say that Grace, you know I do and I'll be damned if another man is taking you out. I always get what I want and that's you not with another man."

"Ugh!" I step away. "Don't tell me what to do Thaddaeus, I mean it. I can go to lunch with a coworker if I please. I'm my own person and I make my own money. I'm not one of your toys; you can't boss me around whenever the feeling hits you. You try to tether me down, and trust me, I won't stay with you."

I don't know where it all comes from, but I'm angry. Would I leave? Probably not, but he needs to know that there are boundaries. He can't come in here and just steamroll me to bend my will; it doesn't work that way.

"Fine, I won't tie you then." His cheeks are red as the words leave his mouth, "But you need to remember that you've never met another man like me, cara. I'm not joe-fucking-schmo from down the way. I expect things, and one thing I won't tolerate is another man hitting on you. Independent woman and all, then you won't mind if I stay and have lunch with you and your boss, especially if it's as innocent as you claim."

I can tell he's pissed, and it's taking everything in him to hold back from exploding and getting into a full-blown argument. I have an inkling that if it were anyone other than me asking him for patience, that David would already be eating his teeth right now.

"Fine. But be nice to my boss," I mutter and make my way back to the table with Thaddaeus hot on my heels. I can feel the heat pouring from him. He doesn't have to be right beside me for me to sense his overheated body, not setting me straight for essentially ordering him to do something.

"Everything okay?" David asks as we sit back down, curiously watching Thaddaeus fill the seat beside me, uninvited.

"Yes, thank you," I nod and take a drink of my water with lemon slice.

"So, how do you two know each other?" He gazes nosily between us, and Thaddaeus answers immediately.

"She's my wife."

"I am not!" I turn to him, shocked that it came from him and sounded so natural.

"Fine," he growls, "but you will be one day."

Stubborn isn't a strong enough word I'd use for him today, maybe jerk or hardheaded. He's so sure of himself, and, honestly, it's hot as hell. My panties are soaked witnessing him act so possessive and confident.

"She's my girlfriend or significant other," he begins again. "Or my favorite term I prefer to use … *mine*."

Rolling my eyes, I just shake my head. There's no use in arguing about it; I know he won't stop. He's way too used to getting whatever he wants. He said it himself. It's been a month of us 'seeing' each other. I can only imagine how he'll act further down the road. I can envision him attempting to lock me in a tower away from anyone male within a hundred feet.

"I had no idea you were seeing someone." David swallows, his face scrunching up, not fond of the turn of events.

"It's new." I smile pleasantly and hope it smooths away some of our earlier display.

Surely, he's married and understands the bumps of a fresh relationship. Heh, I didn't even know that's what we have until a few seconds ago. Sure I had hoped that Thaddaeus wouldn't just screw with my heart and mind, but I wasn't certain if that would happen or not.

"Why did you ask my Grace out to lunch?"

Really, his Grace? This is going to be a long hour.

"I thought it'd be a good chance for us to catch up," David responds, a bit uneasy, nervously tapping his fingers against the table.

"I suspect it's really because you have a thing for my woman. Just admit it; you were bringing her to lunch to ask her out again. I walked right into that moment though, didn't I?"

Embarrassed, I squeeze his thigh and mumble, "Thaddaeus,

please!" This is my career he's messing with at this point and he needs to stop before I'm fired.

"Just admit it, David." He keeps pressuring. "Tell Grace your real motivation for today."

A few intense moments pass before he blurts, "All right, I-I'll say it." David stutters, frustrated. "I was going to see if you want to have dinner and maybe see the opera next weekend." He directs his questions toward me, while also wearily watching Thaddaeus. I know then that he's realized who the man sitting next to me really is, his real name, and what he's known for and capable of doing to people.

I can't believe my ears. My boss does want to date me! And that's terrible for my future with the company, especially now, after Thaddaeus has badgered him into admitting his true intentions. Why did this have to happen today? I just wanted to eat a sandwich and text this hardheaded man later tonight.

"See. That wasn't so hard." Thaddaeus responds nearly in a taunt, growing more intimidating with each fleeting minute, and I feel heat at my back. David swallows and looks at the table as our food's placed in front of us. "You won't mind if a few of my friends join us, I hope?"

Thaddaeus's boys surround the table; hence the body heat I felt coming from behind me.

It's a loaded question. If David says they can't sit with us, he'll be in deep shit, but if he agrees then he'll have even more guys around to mess with him. Throwing a quick look over my shoulder, I discover that I'm feeling warmer because Max and Cage are standing directly behind me. They both glare menacingly at my boss.

"The more the merrier," he replies and I nearly choke on my bite of sandwich as the guys take the remaining three seats.

Cage sits beside me and Max takes the spot next to David, with Dillion on the other side of Thaddaeus. The tension's grown so thick with the intimidating, powerful men sitting around us, and thank God I wasn't too hungry because I don't know if I can eat much of anything now.

"Bring us what they're having," Thaddaeus orders and the server scampers away, no doubt to have the cook make their food right this very minute. No waiting for the infamous Joker and his crew.

"You don't work?" I turn to my annoying lunch date and question.

He gets a goofy look on his face as if he's never been asked that before. "Of course, I work. But once I heard you were going out to eat, I figured this was way more important. It's not every day that I get to eat a meal with *my* Bella." He rubs the word in again, and so what if I like the way it sounds. This is not the time and place for him to whip out his dick in a pissing contest.

"And your boss was okay with that excuse?" Everyone at the table stares at us in silence, his friends all thoroughly entertained that he's letting me speak to him like this.

"Your consideration is heartwarming Grace, but don't worry about me. How about instead, you enlighten your boss here that you won't be seeing him again outside of work or else I won't be so welcoming next time. This goes for all men. I can come with you when it's necessary, or I can hunt them down."

I think David wheezes, but I ignore him and everyone else for the moment to pass and to get my bearings.

He's so bossy and entitled and freaking arrogant. Instead of replying, I take another bite, chewing and swallowing the delicious sandwich. "I'm full. Ready to head back to work?" I can order something later if I get too hungry.

Good food or not, this situation is entirely too stressful. I'll end up either losing my job or David will get shot or whatever it is that my self-proclaimed significant other does. All because Thaddaeus wants to play games and measure his dick size in front of other males.

David easily nods, obviously ready to get away from my recently declared boyfriend and his well-dressed group of roguish thugs.

A warm hand lands on my thigh, gaining my attention. I meet Thaddaeus' golden irises. "Grace, you won't stay? I would enjoy it if we had lunch together." I swear he's like an entirely different person when he speaks to me. He's rude, yet well-spoken to others but makes them seem like juveniles compared to him.

"We can on another day. We need to get back to the office. We have clients to discuss and we're under contract to keep their accounts private."

He sits back in his chair, his hand pulling away from my thigh in disappointment. "By all means then, I understand." He nods to me, and then turns to David, "I don't have to suggest you remain professional with Grace, do I?"

"Of course not," my boss mumbles and stands, signaling for the check.

"Feel free to take care of our meals as well."

"Thaddaeus!" I scold, embarrassed at his demand, my eyes wide.

"No, no, it's okay," David consoles. "He's right, they are guests and I'll happily get the bill."

"David, really, you don't have to. Let me pay for mine and theirs, please."

"Don't worry, Grace. As your boss, I can just put it on the company account as a working lunch."

"Good idea, fella," Maximillian throws in with a wolfish grin, gaining an annoyed look from me.

David walks toward the server to cash out, and I start to follow behind, but Thaddaeus is quick to snatch my arm.

"Kiss me," he orders.

"Excuse me?" I whisper.

"I said, kiss me."

Not letting him win over the entire situation, I smirk and kiss his cheek quickly, pulling away. It's not enough for him and he propels me toward him again with enough force for me to fall on his lap.

"What are you?" I'm cut off as his lips powerfully land on mine, going for a kiss that's full of ownership and desire.

His mouth gets me so swept up in him, I find myself holding onto his shoulders desperately, following his tongue as my heart begs for him to give me more. It's merely seconds before he's pulling away, his eyes full of pent-up need as they blaze up at me.

"Have a good day at work," he rasps. I can feel his hardness against my bottom as his lips move.

"Thank you," I utter. My senses are on overload as he helps me stand back up.

In a daze, I fix my clothes, completely ignoring his friends and make my way to the front of the restaurant. If anyone says anything, I don't hear them or even notice them for that matter, too consumed by the scotch flavor that Thaddaeus left behind on my tongue.

How that man gets sexier each time we meet is beyond me, but, somehow, he pulls it off. I should've known that a few nights with him could never possibly be enough. In a way, I think he had me hooked from the moment that he touched my chin in that little restaurant the first time we saw each other. Was it the first time? I know it was for me; I never thought to ask him if he'd seen me before then.

Work passes by quickly without David mentioning lunch and completely avoiding me. I don't know if that's a good thing or bad, but there's a chance I may need to start looking for another place to work now. Part of me wants to be pissed at Thaddaeus for pulling the stunt at lunch and possibly jeopardizing my career, but the other side kind of likes it that he was protective and showed up. I should've expected it though; he seems to always know where I am.

Once I'm finally home, all I can think about is calling him and hearing his voice. I shouldn't want to speak to him so badly. Playing with my new phone, the light sparkles off the diamonds around my wrist, pulling my attention to my new bracelet.

It's the first diamond a man's given me. I've bought myself diamond earrings before, but these look different. They somehow seem old, yet in pristine condition. Could they have belonged to a family member or someone else I wonder?

Me: I can't stop thinking about you.

It sounds desperate, but it's the truth. I want to see him sooner rather than later. Staring at the phone for what feels like forever, I get no response. Maybe I should've said something about lunch instead; he'd have probably replied to that one. I guess I could make myself something to eat and watch some TV.

Getting off my bed, I throw on some sweat pants with a plain tank top and make my way to the kitchen. Opening my refrigerator, I bend down to see what I have to eat when there's a knock at the front door.

Weird. I didn't invite anyone over and I didn't get a buzz to let anyone in from the front. Could be a neighbor, but we aren't really the visiting types around here. Closing the fridge, I head over to the door and check the peephole.

Chapter 10

Insured by Mafia.
You hit me, we hit you.
- Funny Meme

Grace

It's him.

What is Thaddaeus doing here? He wouldn't even text me back; now he just shows up on my doorstep out of the blue? I wonder if this is normal for him. And I'm in sweats with my hair up, not at all how I want him to see me. Shit.

"Open the door." It's not a request and for some reason, I immediately comply.

His body fills up my doorframe, not big and bulky, but tall and solid. No matter how infuriating he can be at times, overall he's beautiful. His face resembles one of a model, so proud and gorgeous. It's his stern gaze and biting tongue that lets you know quickly that he's not a man to be crossed or taken lightly. He commands respect.

He's in the leather jacket from the photo—the one that's my favorite. It makes him appear a little more human than his suits do, but still like a complete badass.

"Hi?" My eyebrow quirks with my silent question of what the hell are you doing here.

"You said you miss me." He answers my unspoken question, stepping close enough that my breasts brush against his jacket.

"No, I said that I was thinking of you."

"That you couldn't stop."

"Okay?"

"So, I figured the best way to cure that would be to come over."

"And you don't wait for an invite?"

At my response, he licks his lips, staring at mine. "If I waited, we'd never get anywhere."

"Where do you want to go?" My gaze trains on his mouth also. His lips are sexy, his teeth perfect and white, with the canines a little more pronounced than his others. Each time he speaks and I see them, I imagine him biting me with them.

So fucking hot.

"Here, with you." He replies, using his right hand to shove the door closed behind me, while leaning in and taking my mouth with his.

The door clicks and our kiss deepens. His mouth's an inferno, drawing me in and setting my entire body alight with fire. Each swipe of his tongue is an erotic torment, beckoning me to play. One hand pulls me closer while the other lightly cups my cheek. The only time he breaks contact is to mumble against my mouth, "I want you."

I want him too, more than I'd like to admit. His thumb runs down, over my neck until his hand stops, holding my throat. I don't know if it's the sheer control of his hand holding such a vulnerable part on my body, but the feeling of his large palm against my skin has my body humming all over. This man knows exactly how I need to be touched and does so without haste.

"More," I'm able to utter, barely breaking my lips from his but it's enough to do the trick. His other hand runs underneath my shirt, working it up, over my torso until we have to separate to get me free from the obstructive material.

Once again, I'm pressed against him, his mouth devouring

me as he works my sweat pants down, leaving me in my bra and cheeky panties. You'd think I was made for him, how well he knows my body after only being together for a short time.

He pulls back to gaze down at my body, his eyes hooded with lust. "Mmmm Bella, you're breathtaking. I'm truly a lucky man." His words make me blush. I'm not shy of my body in the least bit, but his intense stare, makes me want to burst with pride that he enjoys what he sees in me.

"You still have your clothes on." I state the obvious and he nods, not taking his gaze away from me and not wanting to remove his hands either.

In a few movements, Thaddaeus' black leather jacket falls to the floor. I almost want to chase after it and put it on. It must smell delicious after being wrapped around him. Next, his white T-shirt is yanked over his head and tossed to my couch. He doesn't waste time in taking his black jeans off, but just unbuttons them, before pulling me into his frame again. His clothes are entirely under classed compared to his usual; he sort of reminds me of James Dean in that outfit. He's a total bad boy with a sinful touch when it comes to my body.

"The bedroom or the couch?" he asks, unlike last week when he brought me pleasure with his mouth right where I was standing.

"Umm…the bedroom?" Silently, he obeys, walking me backward to my room.

Shoving me gently, I land on my back on my bed and he wastes no time, diving in and pulling me free of my underwear. Tossing them somewhere behind him, he leans in, immediately swiping his tongue against my aching sex.

Thaddaeus' exposed back, clad in nothing but his jeans is beyond sexy. The man has muscles there that I didn't know even existed. His only tattoo stands out in stark contrast to his lightly tanned skin, the large, laughing Archangel standing over a pile of dead bodies, seemingly more menacing than the last time I saw it. I questioned him about it before and he told me it's to remind him to be careful when he turns his back. According to him, someone's always there, laughing, waiting and plotting to take his place. It must be a lonely life to live.

Pulling my tender flesh into his mouth, he lightly bites and sucks on my clit, making my hips shoot off the bed, "God!" I moan as he draws on it harder and makes me see stars.

In a flash, the erotic moment is over and he's climbing over my body, pushing his jeans down his thighs, exposing himself. He's long and demands attention just like the rest of him. I only catch a brief glance before his lips are on mine again, my taste still on his tongue.

Thaddaeus has me practically purring. My body vibrates inside with excitement, knowing that thick cock between his thighs will be bringing me even more pleasure. Climbing over me, he pauses on his way up to nibble on each nipple, the tops of my breasts, and then right below my ear.

"You have me so turned on. Your mouth is amazing."

"Tell me, Grace, are you on birth control?" Its growled as his breath comes in quick bursts as his dick caresses my thigh, anxious.

"Yes." Whispering, I nod, gyrating my hips, searching him out.

"Good baby. Are you safe? Can I stick my cock in you bareback?"

Am I safe? Yes. I haven't been with a man in so long. Do I trust him enough to not use some type of protection? I wouldn't have when I first laid eyes on him. After the past few weeks though, I feel like he truly wants the best for me and to make me happy. He told me he would always protect me and while it's naïve to believe everything a man says, he's shown me over the entire time he's been courting me that I'm special to him, that I mean something and that I can trust him.

"Can I trust you, Thaddaeus?"

"Christ, say my name like that again."

"Thaddaeus." It's uttered softly, my eyes fluttering, still a bit blissed out from the miniorgasm his tongue's so kindly provided me.

"Yes." His chest rumbles and he drives into me in one powerful swoop.

"Oh my God."

"Not yet, but I will be someday."

It's obnoxious and conceited and lord does it do things to me. If it could happen to anyone, it'd damn sure be him.

Another strong drive and he rips me open. It's painful and hard, in so many ways like the man himself. Tears crest and the moment he notices them, his eyes widen and his body slows. Kissing my tears away he pushes into me slowly, taking his time so the pain disappears and satisfying tingles replace the discomfort.

"I don't want you to hurt baby, I'm sorry."

"No, it's good, the sting …. You fill me up. Finally, someone that belongs."

"You're getting so wet, Bella. Amazing." His teeth graze my ear lobe, sending goose bumps over my arms and breasts. "I want you every way that I can have you."

I nod, meeting his tender lips as he grinds against me, showing me the stars he's promised the past few times he's been over. "You can go faster; I'm okay."

"You're sure, beautiful cara?"

"Yes, I'm good now." I love it that he cares like he does, making sure I'm comfortable and not hurting. He knows it's been a while and he's doing everything the right way to make me remember him, always.

As the words leave my mouth he pulls back, flipping me over quickly until I'm on my hands and knees, ass directly in line with him. A few beats later and his tongue swipes up from behind. I moan loudly, not expecting him there, like that. His mouth and then the air hitting me leave behind a burst of coolness, soothing the tender area.

He fills me again from behind and I swear he feels much bigger than before. Palming my ass, with one hand, he grips my hip in the other as he pumps into me. Stroke after stroke, needing my full curves, massaging the areas as he holds on to drive deeply inside me.

Running his palm up my back, he reaches around, cupping my breast as he plunges forward, filling me to the hilt. "I'm going to spank you, Bella. I want to leave my hand print on this gorgeous round ass of yours, but I want to warn you, because it may hurt."

"Hell yes, spank me, Thaddaeus! And please go harder."

"Will you come?"

"I'm almost there," I promise and clench my eyes closed, concentrating on the feelings he's inflicting so my orgasm will come on quicker.

Pulling back some, a sharp crack echoes through my tiny room at Thaddaeus' strong palm on my flesh, the spark of pain has me yelling out in ecstasy and excitement. At my voice calling out noisily, he slams into me. He's buried himself inside me while groaning incoherent words in what I assume is Italian. It's the most erogenous thing I've ever heard in my entire fucking life. That man is pure perfection.

Another smack leaves behind a harsh burst of pain being followed up with a bite, his canines sinking into my shoulder leave me dizzy with passion. He thrusts quickly, full of strength and need and urgency.

It's blissful.

It's utterly mind-shattering and has my body careening out of control, my heart racing with each stroke as my orgasm washes over me, leaving me sated and sleepy.

He's on a whole other level when it comes to lovemaking. The man struts with a swagger that I now know he's earned. The fucker deserves to walk like a cocky bastard because he can own his shit.

My body's laid down gently on my tummy and a few beats later, Thaddaeus has a wet cloth between my legs, taking care of me after treating me to multiple orgasms. He washes up and joins me, crawling into bed and pulling me to his chest.

"My Bella," is whispered sweetly into the back of my neck as he inhales my scent there.

He's warm and feels like home.

It's the last thing to cross my mind as I drift off into a deep sleep, feeling safe and happy wrapped in his strong embrace.

Thaddaeus

The line rings a few times as I wait anxiously.

"Hello?"

"Bella."

"Hi."

"I need to see you tonight."

It's been three days since I was last near her. I can wait no longer. This is getting harder. The more I become consumed with her, the more I miss her. She needs to move in with me. I'm not a patient man and I want her close all the time. I don't like not having my eyes on her all the time.

"Okay, I would love that."

"I'll pick you up tonight. It'll be late though."

"Is everything all right?"

"Yes, baby. I have to work, but I'll stop by."

"I'll be naked," she says quietly, drawing a chuckle from me.

"Don't tell me that or I'll have to hurt someone to get to you faster."

"Don't do that. I'll be in pajamas then and naked after you get there."

I have to pull the phone away for a second to clear my throat. Just hearing the words has me growing hard under my desk.

"Tonight then," I reply and hang up before she can entice me further.

A knock draws my attention from my cell. Glancing up, I find Dillon—my friend and my usual driver.

"Joker."

I nod and he enters.

"D? You have news?"

"Yep. You were right. Franco's been following us. Word around is that he wants more territory."

I knew it. I can always tell when something's about to go down. The thing about it now is I have a woman to protect first and foremost.

"Fuck him. Find out what he's up to today. I may pay him a little visit."

"I figured, so I did a little digging. He's supposed to meet an associate for dinner tonight at Caveralli's Steakhouse."

"Good. How did you come across that tidbit?"

"I fucked his new personal assistant. She sang like she be-longed in an acapella group."

I snicker at his comparison. Smart fucker was a regular col-lege boy before he came to me and started cooking mine and my familia's books for us.

I need to get to Franco before he has time to get anything in motion and starts a new turf war. This is Chicago; there's already enough violence and people dying around here, I don't want a war of all things when I'm barely getting Grace comfortable with my lifestyle.

Who am I kidding? She has no fucking idea about my life. I'll get her to move in first.

If he's been following me around, then he probably knows about her. I won't have any threats to her safety—now or in the future. It's time to snuff out the source before it becomes a real problem.

"Did you already burn that bridge with her or can we still use her?"

"Nope, we're good. She's been texting me like crazy."

"Hope Franco doesn't catch onto that."

"He won't have a chance if we get to him tonight."

"Agreed. Do you know if he was around at all when I was with Grace?"

"I don't know, but I wouldn't doubt it. You've been out and about with her a fair bit and everyone's starting to talk."

"What do you mean?"

"There's been word that *Joker's locked some pussy down* and there's a cool million on her head at the moment."

Stunned, I sputter, "Are you fucking kidding me right now with this shit?"

"No. Look, I'm sorry. I just found this out last night."

"And you didn't think I should know about it *last night?*"

"You were on the phone with Grace..." He trails off and I growl in frustration.

I told them all that they better not call or bother me when I'm around her or speaking with her. Even texting, I want my focus to be completely on her as she deserves. And only notify me if it's a fucking war on my hands or someone in my familia dies. Clearly, I should've specified that they call or give me a heads-up when it comes to Grace's safety as well. Fuck. I could've already been dealing with this last night.

"Does Max know?"

He nods.

Double fuck. Maximillian must still be butt hurt because I know he would've chanced interrupting me had he heard.

"Is he here?"

"I think everyone is right now."

"Call them all to the bar."

"You got it," he replies and hurries out of the room to find the crew.

I have to figure out something to say to get them all on board with me again. This rift that's grown between us will do nothing but destroy everything I've worked so hard to accomplish. I refuse to live like a gutter rat. My ties are too deep in this city. They must learn to respect me again whether I have a woman beside me or not. I won't live in fear, and I refuse for her to as well.

Making my way to my home bar, I pour a hefty glass of scotch and take a seat on one of the large, plush leather couches and wait.

One by one, the guys file in, each making their own drink and taking a seat. This is standard for when we have a sit-down to discuss business matters.

"Thank you for coming," I begin.

Once they've acknowledged my statement, I fill them in on everything Dillion shared with me, drawing a few surprised expressions. It's a big fucking deal when someone threatens me, especially when they have the fucking balls to put a threat on my woman's head.

"What do you wanna do?" Cage asks and chews on the inside of his cheek, mind going a million miles per minute. No doubt, thinking of effective ways to snuff out the threat.

"I'll see what I can get out of Franco tonight; hopefully, it'll help squash the search for whoever took out the hit against Grace. This can't touch her."

Dillion rubs his jaw. "We could bring her here for the time being to keep her safe."

I'm surprised he's the one to suggest it. I've thought about it, but figured they'd all throw a fit over the idea. I want her to live with me and this could be a way to get them onboard with it at first.

"I can drive her to and from work too. You know I won't let anyone hurt her."

My respect for Dillion increases to an entirely different level. Knowing that he values our friendship to protect someone I care about means everything to me. While I'm grateful, he's not the one I need to be devoted to her. It's Maximillian.

He became my best friend for a reason. He's a very dangerous man, and he's built bigger than me, not to mention, smart as a whip when he's not fucking off. He could ultimately protect her if something were to happen to me, and I know his loyalty. Once she has it, she'll have it for life.

Cage chugs half of his water, then grumbles. "I could probably get a few of the fighters to help out. Pretty boy Blake Adonis is looking to earn some extra cash. Fucker can spar too. They'd be stupid to come at Grace with him guarding her."

Just the thought of another man around her that isn't my crew has my anger rising. A growl escapes before I can tone it down. "No. No one but us gets near her. We can use the fighters to roll with us if needed, but I prefer to keep them separate. They're business. We make a lot of money off them and that'll end if they're dead in a gang war."

Max is quiet, his hand moving to make the gin and tonic in his tumbler swish around in circles with the few cubes of ice.

"Max?"

His irritated blue gaze meets mine. "What would you have me do, T? This isn't my lady; I'm not fucking her like you are. You want me to respect her and guard her as mine, am I correct?"

I nod.

"Do I get to fuck her as if she were mine as well?"

He's more evil then even I am. Before I'd find it amusing that he expects such a payment, but it's infuriating now. Picturing him with her, naked, has a rage like no other building inside me. She's mine; she's supposed to be my wife someday. I know this and so do they. It's why he pushes me. As much as it will tear me a part inside, I know what I must do. I have to protect her anyway that I can.

"If, and I mean IF she comes to you, offering herself, then yes, Maximillian. You can fuck her." It takes every bit of discipline I hone to say it without tearing him apart, piece by bloody piece.

He sits back, a pleased smile resting on his face. "Well then, consider her safe, my old friend."

Chapter 11

Snitches get stitches.

Grace

Thaddaeus never specified a time or anything that he'd be here tonight, so when he finally shows up at eleven p.m. I'm stretched across my couch in comfy yoga pants and an oversized sweater. I'd vegged out all evening and it's surprising that I didn't end up dozing off.

He waltzes right in like he owns the place, an excited grin tugging at his lips.

"Shit! You gave me a heart attack!" I clutch my chest, my heart thundering with his random entrance. "How did you get in here? I swore I locked the door when I got home."

He smirks. "You did, but I have a key."

"What? How did you get a key?"

"I have ways." He winks, and while stunned, I'm enjoying this good mood he's in.

He actually grinned, which is a leap up from just the trademark smirk he always shares with me. It completely transforms his face. I'd thought him handsome before, but to see such happiness, he radiates. He's beautiful.

Hopping off the couch, I practically bounce over to him, pressing a kiss against his mouth. "I missed you today."

"Me too, baby. Shall we go?"

"Go? Where?"

"It's a surprise."

"Okay, let me change."

"No need, Bella. Grab some shoes."

"Okay." Glancing over my outfit, I can't help but wonder if I shouldn't change anyhow. Unless he's taking me to get drive-through tacos. I look like a bum compared to his usual spots. Pulling on my furry boots and a scarf, I grab my wallet and nod, smiling as I get excited too.

He takes my hand in his much larger one, pulling me along, pausing briefly to close and lock my front door for me.

The cool air hits me as we exit my building, my hand warm in his and at the curb, Dillion's standing next to a gray masterpiece. He looks all too pleased with himself as well. These two must've been up to something today, or perhaps the car's new and they're just overly zealous about it.

He beams at Thaddaeus and tosses him the keys.

"Thanks, D."

"No problem, text me when you're ready."

Thaddaeus nods, turning to me, anticipation lighting his golden irises, "Come on, baby." He opens the door to the sporty number, holding my hand sweetly while I sink low to the ground. Closing my door, he jogs around the front, climbing in and cranking the engine over. It whirs to life, and rap starts blaring through the speakers, bass vibrating my butt.

"I didn't know you listened to this stuff?" I practically yell.

He shrugs. "Different car, different music."

I barely get my seatbelt on before my back's sunken into the creamy soft leather bucket seats. "Oh my God! What is this?"

"Aston Martin." He grins, chuckling at my stunned outburst and hits another gear, the speedometer climbing as he races through Chicago. It's late and he's taking full advantage of the open roadway.

I love when he calls me Bella, but hearing the pet name baby leave his lips has an entirely new range of emotions coursing through my blood. It fills me full of excitement along with the easygoing grin he's flashed me a few times tonight already.

A new song starts, and I can't help but giggle. It could be his theme song. Glancing at the center console, it brightly reads, *Ghetto Cowboy* by Bone Thugs-N-Harmony. Never heard of them, but the song is awesome, especially hearing it on speakers like these. He's normally so refined that I'd never guess he'd ever listen to something like this. I don't mind though; if anything, it gives me a glimpse at another side of him.

The drive goes by quickly, and I find myself wishing he'd keep going. The ride's smooth, the speed addicting, and I'm not even the one driving. We pull off outside of the city in the middle of nowhere. I've never been out here, and the stars are more pronounced allowing the sky to twinkle enchantingly. It's serene and kind of spooky, the stark quietness compared to the noisy, busy city we just came from even if it is late.

He opens his door, leaving the car running with the stereo blaring loudly out into the open air. The headlights illuminate brightly out into a field full of nothingness—only dead grass and old snow. Thaddaeus rounds the car, opening my door and helping me out. He's always chivalrous and caring when it comes to his actions with me.

"What are we doing?"

"Shh, my Bella."

With a firm hold on my hand, he tugs me around the front of the still-running vehicle and immediately starts pulling my sweater free.

"Hey!" It's freezing and he's taking my clothes off! A giggle escapes me and he flashes a wolfish smile, chuckling at my exaggerated shiver.

"Trust me?"

I nod. "Always."

He beams brightly against the night, pleased. Laying me down against the hood of the car, his warm fingers work my boots and yogas free. I'm left naked, panty and braless, as I was expecting him sometime so I never put any on earlier.

He swallows roughly and curses at his discovery. He wastes no time, drawing my stiff nipples into his mouth, loving every part of my body with his palms and warm, wet mouth. My head falls back, my eyes staring out into the exquisite sky. The heat from the car's hood provides a teeny bit of heat, the rest from Thaddaeus and the unbelievable sensations he's inflicting upon my flesh.

His tongue explores, making its way to the juncture between my thighs. His skills with his mouth have fast become one of the many things I thoroughly enjoy about his lovemaking skills. Thaddaeus gets a few licks in when delicate white snowflakes begin to flutter down from the sky. It's chilly, but at the same time warm. The night's quiet but the music vibrates loudly from the car. The sky's black, with a million stars and white snowflakes thrown in.

It's unlike anything I've ever experienced and it's special because it's with *him*. The night's serene and being in his arms only makes me fall helplessly for him, offering up anything he wishes to take.

It seems like merely a flash before he has my body humming from my first orgasm. Without hesitation, he's climbing over my frame. Pushing his jeans down his thighs, he exposes himself to the cool evening air. It does nothing to deter his hardness. He's long and demands attention just like the rest of him. I only catch a brief glance before his lips are on mine again, my taste coating his tongue.

Thaddaeus' drive is powerful, as the radio screams about 'making me a believer.' He enters me on one hard swoop, forcing me to moan into his mouth. I didn't see him put on a condom, and we need to wear one. I'm out of birth control at the moment. I'd run out yesterday and my doctor couldn't squeeze me in for another week. I never imagined I'd need it though or I'd have refilled it sooner. I don't go out randomly having sex with gorgeous men. Thaddaeus was very unexpected and the only time we had sex, I was taking the tablets each morning like clockwork.

"Wait," I whisper, not wanting him to really stop. I turn my head to the side so I can speak. He lets me, passionately kissing down my neck and sending little goose bumps all over my body as the frosty air follows in his wake. "We-we need a condom, Thaddaeus." It comes out in a blissful groan as he drills into me again, full of hunger.

"No," he objects, rasping against my throat, trailing his lips over my chest until he reaches my breast where he nibbles, while pivoting his hips deliciously. The movements make me delirious with desire for him.

"Yes. We have to; my birth control ran out. We have to stop." My protest is there even though it's weak. I know I can't afford to get pregnant. Especially by a man who I've not known for long, no matter how attracted to him I am or how much my feelings grow with each day that passes us.

"I said no, Bella Grace. You're mine, sweetheart."

"Thaddaeus, I can't. I can't afford to be pregnant." Not cost wise, but in general, my heart would never make it if I ended up having to do it all alone. Some people are strong enough to handle being a single parent; I'm not one of them. I have to think rationally, no matter how strongly the passion chases the thoughts away.

"Shh," he mutters against my skin, rotating his hips until I begin to see sparks.

"God," I call out again as my orgasm starts to tumble through me, blurring any previous worries I'd had.

"Yes, baby, feel me," he orders, seating himself inside me fully, bringing his mouth to my jaw. He peppers tiny kisses along it and it's just the small dose of sweetness I need to send my body spiraling into pure madness.

The amazing feelings erase the prior warnings of caution I had and I grab his ass, wrapping my legs around his hips and pull him into me deeply, riding the tide of pleasure. My sighs of satisfaction and excitement tip him over, and he follows my moments of bliss with his own.

Luckily, he's smart enough to pull himself out of me right as he comes to empty himself on top of my stomach. Watching his ember irises flash with each stroke of his hand as he expels every last drop onto my skin has to be one of the most erotically satisfying things I've witnessed from a man—from him. He doesn't hide himself from me in these moments, showcasing each emotion cascading through him as he stares intently into my eyes. They say that they're the windows to your soul; if that's true, I saw myself rooted in his.

"That was for you. Next time, I won't stop," he declares and I clench wantonly. I know it was for me. His blistering gaze told me so.

Fuck. I want it too—him filling me, giving me everything. Some day.

He finds a package of tissues in the car to clean me up with and helps me get dressed again. The only thing I don't understand is that he's kept the radio blaring this music that he doesn't normally listen to. I'm not complaining; it's all just a bit odd.

"Now what?" Her eyes twinkle, sated from the lovemaking.

"Now," I reply, smiling, digging out the gas can from the behind the driver's seat and some long fireplace matches. "We torch it."

She sputters. "Excuse me?"

The laugh in my chest bursts free. "Yep, you heard me Bella."

She makes me feel lighter, happier than I have in many years.

I start pouring the gasoline all over the car, including the inside. The liquid coats the surfaces, sinking into the creases of the smooth leather seats. Thankfully, she never tried to turn the radio down or she could've heard Franco. I caught the idiot climbing into his car in the parking garage after his meeting. He should've learned that to be a player in this game, you never go anywhere alone. I learned that long ago—the hard way. Now he can too.

Dillion and I tried getting information out of him but he wasn't too cooperative so we stuffed him in his own trunk and I got to go for a joyride. I needed to see Grace, so I just knocked out two birds with one stone. Never mind that she has no idea of what we're really doing here—disposing a body.

"You're serious?"

"Yes."

"But it's so lovely. It must've cost a fortune."

I shrug "I don't know, but you're probably right."

"Wait, you didn't buy it?"

My eyes meet hers and I shake my head. I won't lie to her. *Ever.*

Her eyes grow a little fearful, but I see the underlying bit of excitement as well. The thrill of doing something out of the norm spikes her adrenaline and if I hadn't just poured gas all over everything, I'd fuck her again.

"Is it even yours?"

"No, Grace, it's not. It belonged to a corrupt man, so I'm getting rid of it." Tossing the empty gas can inside. I push her backward a few steps so she's safely out of the way.

She chews on her bottom lip, watching me light matches and toss them inside. Once I'm finished and stride back over to her, she pulls me in tight. Tearful, she gazes up at me, drawing my face to hers so she can whisper sadly, "But you'll go to jail and I'll miss you. I've barely found you."

"Baby." I draw her into my chest. "I won't go anywhere. I promise you." Her words are endearing, she's come to mean so much to me as well. Maybe she'll be open to moving in with me now that some time has passed and we've gotten to know each other some more.

"You can't promise someone that."

"I can. I don't do time. Ever."

"The google articles; they were true then. You did those things and got away with it."

I tip her chin up so she can see that I'm serious. Licking my bottom lip, nervous that for once I don't feel so proud of the shit I've done, I confirm. "Yes. Most of them are true."

I can hear Franco making noise, so I pull her farther away while holding her head to my chest so she can't hear him. I think she's too upset to pay attention now anyhow. I'm merely offering her comfort in her eyes. Pity, I'm covering up a crime so she doesn't have nightmares later from the burning body left inside.

She's read the articles about me, she knows who I am. She just refused to believe it. I'm not a good man and when it comes to her, I'll do whatever it takes to make sure she's safe. It's not all about me and money anymore; she's much too precious.

"I don't want you frightened of me." I haven't really come out in the past and said those words; if anything, I wanted the opposite. I wanted her scared, but now I can't imagine the pain I'd feel if she looked at me with true fear in her eyes.

"I'm not, really. You don't seem that way to me, I guess that's why I blew the warnings off. The only thing I'm scared of now, is them catching you and me not being able to see you anymore."

"It's amazing how life can change so quickly, no?" I press a soft kiss to the top of her head and signal for Dillion. I can see the sedan parked a short way down the road we came from. He followed us and has been patiently waiting for me to dispose of the car. He likes doing it himself when we get a chance to destroy evidence, but I wanted to take Grace for a ride so he backed off.

The Mercedes lights come to life and he makes his way over.

"Who's that? Oh God, I hope it's not a cop." She clutches me tighter and I chuckle.

"It's Dillion. He's giving us a ride home."

"Did he … you know?" She trails off and I smirk.

"Probably had a good show while he was waiting."

"Ohmygawd." It comes out as one word and I laugh at her again.

"No need to be embarrassed, he didn't mind, I'm sure of it."

He stops in front of us and I open the door. Grace ducks in, not looking at him and I want to laugh even more. The feelings that this woman give me are like no other.

"Home?" D asks.

"Yes, thanks."

"Wait, we're going to your house or mine?" Grace asks, resting her cheek against my chest.

"Mine, cuore mio."

Chapter 12

Blood makes you related.
Loyalty makes you familia.

Grace

Out of all the times we've been fortunate to spend time together, he's never brought me to his place. I think I'd be more excited about it if we hadn't just lit a car on fire. Is this the sort of thing I should start to expect from him? Sure, we're in the 'new' faze with each other, but we should start moving into different territory now where we find out a bit more about the other.

That thought has me curious and a bit nervous about what will be exposed. Thaddaeus' life is no doubt very different than mine. I'm just hoping that we can find a middle ground and compromise when needed. I could tell he enjoyed lighting the car on fire; hopefully, he doesn't do too much more of it in the future though. I feel as if he's barely come into my life, and I don't want anything to jeopardize that for us.

We ride along for a while and pull up to an estate. I knew he had money, but this is more than what I was expecting.

"You live here?"

"Yes."

"Alone?"

"Not exactly. Dillion, Cage, and Maximillian live here as well, along with a few household staff."

I don't know how this subject was never brought up prior to

this moment, but I'm kicking myself. "They're all here, now?" My voice is shriller than usual, but Maximillian freaks me out and the guys are so intimidating when they're all together. It's like a group of bears just waiting to be poked.

"D, is everyone home?" Thaddaeus directs toward the front.

"I think they will be. They were a tad curious with you bringing Grace home for the first time."

Fuck my life. We should've just gone back to my place. But how did they know I'd be here for the first time? Did he plan this already? He must have, and knowing that he's spoken about it to his friends is a bit thrilling. I wonder what they said about it. I'm hoping they don't mind me being in their space, since they're all supposed to be home.

Ah, to be a fly on the wall during the conversation they had about me; would've been surreal no doubt.

I send out a quick text to Kaleigh just in case she was going to stop by my apartment in the morning. She does that sometimes to see if I want to go to yoga with her or eat donuts.

Me: I'm staying at Thaddaeus' house tonight, so I won't be at my place if you stop by tomorrow.

Kaleigh: OMG he invited you over? Are you freaking out?

A chuckle comes from over my shoulder as he reads our conversation. I shoot him a small smile then type out my reply.

Me: Nope, just happy. I'll call you Monday when I have a break at work.

Kaleigh: Okay, but if you don't, I'm calling the police on your behalf.

My eyes automatically roll at her being overly dramatic. Although, after what I've realized tonight, maybe her fears aren't so farfetched. I don't believe anything bad would happen to me, but I wouldn't be too surprised to hear of others disappearing.

Why doesn't that bother me as badly as it should? Maybe because he keeps me away from it and keeps me safe? Who knows; I'm just glad he cares for me deep enough to share himself. While he may be ruthless where some are concerned, he's changed my life and for the good.

Me: I'll be having multiple orgasms, so don't worry lol. xoxo

Kaleigh: Only you would fall for a gangster and get the decent side of him.

He snorts behind me. "She's right, you know."

I shrug. "As long as I get the good side; that's all I care about."

"Jesus Bella, how did I get so lucky with you?" His gaze softens and he presses his lips to my temple. My eyes close with his tender show of affection. I'm the fortunate one.

Kaleigh: Make him wrap it up or put a ring on that left finger. Remember the one year rule. XO

I shake my head and silently hope the gorgeous man next to me didn't see that last part. She's dishing out the same line I give her when she's out on a date.

"Wrap it up, huh?" He sounds amused.

Shit. He did read it.

"Or put a ring on it? What does that mean exactly?"

"We have this thing about dating a guy. When she meets someone new, I always tell her to make sure he wraps his dick up and that he has a year to put a ring on her left hand. If the ring doesn't come by month number twelve, then it's time to go."

"That's not rushing? What if he's the one, but needs a little longer than a year?"

Shrugging, I smile brightly. "Don't worry; you're only on month number one, eleven more to go before you get kicked to the side." Winking, I stare up at him amused.

His head tips back as he laughs outright at me and drawing a surprised look from Dillion. I'm guessing they don't hear him laugh like that? He smiles and laughs for me though…

"I'm not worried, baby; if anything, I'd expect you to be the stubborn one," he says after he stops chuckling.

"If it's right, then why waste time?" I can't believe I answer him so honestly, but that's how I feel with him—free and happy—like anything's possible.

"My thoughts exactly, cara. You surprise me every day."

"I hope that's good?"

"You have no idea."

The car stops in front of the massive home and we all get out. The large gray stone steps leading to the entryway make it appear even grander—there are only six, but it's enough to do the job. I wish it were daytime so I could see everything better. There's up lighting along the house and throughout the grounds, but I know it has to be far more striking in the daylight.

"This place is amazing," I mutter, following them through the massive-sized front door. It looks like it belongs to a castle, all richly-stained wood with black decorative iron.

"Not nearly as stunning as you, my Bella." Thaddaeus grabs my hand as we come to an impressive foyer.

The floors are made of white marble, confirming the notion that Thaddaeus is indeed wealthier than I'd originally imagined. No wonder he needs house staff; these floors would be hell to keep clean. The chandelier lighting up the area is magnificent with probably close to a thousand crystal shards reflecting the beams in every direction.

Dillion sends me a wink and takes off to the right down an expansive hallway. The walls are decorated with a few pieces of exquisitely painted art. It reminds me of something you'd see at an art gala or somewhere similar.

"Dillion's not being rude. He just likes to eat at night. He has a habit of eating healthy all day then like five bowls of cereal before bed."

A giggle escapes. I love knowing these menacing men can be somewhat normal at times. Dillion is by far the nicest one to me that I've met. "When we first saw each other, there was another guy with you. He's not here? Come to think of it, I haven't seen him since that day."

"You were observant as well, I see," he remarks. "You're right. He does a lot of traveling though, so he's not home much. You caught us on a rare day when we were all out together."

"Does he know about me too?"

"Of course, Grace. Everyone knows about you, Tyson included."

His words fill me with sweet warmth. He's told everyone about me. It's no doubt one of the nicest things he could've said, knowing that I mean enough to him that he'd want to talk about me. I don't feel so foolish now defending him to Keisha and Kaleigh. He does have a heart, a big one. He just keeps it well hidden from others. How I got fortunate enough for him to open it to me is baffling, but I'll be sure to cherish it.

There's laughing coming from the corridor to the left. Thaddaeus flashes a grin at me and then I'm faced with Maximillian's striking gaze, along with Cage.

Max's smirk's contagious as he approaches us. "I see Joker was able to successfully capture you." He winks and smiles wide. It's a little freaky considering he's normally quite cold toward me.

Fluttering my lashes at him, I glance to the floor and nod— not sure how to approach him. He normally doesn't speak to me whenever he's around.

His large hand grasps mine as he tsks. My gaze meets his again, "Grace, you're looking exceptionally beautiful tonight." My eyes widen when his compliment registers. This is literally the worst he's seen me. I'm in lounge clothes, my hair's a mess and I'm makeup free. This man confuses me each time he speaks, I swear it.

Thaddaeus clears his throat beside me and Cage steps forward breaking the spell Max briefly has over me. "Grace, good to see you again."

I blink, staring over at him. He's genuine, so I smile. "You too, Cage. Thank you all for welcoming me." My irises flitter over to catch Maximillian still staring at me intently.

I feel like I'm in the damn twilight zone or something.

"Tell me, Grace." Max takes up my hand again and pulls me off to the right; I hear the other two following us behind. "Do you like sweets?"

"Um...I suppose, just depends."

"I have some chocolate I got last time I was in the UK; would you like some?"

I don't want to be rude; for once, this guy's being friendly to me. "Sure, I'd love some."

Thaddaeus growls behind us while Max smiles triumphantly. I have no idea what he's up too, but it's something. In the meantime, I'll bite my tongue and keep an eye on him. If it weren't for his close friendship with Thaddaeus, I wouldn't give him the time of day after how frightened he made me at the police station.

He leads me into a massive-sized kitchen, over to a barstool next to Dillon, who's currently inhaling the largest bowl of cereal I've ever seen.

"How can you stay looking like that eating all that cereal?"

"How do I look?" Dillion asks quizzically. His dark hair's still perfectly styled. He's in the same jeans as earlier, but his jackets gone, leaving him in a red shirt that appears to be specifically tailored to his body.

Um ... like GQ? I don't say that, but it's on the tip of my tongue. Even Cage is freaking gorgeous. Scary, but hot nonetheless.

"I just mean in shape and by shape, not round."

He snickers. "Well thank you, I think." He takes another bite, not answering my question and it makes me even more curious as to what these guys are up to.

Maximillian brings over a sleeve of individually wrapped little squares of chocolate. "Enjoy, Poppet."

And now he's given me a nickname? I'm beginning to wonder if he's going to poison me or something next—perhaps smother me in my sleep. I'm sure it wouldn't be the first time he's done something of the sort.

"One," Thaddaeus grumbles, removing a chocolate quickly. He snatches up my hand and starts to pull me away.

"Thanks, I guess I'll see you guys later!" I call, trailing behind and they chuckle.

"Everything okay?" I ask, moving my legs quickly to catch up to Thaddaeus and walk beside him.

"It's fine."

His good mood from earlier has dispersed and I'm sad to see it go. Something clearly has him agitated and I need to get to the root of it.

"So, that was weird back there."

He grunts, starting up a staircase with exquisite hand-carved banisters. I feel a bit like Belle in *Beauty and the Beast* and I've just gotten caught going into the wrong wing. Will he punish me? But for what?

"Please talk to me." I don't like this. It's my first time here and something is evidently bothering him.

After a trek down another long hallway, we come to the end where he throws the door open, towing me into a room.

Once the door's closed and locked, he pitches my piece of chocolate at the wall right inside the door. It's tossed so hard that I'm surprised it didn't dent up the drywall.

"Explain or I'm going home." Shit better be serious; he just wasted perfectly good chocolate. Or was it poison like I'd thought? Surely Max wouldn't do it right in front of Thaddaeus.

"They were flirting." He sounds like an angry child whose toy was just taken away from him.

"I wasn't flirting back, and that was *my* chocolate!"

"No, but Max was and I had to grit my teeth as to not shove his hand into the garbage disposal."

That image is enough to give me shivers and have me cringing. "Gross! I'll never look at a disposal the same again. They're your friends, right?"

"Even more of a reason they shouldn't do it."

I agree, but keep that opinion to myself as to not stir him up more.

"Can't we just be happy that they were all nice to me for once? It was progress and you're being way over-the-top alpha at the moment."

He nods, "You're right. I just don't want anyone to come between us is all."

This crazy man has lost it if he thinks his friends are any competition when it comes to him, or anyone else being competition for that matter. I can't believe he just admitted that I'm right as well. Each little chink of armor he removes between us brings me closer and closer to him.

"No one can take that place. We'd have to let them, and I refuse too. You mean too much to me already."

His lips turn up a bit, pulling me to his chest. Once he has his arms tightly wrapped around me, he mutters into my hair, "You're everything, Bella." He holds me close for a few moments before finally ridding himself of his shirt and jeans, setting them into a hamper under his massive bathroom counter. "You can put your clothes in here to be washed. I'll have Dillion get you some in the morning or you can wear a T-shirt and pajama pants of mine until housekeeping has them clean."

"You have a maid?"

"Yes, one who does all the cooking and two others who clean up around here; they make up my staff. Five men living in the same house can get messy and someone's always hungry."

"That makes sense. Can I just borrow something to sleep in though? I don't have panties, remember?"

"Fuck no, you can't. You can sleep beside me naked."

Grinning, I kick off my boots. I absolutely love his body and to have it pressed up against me all night will be pure heaven.

"Fine." I pull my shirt free and step out of my pants then wag my eyebrows toward him. "Don't threaten me with a good time."

Before I can register him moving, he has me against his solid bare chest, carting me to his king size bed. He lays me right in the center.

"Stunning, absolutely exquisite, ciccia."

"Thank you." I respond, growing bashful with his lingering gaze. His whispers of Italian transport me to another world entirely where no one else exists but the two of us.

I expect him to ravish me, but he does the opposite, climbing into bed beside me and pulling my body into his large frame. The man has the control of a saint I tell you.

"You're not going to make love to me?"

"Yes, Bella Grace, that's exactly what I plan to do. No fucking tonight, baby; just you and me and bliss."

His lips sprinkle kisses over my shoulders and neck and he does as he promises. He makes sweet, tender, passionate love to me off and on all night long with more whispers in Italian that I swear are words of love.

Maximillian

Watching the little minx sit across from me eating her brekky with her hair in a loose bun, clad in my best friend's pajamas and a white T-shirt is making me stiff as a fucking log. I can see her nipples for Christ's sake as she isn't wearing a bra under the thin tee. The view is straight on and has my cock twitching with every move she makes.

Her tits bounce and rub against the material; she doesn't have a clue that we can all see her nipples in stiff peaks? She's liable to have every lad in the house coming in their fucking briefs by lunch at this rate.

My best mate never should've given me the go ahead on a chance with her. Now it's like a challenge, but I also know if I land her that he'll hate me forever. How the hell do you be friendly with one of the most stunning women you've ever seen, who'll end up being your boyo's wife when you want to fuck her so badly?

Lord give me strength, because I'll sure as fuck be needing it.

Thaddaeus

I told her last night that I love her in Italian. She has no idea what I was saying, but it happened. It came out right in the middle of me making love to her; I couldn't stop myself. I came in her as well.

Grace was too far gone to register what I did. If she knew that I came in her on purpose she'd probably hate me. But just the possibility of her having my child has me wanting to lock her up in my room and never let her out.

If she's pregnant, she won't leave me. She won't give Max a chance, and she'll be mine forever. She may hate me at first, but it's a risk I'm willing to take. I'm a selfish man; I always have been when it comes to taking what I want. I'm not against doing what I can to shuffle the cards in my favor.

"Anyone have any updates on the turf war?" I ask everyone sitting at the table, and Grace glances my way, stunned.

She probably can't believe that I'm speaking about it in front of her, but this discussion has to be had and touch over the threat about her. She needs to have a small idea of what's going on so she doesn't trip out later this evening when I ask her to move in with us. I don't like her knowing about any of my business, and I don't plan on sharing future work stuff with her, but this is important. I refuse to have her get injured in any way simply because she was unaware of the threat.

Grace will move in; I'll do whatever I can to make sure of it. She can have her own room if she wishes, but I hope that's not the case. I won't offer it to her, but I'm not above using it as a bargaining tool. If I really wanted to be a dick about it, I could just make her stay here. I could send one of the guys to collect her little friend and bring her as well. They'd disappear and no one would have the slightest idea where to look.

I'm not going to put her through that though; I don't want to have to fight her hating me in this. If I have to come and stake out her apartment or what not to keep her safe, I will. I'll do anything to make sure whoever's hunting her down gets nowhere near her and I take their life from them.

"T-turf war?" she stutters around her piece of toast and I nod. I'm confident she's never been around such threats, and I'll have to do whatever I can to reassure her of her safety.

Cage grumbles, pissed that I mentioned our business in front of her, but he can get the fuck over it. This is my operation and who I bring in or out is up to me. I'm aware of his feelings with me involving her in our conversation, but I think it'll be key in persuading her.

"Yes, Bella. Someone always wants to take over what you've got in this world. You have to stay on your toes, always." I told her damn near the exact same thing when she first discovered my tattoo. There's always someone waiting for their turn.

"That must be exhausting; how do you guys deal with it?"

Cage's glower shoots to her as he responds, "I fight. It helps." He's not being an asshole about it; he's always grouchy in the mornings, so this is just who he is.

Dillion smirks, "Driving clears my head."

"Oh, so that's why you always drive Thaddaeus around?"

"That, amongst other reasons." He takes a drink of his freshly-squeezed orange juice.

Thankfully, he leaves the part out about my brother dying because he was alone so Dillion or someone else is always around me. Paranoid? No. Cautious? Yes. Grace needs to adopt the same way of thinking too. I don't want her going anywhere without one of us in tow to protect her.

"I fuck. A lot," Max inserts, sending her a wink that has me wanting to stab him in his eye.

Her cheeks and neck flush so I draw her attention back to me. "You give me peace, Bella."

"Me?" Her brows rise, caught off guard with my admission, probably more so with me sharing it in front of my crew.

So innocent, yet she hasn't the slightest clue. She thinks she's a tough one and she is in ways, but in my life, she's untouched, and it makes her a thing of beauty. It's been so long since any of us have known a life like that, if we had the chance at all. To see her so happy and sweet, it's like being able to breathe again.

Chapter 13

I swallow my blood before
I swallow my pride.
- Al Capone

Grace

To say breakfast was interesting would be an understatement. I wasn't too frightened by Thaddaeus' lifestyle before, but after everything that I've heard straight from the horse's mouth, I can't help but feel intimidated. There are people out there who want to kill him all because of the money he makes. And he swears that he's not even the worst one in this area. Apparently, he has family that runs the mob, and if I'm scared of anyone, it should be them.

Gee, I feel so much better now. Said no one ever! Kaleigh would've straight up shit her pants if she were here right now or if this were happening to her.

I have to give it to my man, though, after hearing their discussion, I sort of went mute. Drawing into myself to process everything and how I felt about it all. This is his life—his normal—and if I want to be with him, then this is something I have to get used to. He took me to his movie room, put on a chick flick, gave me a blanket, and left me alone for two hours. Somehow, he knew exactly what I needed to bounce back. Is that what he meant by me bringing him peace? Do I make him bounce back?

"Look, Bella, like I told you earlier; this sort of thing is common. It happens more than you'd think, there's always someone stirring up trouble. My crew will handle it. In fact, the asshole who started it all is already gone."

"Gone as in on permanent vacation or six feet under?" Do I even want to know the answer to that? The real one and not some made-up fluff?

"Enough. I'm not deliberating about the actions I took with him to you. He's not the one I'm worried about. There is something serious going on, and I need to discuss it with you. It's the real reason why I let you know about the turf war, so you could see how it's come to this."

"Okaaay." I draw out the word and stare at him intently, waiting for whatever news he has to share this time.

"I'm not the only one they want dead."

I swallow. Take a deep breath and swallow again.

"Excuse me?" Please don't mean what I think it means.

"They know about you too."

"Who is 'they' exactly, anyhow?"

"Dillion and Cage are helping me figure it out. We'll fix it, I promise."

"So, I'm in danger." It's a statement, because I already know that's the case. He probably never would've brought me to see his home had this never happened.

"Yes, you are. I need to protect you. Would your boss mind if you took some time off?"

"I mean, I have some vacation saved up. I can say an emergency came up and see if he'll let me use it."

"Good, that's perfect, Tesoro." He kisses me on my forehead and I can't help but bring up the thoughts bothering me even more than knowing someone may want to hurt me as well as him. If I'm honest about the whole threat thing against me, I'm not too worried anymore. Thaddaeus won't let his best friends too close to me; no way is he going to let someone near me to hurt me.

"Is that the only reason why you brought me here?" I have to know. Is it the danger or is this thing between us as real as I keep painting it out to be. I like to think what we have is more and lasting, but I need to hear it from him as well.

"It's one of them."

"So, you wouldn't have if there wasn't some lunatic out there after the two of us?"

He reaches for me, the pad of his thumb trailing over my bottom lip. The caress has my eyelids fluttering closed, my body already trained to his touch, in tune with his movements.

"Of course I would have, Grace. I've wanted you here since the moment I sent you those flowers. I couldn't stop picturing you everywhere."

My gaze finds his, so full of warmth, and dare I say love? He always looks at me as if I'm the most precious thing there is. "Everywhere?"

"Yes. It's how I knew I needed to court you. Every time I closed my eyes, there you were. That sexy little nose turned up, pretending to ignore me, while your body screamed something else entirely. The flowers were merely the beginning. I had to keep contacting you in some way; I couldn't stop myself. Then we had dinner and I tasted you … I knew then you were made for me."

"It is? What was so different about it?"

"You wanted me, baby, and no matter how hard you tried to act like you didn't, your body told on you—loud and clear. The way your throat was splotched with pink, your breasts pushed out, begging to be cupped and then your sweet little breaths as you panted. I only used two fingers to touch you that first meeting, yet you responded like I'd thrust my cock inside you. I knew I had to have you and that only grew each time I came face-to-face with you, the desire, the longing. I couldn't get enough of you."

What he says is completely true. I wanted him so fucking bad; I just wouldn't admit it to myself, let alone anyone else. I tried to be stubborn, to fight it, but I didn't even have a chance. It was over the moment he walked through the door to the restaurant that day. No one that I could've met afterward would've done it for me, because, like him, I would've pictured his face each time too.

He brings my fingers to his lips, brushing a kiss across my knuckles, making me feel worshiped and cherished. "So, what's going to happen if I'm allowed to take vacation time?"

"Then you can relax here with all of us. We'll keep you safe and I'll make sure you have whatever you want. I can hire some of those nail ladies to paint your toes or give you massages if you'd like …Whatever you want, just name it."

"I don't need anything besides some of my clothes. I'm just afraid that if I take time away from work, then I won't be able to visit my mom down the road." He bought me that ticket to visit her and I'm beyond grateful for his generosity. The man really is kind hearted when it comes to me.

"Don't worry about it. If I have to fly your familia here or talk to your boss personally, I will."

I figured he was going to tell me to quit, because I know he hates my boss. I nod, putting him at ease. It's the least I can do when he has so much else going on. I know he does, no matter how well he hides it from me. "Okay, Thaddaeus, I'm yours. I just need to call my boss really quick and confirm it."

Thaddaeus

I wasn't expecting her to give in so easily. Hence why I started sprouting off things she could do while she's here. I can't believe I offered to hire her own nail tech and masseuse. Yes, I can believe it. Because I would in a heartbeat if she requested either of them. I've already filled in the cook to make Grace's favorites each night for dinner for the rest of the week and am having one of the maids clean up a guest room especially for her. Not that I'm offering it up for her to sleep in, but to keep her things in that won't fit in my bedroom. Eventually I'll have my room remodeled to give her all the space she needs. Hell, she can redo the entire house if she pleases. I really don't care, as long as she's here with me each day.

Step one toward getting her belongings here is complete. I've put Dillion in charge of retrieving them. He'll have the guys bring over way more of her belongings than she needs because by the time this is over with, I don't plan for her to ever go back to her apartment.

This will be her home. Our home. Together.

I'll wed her, fill her with my babies, and we'll grow old together—here. I know it's all very demanding and pigheaded of me, but it's my plan. I was telling the truth about her bringing me peace, and I don't plan to let that serenity slip through my fingers.

The crew will think I've lost it when I admit to them that this is far more than her staying around until the threat's snuffed out. Frankly, I don't give two shits about what anyone thinks, except her. When did that happen? I knew I wanted her from the very start, unlike anything I've felt before toward a woman, but it was purely primal. Now I'm over here simply thinking of her overall welfare in the scheme of things and not considering what could happen to me or the guys who've devoted their lives to keeping me safe. I wish it were entirely true; I know they're mainly here for the money. I did save them after all, not the other way around.

Could Grace be happy here, holed up in a house full of men? Or better yet, could I stand her being around them all the time? I'm jealous when it comes to her, and I wouldn't put it past myself to sink a bullet into someone's skull if they tried to take what's mine.

Grace steps into my office without knocking and I have to grit my teeth to keep my cool. This is the one place in the house that if the door's shut, you need to knock. I deal with a lot of business in here and the majority of it, no one needs to hear about. That's one of the many reasons why there's a thick ass barrier on the hinges to enter. I've got to talk to her and also bite my tongue to learn patience. I'm not used to having a woman in my space and a strong willed one at that.

"He wasn't too thrilled about me needing time off on such short notice, especially with how busy we've been this last week. But, I promised to make calls from home to check on clients and correspond through email."

"Good. Do you need me to have a laptop delivered here for you?" She could always just quit the useless job and tell that dickweed to screw off. Or better yet, let me do it for her.

"Actually, would Dillion mind grabbing my laptop off my kitchen counter when he gets my other stuff? It has the account information for my clients already on it."

"I'll let him know. He'll take care of everything." Including packing up all her other belongings; I want everything here in my home.

"I still don't like the idea of him going through my drawers."

"Bella, I told you, we can order whatever you'd like offline and have it overnighted. Him digging through your things doesn't have to be so in-depth."

She lightly bites her bottom lip. "I have a budget and that doesn't really fit in with draining my savings account."

"I wouldn't dream of letting you pay for anything. I can give you a card and you can order whatever you want."

"I don't like that, Thaddaeus. I appreciate everything you've done, really, but I don't need your money. I can pay my own way, this is just a time that I have to use my better judgment and I have clothes at home that will work just fine."

"Suit yourself. We'll be lying low for the week anyhow, no need for anything past sweat pants and T-shirts." There's also the fact that I don't want anyone checking her out while we're cramped up in this house all week long or an artery may explode.

"Joker?" Cage makes his way into my office as well and I gesture for Grace to take a seat.

"Anything?"

He shakes his head.

"This is utter fucking bullshit. You're not digging enough; find me something damn it."

Cage has been making calls since breakfast, trying to find out if anyone knows who's after Grace. I made it loud and clear that my guys make it known that if anyone touches a fucking hair on this woman's head, that half a million won't be enough for what I'll do to them. The gods themselves wouldn't be able to save them from my wrath.

I rarely issue citywide threats, but I had to take some sort of action immediately. My declaration will stave off a few that go looking for her, but not all. I'll have to make one hell of an example to fend off the others. Can't say I mind that bit, being locked up here for a full week will no doubt feed into me needing to relieve some pressure. Sex can only do so much in that department.

Marrying Grace would do the trick. No one would have balls large enough to come after her with my ring on her finger, but I know she won't go for it. Like she said about her twelve-month rule; ring needs to be on her finger, but we've only been seeing each other for a month so no rush. I know what that means. She wants it to happen eventually, but not necessarily tomorrow. I'm not a man to pussyfoot around. I know what I want even if it has been four short weeks with her in my life. I need to figure out a way to speed up time or her thought process on it all.

"I'm doing my best."

I blow out an irritated breath. "Fine ... okay, keep checking around and passing along the word. I'll fucking scalp them."

"The word?" Grace interrupts, her eyes wide at my last threat and Cage grunts. He's still not a fan of her knowing our business. He can shut his trap or fuck off too. This is her life and she means too much to me, already.

"Yes, baby." I trail my finger lightly over the side of her beautiful face, before I take my seat again. She's exquisite, nothing I've ever had finer than her. "I'm letting it be known that if anyone has a nut sack big enough to harm you, that I'll be sure and feed their cock to a meat grinder while it's still attached to their body."

Her mouth falls open in a small 'o' and fuck if I don't picture what I could stick in there. She has perfect lips My guys would call them dick-sucking lips, but I'd never let her hear them speaking that way. Cage snickers, shaking his head. He's used to me like this; her, not so much.

"That's, um some threat."

"I'm glad you think so." I wink and Cage snorts.

"I'm going to my office," he grumbles and I return his nod.

"He has an office too?" She peers over at me curiously, her questions coming more freely as she warms up to everything going on.

"We all do. Once your laptop gets here, I'll set one up for you too. Anything you need, cara, you say the word."

"Oh, I don't need my own office, really. I'm fine. Thank you though, that's very kind of you. I can just sit on the sofa or your bed, kitchen stool, you know, anywhere." She giggles and the soft tinkle makes me grin. Something about this woman, I swear.

"Nonsense, Bella. This is your home now too. You'll have your own place to work and anything else you need, no arguing about it."

The sweet smile she sends me is enough to make me feel like I've just bought her the moon and trust me, if I could, I would. I'd do damn near anything to keep her looking like she does right now. My chest swells with pride, my mind quickly running over what else I could possibly do to make her happy.

"I like having you here like this," I admit outright, not wanting to close myself off from her like I do with everyone else. I want her to know me—the real man inside. I think he's the only one she could ever possibly love, not this hard exterior that I've worked so meticulously over time to form.

"Yeah?" She perks up, climbing to her feet and approaches my desk. "I haven't gotten on your nerves yet?"

"Maybe just a little, but not bad."

She laughs, leaning her hip against the smooth dark wood, right beside my thigh. "You're so charming." It's sarcastic, but I find myself smirking again. I feel like a fucking fruit loop smiling around her so much. It's like I turn into a giant pussy when it comes to her.

"It comes natural with you and that smart mouth."

"I've toned it down with you, a lot." I open my arms and she sits on my lap, snuggling in until her feet are pulled up into my lap and she's comfortable.

Meeting my amused gaze, she grows serious. "I didn't understand how to act when I first saw you and I apologize. I didn't give you any respect or even a chance. You've earned it with me and now I see that I was wrong. The way that I treated you in that restaurant was unbelievably rude. You've quickly become the most caring, giving, thoughtful man I've met, and I wish I could go back to change the way I behaved."

"I don't." Kissing the top of her head, I brush my nose against hers. "I loved every damn minute I was in that restaurant. You weren't some little meek thing, cowering down to me. You stood your ground, and in return, you, amore, earned *my* respect."

Her lips seek mine out, lost, wanting to be found and ravished. So I do exactly that. I kiss her like she's the breath that my lungs need to keep me alive. In a sense, now she is. Without her, my life would be mundane. The killing, the fucking all the same boring cycle that I'd been stuck in without realizing it before. She's opened not only my eyes but also my heart.

As I feel Grace's body surrender, offering up more pieces of her to me, I fall a little deeper than before the kiss began. It's like Alice in Wonderland—the falling. I feel like we're spiraling down, dropping helplessly into the unknown and not the faintest idea as to where we'll end up.

That night I put in a call to the familia. Yes, I have cousins everywhere throughout the city. My familia is a lot larger than most know and my ties to the mob run deep. I grew up in the lifestyle, surrounded by mobsters. The real kind of mobsters that'd hunt you down to the ends of the earth if you threaten their organization.

Everyone I knew was uncle or cousin so and so. You didn't let anyone near that wasn't familia. I was young and dumb, believing I'd eventually join them and pledge my loyalty to the Italian Mafia.

It changed the moment I witnessed my father shoot my mother in cold blood—a Mafia-ordered hit. She'd fallen in love with one of my so-called uncles. Turns out, he was a friend of the familia. She stayed true to my father, but knowing that her heart was elsewhere drove him completely mad. The mob found out about it and ordered a hit on her. My father was distracted with his wife and in the Mafia life, Mafia comes first. Familia is second, no matter how much they claim differently.

Seeing him murder her to follow orders flipped a switch inside me. I refused to be one of them. I wouldn't go against my familia, but I wouldn't show them my loyalty either. I was done with the mob and their ways. I decided to carve out my own path, make my own crew and earn their loyalties. I still love my familia when they're being my actual familia and not being the mob. To this day, I would open my home to any of them, but I will not pledge myself to their way of life.

At my request, my cousin—a man I grew up with—will alert my uncles as to what's going on right now. They need to know that Grace is mine and that she will be forever, if I have any say in it. And, they also need to know that I'll go to war for her. I'll tear this city apart to find anyone that poses a threat toward her. My life is one thing, but I won't tolerate it toward her.

Hopefully with them informed, they'll be able to help weed

out whoever is testing my sanity. Because that's exactly what she is. Anything happens to Grace—and I'm so far gone for her— I'll completely lose it. There will be no more attempting to keep the peace. No mercy. No nothing. Only me laughing as I watch them all burn, not giving a flying fuck who goes down into the flames.

Chapter 14

If you let a person talk long
enough, you'll hear their true
intentions. Listen twice, speak once.
- 2Pac

Grace

I've been cooped up in this house for five days. Sure, those days have been filled with Thaddaeus' insatiable lovemaking and there are also the perks of shirtless men, but I'm not used to not being able to go out anywhere. I miss my after work and lunch-time walks. Having clients to check up on has helped keep me busy, the time off has also shown me how much I dislike my job. I hadn't paid much attention to it before, but now I know for sure that I need to find something else to do with my life.

"Penny for your thoughts, Poppet?" And Maximillian, he's a whole other story.

I've never met someone so night and day in my life. He seemed unnaturally evil the first time I met him, but ever since I've been here, he's been a complete gentleman. Makes me wonder how he got tied up with the rest of the crew. He doesn't quite fit in with them; it's almost as if he's more selfish. Not necessarily in a bad way. I'd guess it has something to do with how he grew up. Some-times you meet a man and you can tell they weren't loved enough as a child, and that's what I get from him. Part of me wants to hate him while the other piece of me just wants to hug him and tell him it's okay. Stupid? Probably, but we'll see how it plays out with time.

Dillion's funny and nice, but he's a criminal and doesn't hide the fact that he specializes in tax fraud and destroying evidence. Cage, he's like a momma bear all the time. He eats a lot, is insanely buff, and is constantly grouchy. Not just toward me, but in general. It's baffling how four completely different men can come together and form such a strong type of brotherhood with each other. I wonder how Tyson is. Could he be more like Thaddaeus? He's a wanderer, that's all I've really heard. I know Thaddaeus is fond of him. though. I can tell just by the way he says the guy's name that he's more like a brother.

"I was just thinking that I'm tired of being stuck in the house."

"We could go for a stroll, maybe check the gardens. You need a smile on that gorgeous face."

Ah, the gardens have been my saving grace. Even in the cold weather they're beautiful and peaceful. I can sit in Thaddaeus' gardens for hours and do absolutely nothing it seems. I can only imagine this place in the spring and summer. Especially with the pool, I'm sure it's breathtaking.

"Thank you, that's kind of you to offer, but I've already been out there twice today."

Truth is, it's close to my cycle and I'm craving chocolate cake and cinnamon rolls and anything sugary I can get my hands on. The guys have offered several times that if I want anything specific they'll go pick it up or the cook will make it. I feel guilty asking though. They've already done so much for me, like making sure I'm protected all the time. I don't want to bother them unless it's necessary and the lurking danger is another motivating factor to not leave the premises.

"I'm wanting a cinnamon roll and Frappuccino something fierce," I nearly groan, just thinking of it and imagining the smells from each of them.

He chuckles. "Have you stopped in Beanery Bliss?"

"Oh, my God, I love that place!"

I smile and he takes my hand, pressing a kiss to the middle of my palm. My mouth grows dry at his affection just as a throat clears from behind me.

Pulling my hand away, I turn to find Thaddaeus behind us, glowering at the very spot Max just had to his lips. I nearly blurt out that it was platonic and swear that it wasn't me, but stop myself. I have no reason to feel guilty. Thaddaeus owns my heart.

"Um...hi."

"Bella. Maximillian."

"Joker, Grace here was just requesting we head to the Beanery Bliss for a snack." He doesn't seem the least bit bothered that Thaddaeus appears pissed and ready to decapitate him for touching me.

"What?" My eyes snap to his that are full of mischief. "I didn't. I just said that I was craving a cinnamon roll and a Frappuccino. You added in the rest of it!"

"Good idea. I need some fucking air," he growls. "Max, get the crew. We'll take the Denali."

"Give me five to round up the lads." Maximillian strides off, following the order and not giving me a second glance.

Obviously, the possible threat of danger does nothing to deter his need for a snack. I think his sweet tooth is worse than mine. Who am I kidding; every man in this house is addicted to sugar.

I found an entire cabinet loaded down with sugary cereals and snack cakes. It's a wonder how they stay in such great shape. If I hadn't caught Dillion and Cage leaving to run in the mornings, I'd have thought they were super beings or something.

"Thaddaeus, we don't have to go out. I know how important you said it is that we stay here for this week. I really don't mind, I promise. It was just a stupid craving, that's all. I don't want to jeopardize anyone's safety because of me."

Wrapping his arm around my waist, he tugs me along to walk with him. "Bella, I need to get out of the house too, trust me. The ride will be good for us. We can all grab a coffee and a pastry then get back home."

He calls it home as if it's mine as well. I kind of like the sound of it to be honest. The house is lovely, his staff welcoming, and even the guys have been kind to me. I was caught off guard with the way they've treated me. I was expecting them to be rude and annoyed, but it's been the opposite.

"Thank you."

"It's nothing. I want you happy."

"I am happy. Well, except we haven't finished our conversation about my birth control." He was not too thrilled that I brought it up either. "My appointment's for Monday to get a refill and get new lab work done. I talked to Dr. Carrie, and she thinks we'll be fine having sex since I was on my pills for so long."

"I want to come with you on Monday."

"What? Why?"

"Because if those tests come back any differently than you expect, I need to be there for you. You have my support in all things; I meant it when I said I will be your strength when you need me to be."

I have to turn my face away because his words bring tears to my eyes. It means a lot to hear him say that. I know I should automatically assume he'd be there for me, but let's be real here. That's not how life always works. And we haven't been together for too long either; most men would flip out and take off. Him stepping up before it's even necessary says a lot about his character, not only with this, but also with him so willingly offering me protection. He's, no doubt, a very loyal person.

How I ended up with a man as strong as him still has my mind spinning. You won't see me complaining though. If anything, I'll happily be sucking his cock all the damn time if he's always going to treat me like the most important thing in his life. He treats a woman the way she deserves to be treated. Yes, he's a bit overbearing, but he makes up for it tenfold.

The drive's anything but relaxing. Dillion's speeding down the road, driving like we're being chased, and if it weren't for the trust the guys show him, I'd be holding on. Cage is riding shotgun complaining the entire time about anything and everything we pass by. Me? I'm sandwiched between a pissed-off gangster who's busily glowering at the other man next to me who happens to be a flirty Englishman, hell bent on pressing his Boss' buttons until someone finally explodes. If we get pulled over, I sincerely feel bad for the officer having to deal with this crew. I can only imagine how it must be when his other friend isn't out traveling.

Maximillian randomly leans forward, completely in my space, to crank up the radio. I can't help but wonder if he touches me more than necessary. He's up to something; I've been paying attention. The radio's playing Lil' Kim's song *How Many Licks?* It's the cherry on top and I start giggling. It's loud, and tears flow over my cheeks when Cage starts to automatically bop his head to the beat.

She sings about being the night rider and I lose it. It's fucking hilarious to see these grown-ass men listening to this song. And they all stare at me like I'm the crazy one, too. That's the best part. No one in a million years would picture this happening right now and it's freaking awesome. The most entertainment I've had all day.

Pulling up to the café, the guys practically leap out like their fearful of my type of crazy. I think I wigged them out a little with my laughing fit. I couldn't help it. I'll blame it on sugar and exercise deprivation.

Could also partially be my pms kicking in. If so, they'll want to stay away from me tomorrow because they won't be the real threat at that point. Their anger has nothing on a woman at her monthly time with no snacks or Midol in the house. I'm sorta wondering if they have any tranquilizers or whatever with their type of work. If I piss them off too much, there's a chance I could not wake up until next week.

The shop's divine scents of coffee and pastries float throughout the air as we make our way inside, causing my stomach to grumble a bit. I think this is the first time I've seen the guys all out in public during the day and not clad in full suits. They look so hot and intimidating in them. Right now they could almost pass for regular guys; if regular guys traveled in packs and glared at anyone who looked their way, that is.

"What are you having, Bella?" Thaddaeus tucks me into his side securely as I stare at the case full of scrumptious morsels. I want one of nearly everything. Cinnamon rolls, mini cakes, apple turnovers—it all looks fantastic.

"I'd like a cinnamon roll and that chocolate croissant." I point through the glass.

"Very good choices," the older Italian man behind the counter smiles kindly, his face full of wrinkles from living what one would think a happy life. Immediately, I notice that he has the same eyes as Thaddaeus, but his have a bit more of a twinkle in them. I'd bet he's someone's grandpa. He has that feel about him.

"Thank you; can I have a tall Frappuccino as well, please?"

"Such a sweet one, Nephew," he directs beside me and I get drawn in a touch tighter against the solid chest I'm leaning on. It's affectionate, not territorial. Evidently Thaddaeus is at ease around the older gentleman.

"Indeed, she is. I'll have a black coffee and a strawberry cream cheese muffin." I forgot that he loves those muffins. I wonder if I can find a recipe somewhere to bake some he'd like? I know the cook could make some, but I want to do something special for him.

"Two biscuits with the bit of chocolate on them and hot tea with cream, for me." Max points out some delicious cookie looking things in the case. I should get some of those for later too.

"I'll take five of the blueberry cream cheese Danishes and a large Cappuccino," Cage orders, my eyes growing wide, wondering how he'll fit all of that in his stomach. He was just eating a damn sandwich an hour ago back at the house.

"Hazelnut coffee with two sugars and a scone for me, please," Dillion tells the older man and pulls out his wallet to pay.

I've already been scolded not to argue with Thaddaeus or try to pay for anything in public. That was a hard pill to swallow, but he has an image to uphold and the last thing I want is for anyone to think he's become weak, especially because of me. The men are the same way. They don't disagree with him or argue with him about anything in public; they save it for back at the house and one of them is always taking care of the bill wherever they are so Thaddaeus doesn't have to worry about it. In and out, the guys say is the safest way for their leader.

"I need to bring Kaleigh here," I mutter as we take a seat around the largest round table in the small shop. "I should get one of those chocolate things to go too." And one of everything else while I'm at it.

Thaddaeus smirks, leaning over to kiss my head. He finds me amusing, especially when I talk to myself. He acts like he doesn't do it, but I'd bet money he does once that door to his office closes.

After a few moments, the guy from behind the counter comes over, delivering all our order. The drinks are steaming and the pastries have been warmed to the perfect temperature. The aromas are magnificent to the point I may lick my plate when I'm finished.

"Uncle." Thaddaeus directs the man to glance at me. "This is my Bella, Grace. I had you make her a batch of muffins before."

"Ah, yes. I remember. A ciccia; I see why, Nephew."

"Grace, this is my uncle, Roberto Benito Morelli."

"Hi, Mr. Morelli, it's a pleasure."

"Please, Robbie is fine. And the pleasure is mine, pasticcino."

Thaddaeus smiles warmly at whatever his uncle just said, so it must be good. I know he'd never allow anyone to be disrespectful toward me—family or not.

"Robbie, then. Thank you for our delicious treats."

"Enjoy them." He grins, his hand on Thaddaeus' shoulder for a second. He seems pleasantly surprised with the warmth his nephew shows me. It's my understanding Thaddaeus never used to smile at anyone, only when it's something to do with me. His uncle pats his shoulder affectionately before making his way back behind the counter.

"What did he say in Italian?" I ask as soon as Robbie's out of earshot.

He chuckles. "He called you little pastry. It was meant as a compliment."

"Coming from a baker, I definitely agree." I grin and take a big bite of my delicious croissant. It's pure heaven—the flaky layers, light and buttery, drizzled with the perfect amount of chocolate. I could live off these things.

Cage busily inhales a few of his Danishes; I find it mildly amusing watching him fit it all in his mouth. His speed and process is amazing. I wonder if the man even tastes anything.

We're all settled in, happily enjoying our treats when a commotion comes from outside. It happens in what feels like slow motion. One minute we're sitting around the table, content with our snacks and smiling. Okay, so I'm the one smiling. The next second, we're all laid out on the tile floor, the hard surface uncomfortably pressing against my chest while Thaddaeus' massive body shields mine protectively.

The rat-tat-tat of rapid-fire automatic weapons rings out, ruining everything. Glass is shattered, spraying in all different directions as bullets breeze by, hitting anything and everything. A breath catches in my lungs painfully, as my chest constricts in fear.

The beautiful, quaint shop is a disaster zone. The shelves full of sweet treats, the expresso machines and warm Italian decorations have all been mutilated, ripped through with live ammunition.

Thaddaeus' sturdy body creates a curtain of safety. His heart beats powerfully in his chest as it all plays out. I hear nothing around me. The world's gone silent to my ears while it all happens so I concentrate on the movement. The thump-thump, thump-thump, thump-thump of his heart beating against my back, reassuring me that there's still blood pumping through his body and he's alive. Tears cascade down my cheeks. It's hard to stay calm when you don't know what the fuck's happening.

Fingertips on my face coax me to open my eyes and lift my head up until I can meet Maximillian's concerned gaze. He's nodding at Thaddaeus, agreeing with whatever my human guard is saying. His body's overly warm, sheltering me in my own little cocoon. His soft lips graze my cheek and abruptly my hearing comes back. I don't know how it happened, the sudden 'mute' to where I couldn't hear anything. It's like my mind shut everything off and then suddenly decided to be present again.

Thaddaeus isn't speaking quietly to Max like I'd believed. He's shouting, brimming full of fury as he yells at his men, half of his words spill from him in fast Italian. The English pieces I easily understand and he's completely irate.

"Find them, now! They shoot while my woman is with me? Bring me their goddamn hands and hearts! Now!"

There's ringing in my ears as he presses another loving kiss to my temple. The guys scurry around, nodding and agreeing with Thaddaeus' orders. Weapons are drawn, chambers checked and ready as Max takes watch at the front door. Dillion and Cage charge outside, guns out and ready to shoot whoever's threating the infamous Joker.

Chapter 15

Sano E Salvo
- Safe And Sound

Thaddaeus

"He's bleeding," she whispers, and I glance at her making sure I heard her correctly. She's shaken up with an ashy tone to her skin. I don't like that she's upset like this or that she had to witness what just happened. I could skin the assholes alive that're behind this. I have no patience for careless men around my Bella.

"Who, amore?"

She signals toward the doorway where Max stands guard. My eyes scan over him from top to bottom. He has blood running down the back of his calf. I didn't get a chance to see if the others were hurt. I was too angry to think of their well-being; I was only concerned for Grace's. They're well compensated for their injuries if they get them anyhow.

"Maximillian, did you catch fire?"

His irritated gaze flicks towards his leg, annoyed with what just went down. "Just a bit of glass." He shrugs like it's nothing, but I've been stabbed with glass before. No fun there.

Glass wounds aren't like knives. With a blade, it takes more force to drive it through flesh. Glass is so sharp when it's broken, it splits through the skin like butter. Before you realize it, it's sunken in deeper than you'd anticipated and pulling it free hurts like a motherfucker. Cuts like that almost always have to be stitched up tightly too. If not, they seem to bleed forever.

"How's it look out there?"

Max checks all around out the now open doorway, the decorative glass missing from the destruction. The floor's littered with colored shards from the stained glass that was once multiple colors surrounding a coffee cup.

"Whoever stopped over, tucked tail and ran. Bloody bastards, I'd fancy a chance with them."

So the fuck would I. No way I'd let Grace witness the rage I'd have over them though. She'd be scarred for life because I'd make them pay by removing one finger at a time, pausing on their trigger fingers. Those fools will be taught a lesson; you don't fuck with the Joker without repercussions. D and Cage will get them though, and they'll take care of business. And so help me, if I have to hunt down these gutter rat thugs myself, I will.

With a deep breath, I carefully roll off Grace, not wanting to hurt her with my weight. She'll probably have some bruises with the way we all hit the ground. My lungs hurt as I feel like I've already failed her, my heart squeezing with just the thoughts of what could've happened to her today. Five days and yet she could've been murdered on my watch. I have to be more careful with her; she's too precious not to be.

I promised to keep her safe, yet I allowed my jealousy toward my crew and her to drive me out. I stopped thinking rationally, needing to get out of the house. I thought I was going to strangle someone myself and now Grace has paid the price. A cut to Max is nothing compared to what I know she's going to go through dealing with this. She's not used to this life—to my life.

To me, shooting some dick is yesterday's news; to her, it's an entirely new lifestyle. One that I'm afraid she won't be happy to find herself in. I wanted to keep her away from it, keep her oblivious to our business. But no matter what, someone's always waiting, just like I told her before.

"Baby, go sit behind the counter until I can check things out with Maximillian and make sure it's safe."

Her hands clutch onto my shirt tightly, her eyes full of tears. "No," she whispers. "Please stay here, I don't want you to get hurt."

"Grace, I need to make sure it's okay for us to go home. I'll be fine and I won't have you getting hurt. Now, do as I say and get behind the counter." She looks like she wants to argue, so I cut her off. "Let me keep you safe, Bella. Now listen to me."

Taking a deep breath, she complies, carefully stepping over the debris littering the floor to round the counter. My stare stays trained on her the entire way, but it's short lived. Her stunned gaze grows wide, her mouth popping open as her hands fly to her chest. She lets out the loudest scream I've ever heard and I'm Italian. Loudness is in my blood.

In two seconds, I'm at her side. I've never moved so fast before. Glancing to the ground, I see my uncle with two bullets to the chest. He bled out all over the floor behind the counter. It's a fucking mess; no doubt she'll remember it all too.

"It's okay." I lay my hand on her arm, but she doesn't stop. I shake her, but she still doesn't stop the ear-pitching scream. "Stop, Grace, be quiet." I shake her again and she doesn't blink. She's freaking the fuck out and it has something in me wanting to rip the entire store apart to get her to calm.

My hand flies to her face, gripping her chin. I turn her to face me. "I said, shut up, damn it!" I can't help but yell it. I was fine but seeing her like this has me strung out and on edge. I would light the entire fucking city on fire to get her to stop if that's what it took. I need her to calm down so I can take control and fix everything.

After shouting at her and pulling her face to mine, she finally blinks and throws my hand away from her chin. I was holding her tight enough to leave fingerprints, but I wasn't thinking about it. I was only trying to quiet her.

"Don't ever yell at me like that again! I don't care how notorious you may be around here. I'll slap you in front of God and everyone else if you touch me in anger."

Holy shit! A woman's never stood up to me like this. They've tried, but this one makes me think she'd claw my damn eyes out if I pushed her hard enough. I would never hurt her like that; I would never raise a hand to her—ever. She has my full respect, but I had to get her attention somehow and a little bit of force snapped her out of it.

"Look, I'll yell if it gets you under control. I will never hurt you; I apologize if I gave you that impression. I care about you more than you know. Do not cry for my uncle. He was a good man, but now is not the time. It may make me sound cold, but we have to get out of here. I'll make sure my aunt is taken care of."

"You can't compensate someone's death, Thaddaeus. Maybe it's that simple to you, but it's not that way to everyone else."

"Stop it. You're angry, I get that. Now's not the time to have a fucking blowout. You want to fight with me, fine. We'll do it in the safety of my home; not here, not like this."

She grows quiet, arms crossed on her chest and angry. She has so much to say right now no doubt with the adrenaline coursing through her from being scared. She'll have a chance to calm down once we're home and her mind can process. Until then, this is the last place we need to duke it out. The threat could still be waiting us out, and I'm not going down because she wants to be sorrowful for a man she didn't even know.

"Joker?" Max interrupts, so I approach, thankful for the momentarily distraction from Grace's ire.

"What's up?"

"Still nothing. I think we should get back to the house."

"Do you have the keys to the Denali?"

"I do. Dillion tossed them at me when they ran out."

"How will they get home?" Grace speaks up, from the back of the shop. She's sitting on the floor, leaning against the back wall.

She looks frail and exhausted. This sort of thing can do that to anyone though. I know firsthand the toll it takes on the body.

"They have ways and have money if they need it. Don't worry about them. This is what they do."

She turns her face, looking at her hands, still upset with me and not fond of my reply.

"Grab the memory stick for the surveillance, I'll keep watch." Strolling over to the door, I keep my gun pointed to the ground, ready to fire if someone so as much glances at me wrong. I won't hesitate, either.

Maximillian hurries to the back. When he comes out, he grabs Grace's hand leading her to me. We trade places, him on lookout, and I cover her body with mine as much as possible and get to the Denali. It's still in one piece, thanks to the bulletproof upgrade Dillion had put on.

Grace climbs in and I stand in the doorway, keeping watch so Max can run around the vehicle and get in the driver's seat. Once his door's safely shut, I climb in. My door's not even closed all the way and he's peeling out.

We drive our alternate route—the long way home. It's on purpose in case someone's following us. They'd never make it through my security gate at home, but I don't want to have anyone following us regardless. The less people know about me, the better.

"He's dead, Thaddaeus," Grace mutters softly, tears falling over her cheeks.

She mourns for a man she's barely crossed paths with. Some may call her soft. I call her pure, untainted, kindhearted.

Nothing like me. It's one of the things I love most about her. The goodness she has inside draws me in, making me wonder if I can keep something so sweet in my possession without breaking it.

"I know, cara, I know. Now shh," I say sternly. It's the last thing I want, to tell her to be quiet right now, when I know she needs to process it all. But I need to think.

I killed the last asshole to threaten us, which Grace still doesn't know about, thankfully. Who could this be? Perhaps his right-hand man? Those little gangs are like an infestation in the city, popping up everywhere, killing their own and anyone else in their paths. They have no idea what loyalty's about, what respect is. One falls and three more run to take over his spot. The very reason I live and breathe holding my position is because of loyalties. My crew has been with me for many years; my familia stays true to each other, as do I.

It's never just me you deal with; it's four more right behind me, having my back. These idiots want to play games; I'll cut them off at the source, as I did with their last leader. They'll learn the hard way as others have. You don't touch what's mine, and at this point, Grace belongs to me, to my crew. They've placed her on the pedestal she deserves to be on, even if she has no idea. She's got them eating from her palm already and she's not even my wife yet.

"You need to be my wife."

It leaves my lips before I can think over the repercussions. I don't care though; I want her to have my name. She needs to be a Morelli for my sanity and my heart's sake.

"Wh-what?" she sputters, taken off guard. I feel the vehicle swerve, Max obviously listening to our conversation as well. Nosey bastard.

"We need to be married."

"Why would we do that? Did you see what just happened?"

"I did and if we marry they'll back off."

"How can you possibly know that?"

"It just came to me, Bella. I was thinking over my familia's loyalties. Right now, whoever's doing this, is only fucking with me and my crew. You become my wife, you become familia."

"That's not any different than me being your girlfriend, just a piece of paper."

"No, you're wrong. That piece of paper tying you to me does so much more. The threats on your head become a threat to my familia—along with what just happened to my uncle. I may not be Mafia, but my uncle who just passed was. You become familia, and death to a Mafia man declares war. They'll protect you and use you as an example of not to fuck with the mob. Not only will I be protecting you, but half of Chicago will be at your back. It's all because of my uncle; his death is going to keep you alive."

"No, Thaddaeus, I can't. I couldn't use that poor man like that."

"You will. If I have to drug you and forge your signature myself, you will."

Now's not the time for her to be stubborn. I need her in this one hundred percent. It'll save her and tie her to me permanently all at once. This nonsense will be over with. My familia sees me serious about her and the threat linked with her and my uncle will become hell on earth for whomever has the audacity to cause chaos in the city.

"I can't!" she argues, my hands going to her upper arms, shaking her as I yell.

"Yes, you can! You will, damn it. I'm done being easy about this. I've paraded you around town already, everyone knows your mine. A marriage document isn't enough cause for this fight. You should be flattered that I've given you a choice. Most women would be bending over themselves for a marriage proposal from me."

"Newsflash! I'm not most women!" she yells back at me.

"Bloody hell!" comes from the front. "The two of you need to stop the pissin' already; I'm driving for fuck's sake."

My stern gaze meets her petulant one, both of us remaining silent, our eyes saying so much. Hers telling me she's not giving in; mine saying that I'll bend her will until she snaps, giving me what I want.

"We've arrived." Maximillian announces, punching in his own code and signaling to the guy I have watching my gate. "With a headache, no less, and no snacks for later," he adds, irritated. He pulls to a stop at the side entrance, so we're not out in the open.

Grace flies out the Denali, storming toward the gardens. Stubborn-ass woman. The last thing we need is to be out in the open, even if it's in my own damn yard.

"Bella!" I shout, following her. She's quick, even with her strides being smaller than mine; I nearly have to jog to catch her. I'll be damned if I leave her alone though.

Reaching for her, I snatch her bicep to get her to acknowledge me. She twists around so fast, my other hand going to the opposite bicep, and thank God I do because she lays into me. Fists pound against my chest, laying into me, full of hurt and fear.

"Stop it, woman," I growl, holding her tighter and tighter to myself while she beats against me, spending her frustrations on my body.

A weaker man would crumple to the ground. Not me. I stand sturdy and strong, exactly as she needs me to be. I will always be someone she can lean on when she needs it.

Moments later, I'm met with more tears. My poor, broken amore.

Her face pressed against my pecs while she weeps, holding me with every ounce of strength she has—like a lifeline. The first time in an incident like the one at the shop is always nerve-racking. It's hard for your mind and body to understand something so out of your control. Nuzzling the top of her hair, I press a few kisses, showering her in tenderness.

"I thought you were shot when you were on top of me. I couldn't hear anything. The world was silent so I concentrated on feeling your heartbeats against my back. It's what kept me from passing out, I think. I can't believe it happened. And like that, it was so fast and out of nowhere. I didn't know it was coming and you had me to the ground as the first shot rang out; it all happened so fast. Then everything was in slow motion, I thought it was never going to end and in the same breath I was terrified it would end." She babbles on in one huge burst, my heart squeezing for her, my own sadness overshadowing me, hearing how scared she was.

"I know, cara. But you're fine now, you're home and no one will ever hurt you here."

"But-but what about the others? What are we going to do? What if something happens to them?"

"I told you, Grace, the others will be fine. As for us, I told you what we're going to do about that as well."

"You're serious? You want to marry me? But it would ruin your life. Marriage should happen because of love, not because of a circumstance. I don't want you to end up hating me."

"Grace my feelings run very deep for you. You'd make me a very, very happy man if you married me. I think that one day you could even love me."

"I'm just so confused right now; I need to think about everything."

Our conversation's cut off as a taxi approaches. It must be my men, to have gotten through the gate. I hold her to me, her body tightening up, still on alert as I watch the car come to a stop and Dillion and Cage step out, paying one of the few cab drivers we have on call.

They're bloody.

"Well?"

"I know who it is." Cage grumbles, and Grace pulls her face away, wanting to see the guys with her own two eyes.

"See Bella, they're in one piece."

Dillion holds his hands up, grinning, and Cage nods at her. I feel her chest expand with a deep breath. Woman will probably tank soon and pass out from the adrenaline drop.

"Wash up and meet me in my office." I glance at Max. "All of you." They follow my order as I walk Grace into the house, tugging her along. She may as well be dragging her feet with her slow steps. I could carry her, but I don't want her to feel like I'm rushing her.

"How about you lay down for a minute, baby, and get some rest. I'm going to discuss everything with my crew."

"I could use some time alone." I don't agree with her on that, but keep my thoughts to myself. I need to talk to Cage and Dillion too badly to argue.

"You hungry?" I ask as we pass through the kitchen.

"No." She shakes her head and we trek up the stairs.

Once in my bedroom, Grace toes off her shoes and crawls onto the bed fully clothed, curling up into the mountain of pillows. I cover her with a plush white throw and softly place a kiss to her temple.

"I'll be back to check on you as soon as I'm done."

She nods silently.

Chapter 16

Everybody's a gangster, until
a gangster walks in the room.
- Awesome Meme

Thaddaeus

"**Y**ou're marrying her." It's uttered like an accusation rather than a question from Maximillian. With today's events, I'm not in the mood to argue with anyone.

I glance at him, then Cage and lastly Dillion. I wish my brother were still here; he'd understand why I'm doing this, why I'm like this. I like to think I can blame it on a long Italian bloodline full of stubborn men such as my grandfather. These three will never understand as they didn't grow up in my familia.

Things weren't always so black and white, such as they are now. I know what I have to do, what's expected of me. Back when I was a kid, I had the notion that anything was possible. Not so when you grow up surrounded by Mafia. Your fate's sealed early on.

My grandfather let me get away with not joining in the ranks with my cousins, knowing how I felt about my father's actions and the way things were run in the mafia. In the same breath, I was cast out. I was charged with running the streets and only permitted to request help from the mob if it was a life or death situation. I wanted to make my own way so it was no love lost on my part. Even in those times, they didn't help. It was always, "Figure it out and don't bring shame to our name," because Morelli is a real household name.

I learned to get my own crew—one that was loyal to me. The same goes for a woman. She must be able to stand beside me through the street grit, not bow down to the gutter trash around the city and watch my back. The Mafia will do nothing with all this going on right now with Grace. But, with her as my wife and with my uncle deceased, I can work the mob to my benefit—to Grace's benefit.

My crew has no idea what it means to finally find a woman who's strong enough to uphold what's required of me as a Morelli. It means everything and I'm not letting her slip through my grasp for them or some dicks with an automatic weapon.

"Yes. It's been my plan for a while now, you all knew this. I never hid my intentions with her."

"Right. But you promised a fuck in exchange for her safety."

"Are we really going there right now? I told you that if she came to you willingly, that I wouldn't step in the way." Big fucking difference. I never willingly promised she'd fuck any of them, and I never would. I gave him the option to try to coax her to his side; I'm not sure if I would've let him live in the end though. It killed me to promise him even a chance with her, but that's how much she means to me. I'd do anything I had to, to keep her alive and unharmed.

"You're bloody marrying the cunt! It was tough enough before, now she'll never give in. Lass strikes me as a bit too loyal for her own good."

"And she better. You come near her as my wife, and you won't live to see another day, friend. You had your chance—a fair chance."

"I've had five fucking days."

"You're actually pissed over pussy, Maximillian? I never took you for lacking in bedmates."

"It's the significance, not the snatch between her legs that I give a fuck about."

"Oh? How so? Please enlighten me." And, so help me, watch your tongue or I'll cut it out.

"She should belong to all of us. We've been a crew for years— *years*, Joker."

"You had your chance; you pledged your loyalty. Are you renouncing that as well now?"

"Oh, sod off. You know I don't break my word, even if I'm out a bit of pussy."

"Good. I need to know I can count on you, on all of you."

Dillion sips his brandy, lips downturned in a tired frown. "I think it's a smart move, as long as she'll go for it. I'll be honest—I don't mind Grace or even having her around here. She's easy on the eyes and she's kind. Being with you, she could've been a total bitch to us, but she's remained respectful."

I nod. I know she is. She's everything someone like me needs beside him. My mind's already made up; this is all just so they think they're involved in my decisions.

"Cage?"

He shrugs, running a palm over his face. "I don't care as long as you're happy and she stays out of our business. If she makes you all lovey and shit, then fuck it. I don't sleep in your bed at night, you know?"

"Lovely. Guess I'm the only bloke with shit for brains," Max huffs, his tone flat with boredom.

He doesn't like being the odd man out. He prefers having someone in his corner. When it comes to me though, he's usually by himself when confronting me on his contrary opinions. Truth is, he's cocky. He thinks he knows it all, including what's best for me. He's gotten too comfortable in our friendship over the years.

"I should call Tyson." He's my friend with the wandering spirit. I wish he wasn't like that; he's the one who gets me the most.

Max may be closest to me, but that's because Tyson's always gone, handling business for us.

"I've spoken to him," Cage grumbles.

"You have?" I'm surprised. I guess I shouldn't be since we're all friends, but Tyson usually calls me more than the others.

He nods. "Yep, told him all about our girl trouble and the assholes that shot at us today."

"Well shit, you've recently spoken to him then."

"I called him while we were waiting on the cab."

Dillion takes another gulp, finishing off the nasty amber liquor. "Needless to say, Tyson's still your biggest fan."

Good. Makes me want him here, beside me, even more.

"Yep. He thinks we should roll with your plan. Told us to trust you, that you know what you're doing." Cage agrees.

Max scoffs. "You lads should've gotten the idiots who shot at us, not fretted over ringing Tyson."

"We went after them, goddamn it," Cage scowls. "It was Jimmy Fantiome, one of Franco's old boys."

"I gave you an order before. I want their hands cut from their limbs for shooting at us. I want their hearts cut out for attempting to shoot Grace—my heart. Got it?"

"Yep," Cage answers.

"Yes," Dillion agrees.

"Maximillian, I want you with them. See that it's handled. Take whatever you need to get it done. And make a fucking example out of these rats; string them up in the streets if people don't realize that I mean business. You let them know they don't get to fuck with my crew, understand?"

"Got it, Joker."

"And why were you two bloody when you got here?"

Dillion moves so I can see his shoulder, and Cage holds his

arms up so I can see his forearms. They both have a few decent-sized cuts that've been freshly stitched up. They must've been busy sewing up their wounds when I put Grace to bed.

"Shit."

"I'm fine." Cage shrugs and I turn to Dillion.

"Me too."

A scream loud enough to break through my closed door, pierces the air, causing us all to jump to our feet. Goose bumps overtake my flesh, knowing it's my Grace making that sound. I swear to God, I'll castrate whoever's bothering her.

"Go, now! I'll handle whatever's happening; you take care of business." Drawing our guns, I take off toward my bedroom where Grace's voice carries through the hall. The others run off in the other direction toward the stairs to collect my new trophies.

Grace

I wake myself up from my own screaming, my skin slick with a light coat of sweat. The yell must've been loud enough to jolt me from the nightmare I was having, but I'm grateful for it. The dream was awful, replaying what happened earlier at the pastry shop.

Only this time, all the guys had been shot. They were bleeding out all over the floor, surrounding me. I had no idea what to do or how to help. Seeing them all like that completely broke me. I felt helpless and I hated every second of it.

I was busy trying to get Thaddaeus to come back to me when two men entered the shop. They were dressed like evil clowns, their sinister smiles full of razor sharp teeth, staring at me with beady eyes, ready to pounce. One of them came at me with a huge knife full of pointy edges, while the other swung a baseball bat full of nails. I knew the one with the knife was going to saw right through me and that's when I started screaming.

Thank God, I did too; it woke me up at the perfect time. I'm not sure if I could've survived something like that, even if it was just a dream. It felt so real and I know what happened, that alone will haunt me enough.

My mind's groggy and disoriented and I nearly let loose a scream again when Thaddaeus' bedroom door suddenly flies open and he rushes in his room, his chest moving as he heaves breaths. He must've run from the other side of the house.

Eyes wide, his gaze reeks of promises full of murder and torture as his body's strung tight and on alert. He glances around, his gun drawn looking for what, I have no idea. He came to protect me. He's always right there when I need him the most, no matter what the issue is. I feel like I've waited my whole life to meet someone like him. Now I finally have, and I'm willing to let him slip away from me because I'm being stubborn? Not anymore.

"Where are they?" he shouts, frantically scanning the entire room yet again, causing me to wind the throw blanket in my hands nervously. He's freaking me out even more after that dream with his shouting; I need quiet to calm my own nerves.

"Who?"

"Whoever was here. I heard you scream from my office."

Well shit. He did hear me. He really is here to protect me.

"Put your gun away."

"Huh?" His confused gaze meets mine, inhaling and exhaling slowly to compose his breathing.

"Please, you can put your gun away." He trusts me, so a second later the safety's flicked on and his weapon goes back into his holster. "It was only me in here. I'm sorry."

"What do you mean, cara? Tell me what frightened you."

"I had a nightmare. I must've screamed in my dream because it woke me up and apparently brought you in here, guns blazing and all. Did anyone else hear me?"

His face drops. "Oh, my love. Fuck, I'm sorry. The others left to run some errands."

I hold my hands out to him wanting him near me. He complies, coming to me immediately, wrapping me securely in his warmth. He holds me for what seems like forever, but one thing I notice is how safe I feel in his arms. When I think about it, I always feel that way with him.

"The dream is all my fault." He shakes his head, and I can see him beating himself up inside over it. "You never should've been there today, I was careless. I never should've have left you to sleep alone after what went down. I'm so damn sorry."

He makes the nightmare seem like nothing with him here at my side, causing the bad thoughts to disappear with his strength. My skin cools down a few degrees and my chest loosens. I know he'll always do whatever he thinks is best to protect me. He drives me crazy inside, but at the same time he makes me stronger, safer, and happier. I feel like I can face anything when he's next to me. It's all the reassurance I need to make up my mind.

"Okay," I randomly mumble, thinking about the day and my dream—about life and choices that can be made or forgotten.

"Bella?"

"I said okay."

"Okay what? You're not making a lot of sense right now. I'm trying to keep up, but you lost me. Maybe you're still tired."

"I'm talking about our conversation earlier. I'll do it. I'll marry you." I should've just given in when he suggested it, but I had to stand up to him. I can't let him think that he can just walk all over me and command me to do as he wishes.

I'd always thought when I finally met a man and decided to marry him that it would be for love.

I glance at the glimmering diamonds around my wrist. *Loyalty.*

It's not exactly love, but it's the next best thing that I can think of when it comes to marriage. He believes that I can love him someday, but I know I can. I already do, yet I'm not ready to admit it to him. Funny, I'll marry him, but not speak the words just yet. That's not what really frightens me though. It's the fact that he may never love me back. That's the scariest part in this whole plan.

"Yeah? You'll be my wife?"

I can't believe I'm so easily agreeing with him. This is huge—the commitment, feelings, all of it—but it's what my gut tells me. Life is scary. Thaddaeus has shown me that, and if there's one person out there who can and will protect me, it's him. I only hope that over time I can find a way to make him happy, to make him love me in return.

I nod, braced against his chest. It's warm and comforting like there's no other place I should be right now. Somehow, he's so quickly and easily consumed my heart and my thoughts.

"Yes."

"I was wrong, you're not tired. This all makes perfect sense to me." He kisses my forehead. "Non posso vivere senza te." He gruffly whispers into my hair, while laying me backwards.

I have no idea what the Italian words mean, but they sound beautiful the way he says them. His tongue was meant for another language; it pours from his lips like a sweet caress.

He shifts my shirt up over my stomach, his strong hands running over my flesh, knowing their destination like a seasoned lover. His other palm moves under my leggings, rubbing me and pleasuring me with his fingers.

He knows what I need when I haven't the slightest clue. He steals away the unpleasant images from the nightmare, transporting me into another world entirely. This one's full of desire and fulfillment as he hurriedly rids me of my clothes.

There's nothing sweet and slow about our joining; this time's full of Thaddaeus' claiming my body. I've given in, agreed to be his wife, and now he's taking what rightfully belongs to him from this point on.

My bra's shoved underneath my breasts, my thong pushed to the side in haste, and then he's filling me—hard and quick. We've done the soft and gentle, the exploring, and it was all amazing. But sometimes, you need to just fuck. Rough and demanding and overwhelming, his body consumes what it craves.

Thrusting into me hastily with each drive, he overtakes my senses. His smell—so powerful and manly—reminds me of a thunderstorm. It's clean with an undertone of violence, ready to strike at a moment's notice. Words of love are on the tip of my tongue, ready to spill over, but I hold them back. This isn't the right time, even if I did just agree to marry him, to be his for the rest of my life. I'll save it for the right moment.

I'm under him, and then I'm busily pulling him to the side so I can be on top of him. Staring down into his eyes, they're lit up like wildfire, as they watch my hips rock side to side. My body works to bring him pleasure, wanting nothing but to please him in any way that I can.

The feelings are too much, and they begin to overtake my movements and it's not enough to take me where I need to be. Thaddaeus can feel it, me seeking my own sweet surrender to bliss. He stands, holding me to him, our bodies overheated as our primal instinct grows stronger.

With a few quick strides, my back's up against the bedroom wall, the solid surface feeling as if it's digging into my muscles. Thaddaeus' forearms rest against the wall on either side of me, his muscles so hard I want to bite them. Passion crawls its way into my soul, igniting my body. He has me turning to putty with his movements.

He pounds into my body, as my hands clutch around his neck, holding on for dear life. He sweeps me away, my body soaring away as my orgasm hits me full force. His movements grow short as he comes in closer, bracing himself and chasing his own release.

He's magnificent, his body strong enough to hold me while we each seek our pleasure in the other. Seconds feel like minutes

as we clutch to each other forcefully enough to leave bruises behind—love marks or little reminders of what type of animal the
other exposed as we collided in the most beautiful, satisfying way.

"Tell me what you said a few minutes ago." I love his language, only I wish I knew what he was saying when he said it.

"Another time. Right now, I simply want to take you into the
shower. Make love to you under the water and wash you. Then
I want to take you back to my bed and worship you some more.
Tomorrow we pick out your forever diamond and call the priest."

"Tomorrow?"

"Yes, Grace, tomorrow."

Will we marry tomorrow or just set everything up? My forever
diamond. He remembered our conversation from our first dinner
together.

I haven't gotten to call my mother yet or Kaleigh.

"I can see you overthinking everything, Bella. Stop it and just
feel me. Tomorrow you become Grace Morelli, amore."

It's an order spoken full of warmth. His lips meet mine, much
tenderer than before, as he carries me into the bathroom and makes
the world fade away.

Fingers grazing over the skin on my thigh pull me from my dream-
less sleep. With Thaddaeus near, he holds the bad dreams at bay,
letting me sleep blissfully.

A moan leaves my mouth as I stretch my arms above my head,
officially waking up. His gaze is warm as my eyes meet his. He's
been watching me. For how long, he'll never admit.

"Morning." His grin's infectious, spurring my own, even
though I've only just woke up. How can I not be happy seeing his
face first thing?

"Hi."

"Sleep well?"

"Yes. What are you up to?"

His eyebrow quirks and he lets loose a delicious chuckle. "I have to have something up my sleeve, huh?"

"You look like you're bursting to tell me something."

He shrugs, covering something on the other side of his leg.

"Let me see."

"Are you sure?"

"Yes." I sit up, curiosity pulling me from my grogginess.

He twists toward me more, resting his left knee on the bed so he can face me completely. Reaching behind him, he brings a small white box forward. It's about the size of his hand. He's got my full attention as I watch him pull the lid free. He holds the box out for me to inspect its contents.

Nothing fancy about the container or the square of cotton lying inside. It's the three rings, sitting there that have me gasping. They must be the biggest diamond rings I've ever seen in my life.

I know Thaddaeus is rich; he lives in a mansion outside Chicago for God's sake, but this …It's an entirely different level of wealth. Diamond rings like these go for triple digits, maybe even millions—I have no clue. I'm not a jeweler, but I do know they aren't your run-of-the-mill engagement rings you see at the local mall.

"They're stunning," I breathe, meeting his gaze. It's a bit humble, as if he's worried I won't like them.

"You're sure? You like one enough to wear it, then?"

"You want me to wear one of these? I'd get robbed."

He laughs. He freaking laughs! Like they aren't each at least ten carats and then some and I shouldn't be flattered knowing one will grace my finger.

"Trust me, robbed would be the least of your worries. These

make a statement."

"That I launder blood diamonds?"

His jaw grows tight. I obviously struck a nerve or something with that comment. *Oh God, are they blood diamonds? Shit.*

"No, Bella, that you're married to me. Don't fret over where they came from."

Fuck. They are blood diamonds.

Do I ask about it? No. I'd much rather not know. Just like other parts of his business, they are not *my* business. I must learn to keep my nose out of his dealings. After all, I care for the man, not his job. I can ignore it. At least I hope I can to be with him.

So, he wants me to pick one. They're all beyond amazing, but the two super flashy ones don't speak to me. I go with the solitaire. It's ostentatious, but I can't help the excited flutters overtaking my stomach as I point to it. It's the meaning behind the ring, not the dollar amount that makes my heart stutter.

He lifts it out, inspecting it before pushing it on my left ring finger. I swear to God it'll get caught on everything I touch. I don't want to seem ungrateful; the man's offered me so much. Minus his heart.

"It's beautiful, thank you."

"It's nothing compared to you."

The compliment earns him a kiss. It's chaste, but I have to reward his sweetness some way.

"I need to brush my teeth."

"No, you'll give me a proper kiss, and then you may shower and brush them. The priest will be here shortly."

"Already? But I need to call my mother."

"No time, amore. Dress in the gown you wore to dinner. We'll have a big wedding if you wish; right now is for us. You can hire an event planner and organize it all, anything you want."

"You would do that for me?"

"Of course. I want you happy."

"I am happy with you," I honestly reply and his mouth meets mine. This time, it's a full-blown kiss. I welcome it, reassuring myself that he can mouthwash afterward.

The shower and getting ready went by way too quickly for my liking. I wanted to call my mother, but I couldn't bring myself to doing it. I know it would hurt her too badly not being here to witness her only daughter exchanging her vows. I've decided that I'll ask Thaddaeus to transfer my ticket to my mother so she can visit and help me plan a real wedding six months down the road.

I did break down and call Kaleigh. She's in total shock; so much so that she dropped her cell phone when the words left my mouth that I was about to marry one of Chicago's most notorious gangsters. I couldn't explain much, but she's coming. She's terrified, but swears I'm the only person who'd be able to pull off marrying a man like him.

She's scared for my safety, and I understand her concern. When she began to lecture me, well, more like plead with me, I threatened to hang up. I love her and I respect her, but this is my life. I'm doing what has to be done for not only my safety but for Thaddaeus' and his crew. We need to appear united, a strong force, so that's what we're doing.

And then there's the fact I'm also going through with it because inside I know that I love this crazy, overbearing, dominant man. I can only hope one day he loves me in the same fashion.

A brief knock at the bedroom door, pulls me from finishing up applying my mascara.

"Um, Grace?" It's Dillion. His head pops in a crack, flashing me his easy smile. Once he sees me, he opens the door wider. "Hey, wanted to make sure you were decent."

"Not sure how decent I am, but I'm dressed." I wink and his bright white smile grows.

"Your friend's arrived … Kaleigh?" He lets her pass, watching her like he's completely famished as she walks in front of him. I'd not pegged her as his type, but then again most wouldn't see me with my fiancé either. *He'd have to sedate her to get her to go out with him though.* That thought has me snorting to myself.

"Oh, Grace!" She rushes for me, arms open, ready to hug me like it's been years or something. I saw her last week, but she's my best friend, so I smile and return her hug with enthusiasm.

Dillion watches the exchange, a goofy grin on his face the entire time.

"Hey, chick," I say and she releases me.

"Thanks Dillion." He meets my gaze again, his face blanking out as a mask appears.

"No problem. You look great; he'll be pleased." His compliment has my cheeks heating. I love knowing that Thaddaeus will approve, and I know he'll look phenomenal in whatever he chooses as well.

The door closes behind him and Kaleigh turns to me, eyes wide. She's a dork, always dramatic when it comes to them. She whispers, "That man is gorgeous!"

"Who, Dillion?" I reply in my normal voice and she scowls.

"Yes!" she whispers, glancing at the door as if he can hear us. These walls are thick. It's amazing Thaddaeus heard me yell when I had that nightmare. She mock fans herself and I giggle.

"He's cool." I shrug, and put my makeup back into the little bag covered in fuchsia-colored kisses.

Thaddaeus had a fancy makeup holder delivered for me, but I've held myself back from using it just yet. I figure we should be married before I unleash my bathroom crazy on him. The poor guy may never have counter space again and the master bath is huge in comparison to normal bathrooms.

"How can you stand being around them all, and this close? Aren't you scared? I can't believe you're marrying one and not just any of them, but the main dude!" She rambles and the bedroom door opens again.

Dillion's eyes fall to Kaleigh and he clears his throat. "Ah, Grace, they're ready for you." He never looks at me once, his gaze trained on my best friend. She's just as guilty, staring him down with her mouth slightly parted. She looks like she wants to plow him, and he looks like he's ready to rip her damn dress off.

"Okay, if you two screw, it better not get awkward." I come out and say it because at this rate they'll be shredding each other's clothes to pieces in a closet within the hour.

Kaleigh's face turns a bright shade of scarlet and Dillion clears his throat again, adjusting the knot on his tie as if it's suddenly too tight. "Shall we?" he asks and I nod. I slip my feet into the same shoes Thaddaeus sent to me when he was courting me; they're still my favorites.

"I love your something blue." Kaleigh smiles, staring at the earrings Thaddaeus had sent on day number four. The blue glass beads with hearts are also my favorites and perfect for today.

The only other piece of jewelry I have on is the diamond bracelet. I want to be covered in him when he sees me for the first time. Sure, he's seen this dress before, but today's different. It was special the first time, but this time's forever.

Chapter 17

*The rage you feel...listen
to me carefully. It's a gift. Use it,
but don't let anyone see it.*
- Nucky Thompson, Boardwalk Empire

Grace

H e's handsome, dressed to the nines in a dark charcoal suit that I've not yet seen him wear. In a few hours' time, he's had the large sun-room transformed into a spot fit for a ceremony. Large bouquets of bright violet and deep blue lilies are placed on large plant stands around the room that look like mini columns. Matching colors of hydrangea blooms sit centered on a few small round tables covered in heavy white linen with a dark blue lace overlay.

There's long, white lace curtains tied back away from the twelve feet tall windows, letting the natural sunlight flood the entire room. He knows I love the garden here, but it's cold outside. He did this on purpose—for me—and that makes everything mean so much more.

The three chandeliers leading through the middle of the room are lit up. The hundreds of crystal pieces in each one cast different colored reflections everywhere. Small fuchsia-colored blooms line a path straight to the man himself. I'm stunned at the thought he's clearly put into everything. It's like he'd already had this all thought out and simply had to flick his fingers to make it all happen.

At the far side of the room, Thaddaeus waits. The priest, along with Maximillian and Cage, stand beside him. They're in light gray suits, not matching, but close enough. They're handsome and I'm honored they're standing beside him to support us.

Kaleigh showed up in a dark blue dress that ended up being completely fitting. I had no idea they would decorate this room with my favorite colors, and while none of us match exactly, the colors are beautiful, complementing each other. For a last-minute decision to marry, I have to say this far outweighs any expectations I ever had. I really can't wait to see what the full ceremony down the road ends up looking like when we have our families joining us to celebrate.

Dillion and Kaleigh walk on each side of me, not sure if it's in case I have a fleeing desire to bolt or just because they're my friends. Dillion is in Thaddaeus' crew, but he's fast becoming a friend to me as well.

"Grace." My future husband utters, looking over me with awe in his warm gaze. It's tender and I may be imagining it, but I swear it's full of love too. My hands go to his, and he holds them as I step closer to him, linked between us securely. "The father is a friend of the familia's." He nods to the right and I glance to the older gentleman in black.

"Father." I smile. "Thank you for joining us today."

"My pleasure." He returns my smile and surprisingly his is genuine. I wouldn't expect it from someone who's never met me, but from him it is, and I instantly like him. "Now, is everyone ready to start?"

"We are." Thaddaeus answers for us both and I squeeze his palms, enthralled.

"Do you, Grace, take Thaddaeus to be your husband? For life, to have and hold, through sickness and health, until death do you part?" The vows are a little ironic as I think them over. That's essentially what it'll come down to, to separate us—death.

"Yes, I do." No hesitation. I've had time to think it over, and

I've made peace with my decision. I'll devote myself to him for the rest of my life.

At my answer, Thaddaeus stands a bit taller, if that's even possible. Hard to believe that man has any doubts at all, especially about little ol' me not saying I do. I know I'm lucky to have him; I'm not going to let him slip away or embarrass him during such an important event in our lives.

"Do you, Thaddaeus, take Grace to be your wife? For life, to have and hold, through sickness and health, until death do you part?" The priest repeats and I find myself holding my breath.

Tawny orbs meet mine, staring at me like they can see completely through me. He nods, swallowing. "Yes, Father, I do."

Everything else fades away as he leans forward, his hands pulling my palms in closer to him as his lips touch mine. Softness, unlike anything I've felt before overcomes me. He kisses me like I'm a delicate flower, ready to wilt as if he's afraid that too much pressure will push me away.

He's warm and inviting. His scent and his taste consume every thought as I take him in through the kiss. I give him back everything, pouring my heart into the mating of our mouths. I want him to know that I mean it, that he's my forever. Time passes too quickly and he's pulling away, sliding the sparkling diamond ring on my left ring finger.

It doesn't feel too heavy anymore. It feels perfect, like it was meant to be there.

I can barely make out the fuzzy image of the priest in the background. He's simply not here in this moment I'm experiencing with Thaddaeus. This time is for my husband and me—to take him in and really catalog each feature so I can remember this moment for the rest of my life. Nights when I'm left alone because of his business, I'll look back, remembering this right now. How perfect it was and why I wait, no doubt worrying about his safety.

"I now pronounce you husband and wife. I'd say you could kiss your bride, but you've already done that." The older man chuckles quietly.

"That's okay, I don't mind," I reply in a daze and this time I'm met with a scorching kiss. It's urgent and full of unspoken promises of bliss. No doubt this man will be having his fill of me on our wedding night and I look forward to every minute of it.

His embrace loosens as I come back off the cloud his kiss had put me on. I didn't realize he had his arms wrapped around me as I was completely consumed by his mouth.

"You're officially mine, Grace Morelli."

"I like the sound of that."

The ring sparkles beautifully in the lights, as does my bracelet when I peer down at them. The realization that I'm now a married woman isn't lost on me. There were times I believed it would never happen. I can't help but wonder if we'll have children? Will he love me? Perhaps I should've asked him those questions before exchanging our vows, but I won't go back on them now. We were married in front of a Catholic priest, and friends, that mean a great deal to us. In my eyes, this is one hundred percent real.

"You've made me a very happy man, amore," Thaddaeus whispers against my brow, pressing a sweet kiss to my forehead before pulling away and thanking the Father.

I smile and watch as he shakes his friends' hands as they congratulate him. They each move on from him after a moment to embrace me in a strong hug and whisper their support. Kaleigh's last to offer her congratulations, but her hug's genuine and that's all that matters. I'm so grateful she came today and I let her know it.

"I'm happy for you, even if you caught me off guard. I want you to be content, and if you love him, who am I to stand in your way?" She squeezes my bicep affectionately and scopes out Dillion.

"You know, I'm pretty sure he's single."

Her eyes pop back to me. "Huh?"

"Dillion. I'm sure if you made a move, he'd comply."

"Oh no." She giggles nervously and I roll my eyes. She'll never go for it which is a shame because I bet Dillion would show her the time of her life.

One of the housekeepers approaches. "Pardon, the food is ready whenever you all are."

"Thank you, Jenna," Thaddaeus acknowledges and turns to us. "Ready to eat?"

I can't believe he pulled this off and that he's telling me there's more. I assumed he'd only had enough time to have them decorate in here for the ceremony, but there's food too? I'd smelled something walking down to the sun-room but I figured it was for dinner.

Taking my hand, he leads me to the formal dining room with everyone else following along. I've seen this room when I've explored, but we've never actually used it. I'm blown away inside to discover it's been decorated similar to the setup in the sun-room. The exquisitely carved cherry table is set with a white runner down the middle. Hydrangea blooms in my favorite colors accent it with fine china placed in each setting.

On a buffet stand off to the side, there's a freshly-baked Italian crème cake. It's frosted in white swirls for our wedding day and lightly sprinkled along the sides with almonds. It looks delicious. The elegant porcelain dessert plates and petite fuchsia-colored blooms surrounding it all make it appear even more special. I'll never forget this day for the rest of my life, and I'll always be grateful to Thaddaeus and his staff for doing what they could to make this day stand out against all the others.

It's like a fairy tale—one I never imagined would come from a man who's been painted by the city as such a ruthless criminal. As each moment passes, my decision to marry him becomes more and more confident. Clearly, he cares for me to do all of this. I know he wouldn't have thought twice about any of it. This was for me, and each little thing he does makes me surrender a bit more of myself to him.

I was right in the beginning about needing space away or

else he'd consume me in no time. I've been in his home—our home now—for a week, and the man is easily becoming my entire world. Everything from the first bouquet of flowers he's sent has been giving. How did I get so lucky to meet a man with such a big heart?

Thaddaeus

Lunch, the ceremony, the cake—all of it was perfect. Even if I was working on business during most of it, I couldn't be more pleased. The cheeses, meats, breads, meatballs and sauce we had catered in turned out to be a success with everyone. The priest made Grace feel at ease and I couldn't have asked for more. Her friend even sucked up her fear to be there for her best friend. I was impressed and able to take care of some business, so win-win all around. Thankfully, I don't think Grace ever caught on to what was going on during any of it.

Last night when my guys returned empty-handed, I knew I'd have to take matters into my own hands. They say if you want something done right, you must do it yourself. The marriage to Grace was step one. Next, I make an example out of the gutter rat that attempted to kill my wife. Then we'll see if anyone has a nut sack big enough to come at me again.

I received a text from Officer Lancer, one of the cops on my payroll. He spotted Jimmy Fantiome heading into one of Franco's old warehouses. I'm assuming he overtook his crew and is running things now. I usually attempt to stay out of the local gangs' activities as long as they stay far away from me and my business ventures. They've crossed a line, and now everything's fair game.

Immediately, I sent Cage to the pits to round up some more of our crew and to find a handful of fighters to bring with us in case I needed a few people beaten to death. This isn't an after-school special; I'm a criminal in the streets of Chicago. Things don't always end in a handshake; hence, my kind uncle Robbie getting shot down in his freaking bakery.

"Time to celebrate," I say, turning to Dillion and Maximillian.

It's just us. Grace and Kaleigh wanted to catch up so they went to relax in the theatre room and the priest left about an hour ago. Housekeeping has been cleaning everything up, minus the flowers per Grace's request, so everything's getting back to normal.

"You decided on a honeymoon or party after all?"

Shaking my head at Dillion, I take a drink of my scotch and continue. "Nope. I have a location on Jimmy Fantiome."

Max grins wickedly. "Shall we pay him a visit then?"

"I think it's time we show them what a real drive-by is, don't you?" They both eagerly agree. "Load up the weapons; we're meeting Cage right outside the warehouse. I've already called him and put everything into play. And bring both SUVs. I want to roll three deep on this."

"This is serious then," Dillion states and I grunt. No need to answer. I'm done fucking around with wannabe thugs.

We load up and Dillion drives the Denali with me in the back, and Max follows in the Tahoe. Both are all blacked out with bulletproof upgrades, as are all my vehicles. Cage will be in my other Tahoe. I have three at all times, just for reasons such as this, or if I have unexpected business that needs transport. You can fit a lot in an SUV– weapons, drugs, guns … bodies.

After a quick drive, we pull into an empty parking lot. Cage is already waiting with four shredded fighters and six men from our drug crew. They'll know how to shoot, while, if needed, the fighters will know how to fight and provide security. I doubt it'll get to that point, but I stay alive in this business by always being prepared.

"Cage, thanks for being swift." He nods as I scan over the guys beside him. He did a good job.

I take in the leather boots, jeans, and cut. *Biker.* He looks pretty damn mean and buff though, so no argument out of me. I notice his name patch reads 'Cain' on one side. Another I recognize as

Blake 'The Adonis.' He's pro; Cage must've been serious when he said this guy was looking for extra work. Not sure what kind of hole he dug himself into with taking a chance like this against his fighting career in the pros. If he gets popped or injured, his career in MMA will be spent and he'll be fighting in the pit full-time for me. Not that I'd mind, just surprised.

My gaze stops on the last two. They're a few from the pit, our regular fighters. They stare at the ground, not eager to meet my gaze. The other six, from our drug crew know exactly who I am, but we have so many of them, I have no idea who they are. That's Max's department, I just sign their paychecks, so to speak.

"I want the weapons in the back seat. Fighters in the very backs of the SUVs. I want you four out of the firing range." I direct and they head to wait by the hatches of each vehicle. "Cage, Max, Dillion—you three drive. Anyone familiar with heavy artillery equipment, you sit in the back seat. Small arms fire, you take the front seat."

Everyone springs into action, unloading weapons from the backs of the SUVs and taking their directed places. I ride with Dillion again, sitting in the seat directly behind him. One of the drug crew guys takes the front next to D while another sits to the right of me. The biker and one of the other fighters hop in the very back, and then we're moving. We can't waste time; who knows when Jimmy will take off again.

The two guys on the right each start checking their weapons, loading them and preparing for what's about to go down. Franco's old warehouse isn't too far from here, but it feels like it takes forever to get there. I send a quick text to the officer again, confirming Jimmy Fantiome's still there in the building. Once he gives me the thumbs up, I tell him he can leave and promise to send him a payment later this week for his help.

The old, brown building comes into sights. "Lower the windows," I order Dillion. The guy beside me can't. His weapon's in the way for him to reach. It's bad enough that he has to be squished up against me, sitting in the middle to have enough space.

The two black windows on the right begin to lower and the guy beside me slides the Browning M2 .50 cal machine gun out the window enough to give him room not to get in the way of the loading. Glancing behind me, I can see the other vehicles do the same. The SUVs slow down to a comfortable speed around twenty miles per hour, coming up on the building.

Once we're at the halfway point of the building and the other two vehicles are close enough to fire as well, I give the order. "Light them up."

Thank God, we stuck earplugs in; it's so noisy. The guy beside me has his back propped against mine to help withstand the momentum of the machine guns. There's no rat-tat from puny, cheap ass weapons; this sounds like fucking thunder in the truck as each round goes off. Casings fly off to the side and we each hold our breath, hoping like a motherfucker the hot shells don't burn any of us.

Holes filter through the structure, slicing through its walls like a warm knife to butter. Definitely worth the nine grand I shelled out per .50 cal to keep in each of my SUVs. I like to be prepared.

As the debris from the building flies in every direction, a loud, booming laugh leaves me. Revenge is best served with brass casings involved. Glad I could teach these wannabes a little lesson in what happens when you cross a Morelli.

If Jimmy or any of his boys survive this, one thing's for certain, they'll know to not fuck with what's mine.

Chapter 18

Mozzafiato
- (adj) breathtaking, majestic.
Literally to chop off one's breath.

Thaddaeus

"**W**hat are we doing?"

Adjusting my suit shirt a bit, I take her in. "We're going to dinner."

She looks stunning in her red wrap dress. Don't get me wrong, I love when she's in yoga pants; but this, I can slide my hands under when we're at the dinner table. It's like enticing a bull and I'm ready to charge.

"But what about last time? Is it safe?"

"Yes, amore. You're my familia now—my wife. Everyone needs to see that ring on your finger and know the rumors are accurate. They'd be signing they're death certificates if they went against you."

There's also the part where I sent one hell of a message last week. I'm still thinking about those machine guns. I should order more; they take retribution to an entirely new level. Maybe I should have my crew hit the range with me so we can have some fun with the .50 cals. We could make a guy's day out of it; they've earned it by putting up with my mood swings lately.

"I won't let anyone harm you."

"I trust you."

Grace's faith in me makes me feel as if I'm twenty feet tall and made of steel. I'll break someone in half before they get to her. Pulling her to me, my arms tightly wrap around her frame. I can never touch her enough or be close enough to this woman it seems.

Grace

We get to the restaurant and everyone openly gawks. Usually people shy away from looking at him so brazenly, but not tonight. They practically gape as his fingers wind with mine; my left hand on full display with my new diamond sparkling magnificently. He's proud too; I can see it written all over his profile. I think he's silently beating on his chest as we cross the room.

Thaddaeus nearly glows as he shows me off, walking past table after table. The place is full of people as the hostess leads the way to our own private area set toward the back of the room. He seems elated to have me at his side, and that, in return, makes me overly happy inside.

Dillion follows us along, making himself comfortable by propping up in a nearby corner, scanning the entire place for potential threats. There's no doubt in my mind that everyone here knows exactly who Thaddaeus is, and it's a bit nerve-racking.

The hostess flashes a friendly smile my way and places the menu down, letting us know that our server will be right with us to get our drink order.

"What are you thinking right now?" Thaddaeus leans in, his manly scent overpowering the lingering traces of tomatoes, oregano, and cheeses left floating through the air. He's so handsome like this, dressed in his suit, all nicely put together and gazing at me like I'm the most important person in the room.

"That everyone's watching us and I'd bet money they know who you are."

"They weren't staring at me, Bella." He watches me intently, his gaze lingering on my lips a bit longer than the rest of my features. I wore some darker lipstick tonight; it's a deep red and daring. I love it, and it seems that my new husband is fond of it as well.

"No? I could've sworn they were looking."

"Oh, they were, and that was the whole point of coming when it's so packed. But it wasn't me they were so curious about; it was you. My crew's been spreading rumors that I've taken a wife, then we show up, ring on your finger. I'm sure there's plenty of gossip going on at the moment."

"You want them to talk about us?"

"Yes, cara. The faster it gets around, the safer you'll be from any lingering threats out there."

"Oh. And here I was hoping you just wanted to have dinner with me."

"I do, above all, I do. But I would've taken you someplace quiet, someplace that if I wanted, I could lay you over the table and feast on that sweet pussy between your legs." His declaration has me clenching my legs together, already feeling him there. He's the most experienced man I've been with when it comes to sex. I don't mean that in a bad way either. The man knows how to please me over and over and I'm grateful for it.

"So, you're saying that if I wanted your tongue on me right now, you wouldn't do it in front of all these people?" I issue the small challenge; I love keeping him on his toes.

A low noise leaves his throat, something close to a growl as his eyes grow darker, "Don't tempt me, because I would. People be damned, I'd give them one hell of a show. Just say the word."

I know what he says is true and it has me growing warm all over. His hand finds my thigh, sliding up under my dress until his fingers lightly graze over the black lace thong I'd worn especially for him to discover later.

The server takes our order, leaving glasses of water behind

and Thaddaeus never skipped a beat stroking me the entire time. Ordering for us both while his fingers kept gently grazing my lips. I was growing wetter by the minute and couldn't contain the soft moan from leaving me when he pushed the fabric to the side and barely dipped his fingers inside me. I contracted instantly, grabbing for his fingers, begging for more.

It was like an igniter to a flame. He scooted closer, pushing his finger inside me fully. One at first and then he added a second digit to the sweet torture, rhythmically pumping them in and out. I couldn't do anything but go with it. I wasn't about to tell him to stop. It felt too good.

I squirmed through the server dropping off my wine and Thaddaeus' Scotch. He was smart enough to act like he didn't notice me quietly panting as my orgasm started to build. The refreshing, chilled glass of wine did nothing to cool me off, just complemented the amazing feelings perfectly.

Reaching out to treat Thaddaeus to the same bit of bliss, he captures my wrist with his other hand. He holds me still until I finally stop trying, my hips rolling each time his palm presses against my clit. He watches me closely, waiting on bated breath for me to crest the top of the spiraling mountain of my orgasm.

A soft mewl spills from my lips as I bite down on the inside of my cheek, attempting to tamper down the need to moan. It's like he can read it, his mouth slamming down on mine. His free hand finds the back of my neck, holding me to him so he can kiss me like a man dying from thirst.

Mimicking his fingers with his tongue, it pushes me over. The entire restaurant would hear me call out in wonderment if it wasn't for his mouth drowning the sound. I lose myself as he pumps his fingers into me with more force, finishing me off.

After a few moments, his hand leaves my private area. He fixes my panties back into place and my lids part, still panting, my dazed irises meet his amused gaze. My entire body's scorching overcome with heat, humming in a postorgasmic state.

"Do you believe me now when I say that I'll tongue fuck you, right here if you wanted?"

My head bobs, imagining that scene in my mind. "We should go home."

"Indeed, amore; we should. I'll get our entrees to go. I'm sure we've made enough of a lasting impression here tonight."

My stare breaks, quickly glancing around to see everyone watching us. They just saw me come—an entire restaurant. The crazy part is that I couldn't care less; I thoroughly enjoyed myself and would do it again.

"I think they're just jealous." I shrug, a naughty grin overtaking me and making him smirk in return.

"Ah, Grace, you're already making the Morelli name proud." He winks and I laugh. This city has no idea what's about to hit them, because now Thaddaeus has a wife to be bad with him.

Thaddaeus

Opening the door, I'm surprised to be faced with my uncle himself. He smiles wolfishly as I step out of the way for him to enter.

"Uncle."

"Nephew," he greets. "It's coming down out there, huh?" He gestures behind him toward the blanketing rain. It'll no doubt turn to snow at some point during the night. There's nothing enjoyable about Chicago weather this time of year; it's miserable, plain and simple.

"Thaddaeus?" I hear Grace behind me obviously checking to make sure I'm okay. It's sweet, but I need to have a chat with her about coming downstairs when uninvited guests show up. If he wasn't familia, he never would've been automatically buzzed through my gate.

"Come here, amore. I want to introduce you."

She's by my side immediately, and my arm circles her protectively. It's late, and I'm in a T-shirt and pajama pants while she's in a silk nightgown wrapped up in a matching robe—a gift I ordered for her the other day. It was worth every penny I spent on it too. She looks phenomenal. After our little show at the restaurant, we came home and I made love to her on the kitchen counter while we ate our dinner. It brought new meaning to the term, 'eating out' for us both.

"This darling creature must be your new wife that I've heard so much about." My uncle holds out a small ice chest to me and I take it. Freeing his hands, he grabs for Grace's hands, holding them carefully to bring them to his mouth. He pecks the top of each hand, charming her with his smile. "It's a true pleasure, my dear."

"Oh." Her cheeks flush slightly. My uncle knows what he's doing when it comes to women and business. He's not always so friendly, but I appreciate it being the first time she's ever met him. The last thing I want is for my familia to frighten her.

"Bella, this is my uncle, Sammi Morelli. Uncle, this is my Grace."

"Molto bella, indeed," he purrs. If he wasn't so powerful I'd knock him down a peg. "My apologies for missing the ceremony."

"Thank you, but I'm afraid that's our fault. We wanted something immediate, but we'll have a ceremony for family to come and celebrate in six months or so." Grace smiles, glancing at me and I nod. She's doing the right thing, inviting him. He is after all, the head of the familia. She just has no idea of the fact. Our wedding ceremony will be overrun with so many Morellis she'll never keep up with who's who.

"Wonderful, I'd love to come. Consider this as my RSVP." I nearly chuckle at his response. Normally, my familia has to practically beg to get him in attendance, but he was close to my grandfather, as was I at a time.

"Great!"

"Regardless of the formal ceremony, it's custom to give the

214 | Sapphire Knight

newlyweds a gift, as I've brought one that pertains to you both."
He gestures to the ice chest I'm holding. "Open it, Nephew. I know
you'll be pleased."

I don't know why I turn away from Grace, call it gut intuition
from being in this type of lifestyle for so long, but I'm glad I do.

Inside rests six severed hands and three hearts. It's a bloody
mess, and if Grace saw it, I have a feeling my new wife would be
passing out on us.

My gaze meets his. "How thoughtful Uncle, may I ask?" I
don't finish the sentence. He knows what I mean. I may not be
in the mob, but I know what a gift like this means—respect and
loyalty. It comes from part of my familia's motto, from the Mafia
side.

"Of course." He turns to Grace. "Kitten, be a gem and get me
some coffee. That rain mixed with the wind wasn't pleasant."

Instantly, I can see Grace feels guilty for not already offering.
She's new to playing hostess though so my uncle will forgive her.
"Oh my gosh, I'm so sorry for not checking sooner. Of course, I'll
be right back with it, and some snacks."

He sends her another predatory grin and she practically jogs
toward the kitchen. Once she's out of sight his stern gaze meets
mine again. "Nephew. These belong to the three men who killed
Roberto. I understand this will also benefit you and your wife.
Consider it a gift, retribution, and an end to what could have turned
into a citywide war for you."

"Grazie." I respond immediately and he accepts my gratitude
by holding his hand out to me. I don't even blink, immediately
bending to kiss the familia ring adorning his middle finger.

He is the head of the familia and the fact that he came to my
home with this is a great honor. It's showing me that I'm in his
favor, and I'm no longer cast out from not joining the ranks.

By the time Grace returns, my uncle's already left. He didn't
really want anything to drink; he asked her so that he could tell me

what was needed without frightening my wife. That means a lot to me as well. He could've been the ruthless mob Boss he normally is to everyone else and not cared about her well-being.

"He's gone, already?" my sweet woman asks, setting the tray of coffee, sugar, and Baileys Irish Cream liquor on the sitting room table. She brought a box of thin mints along with it, her favorites.

"Yes. He got a call and had to leave. I see you brought the Baileys with the coffee."

She nods, watching me curiously as I set the cooler at my feet. I'll have one of the guys dispose of it.

"You'll fit in with this familia just fine."

"I hope so. I thought it might help warm him up with the cof-fee." She shrugs.

"You're smart baby, one of the many things I respect about you."

"Oh yeah?"

I nod.

"What did he bring us?" Her eyes fall to the cooler again.

"Just some fresh lobsters from Maine. Dillion's going to take care of them for us." There's no way in hell I'm telling her it's full of body parts. Not until she's accustomed to this life a bit longer anyway.

"I can do it, it's no problem. I don't want to bother him again today."

"No worries, amore, I've already spoken to him. He wants to use a special season so I told him to go ahead."

"Okay. If he changes his mind, I can do it for us."

"I'll let him know."

"So, he was your uncle. He's younger than Robbie, were they brothers?"

"Yes."

"How many uncles do you have?"

"My grandfather had six sons."

Her eyes widen as she fixes the coffee for herself. "So there are four others I haven't met yet?"

"Yes, but it doesn't matter."

"What do you mean?" She peers at me, confused, and I take the spot on the sofa next to where she stands.

"Because you just met the most powerful one. That, Grace, was the head of the Italian Mob."

Her face turns white, as she sinks down to the couch, perching on the edge. "But, he-he was so nice."

"Yes, cara. It appears you have a way with really bad men."

"There's nothing evil about you, Thaddaeus."

A laugh breaks free. "You have no idea how wicked I really am baby, but that's okay. I love that fact." I kiss her forehead. What started out as an obsession, the insatiable need to have her has evolved into love. "And I love you."

She doesn't need to know that I hired the men who put out a hit on her so that I could be the one to protect her. No one does. Jimmy did but my uncle took care of that problem for me. Familia always sticks together, especially when you're Italian.

Grace is mine and that's all that matters. I told you I'd do anything to get what I wanted. If it makes me crazy, then so be it. They call me the Joker for a reason.

Grace

He said it. He loves me. That's all I wanted when we exchanged our vows to each other and he's given it to me. And everyone thinks he's so bad. Not a chance.

Or so she believes!

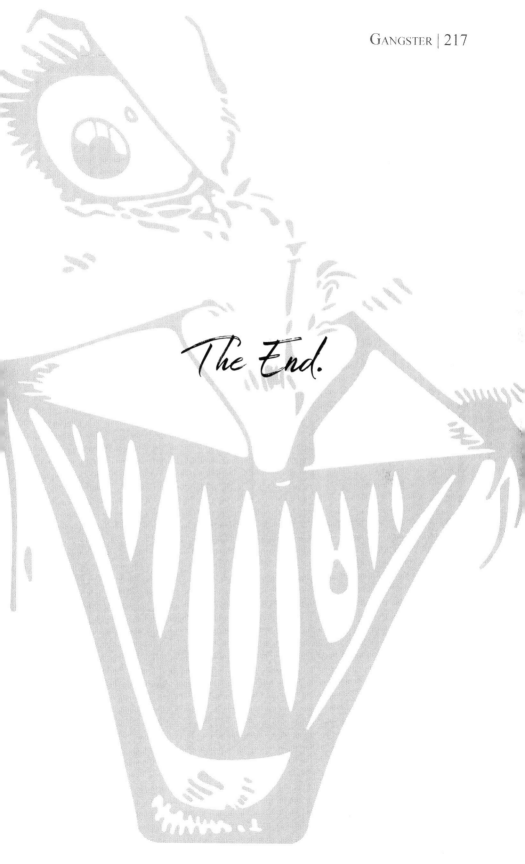

The End.

Hope you enjoyed meeting Grace and Thaddaeus 'Joker' Morelli! These two hit me one day and I couldn't get them out of my head. I quickly fell in love with how stubborn they both were and had to share their story with you all. One song inspired this entire book and my muses. If you'd like to check it out and see who these characters were to me, look up, 'You Don't Own Me' by Grace ft. G-Eazy. So much hotness!

Watch for more Italians in the future! XOXO –Sapphire

Strawberry Cheesecake Streusel Muffins

Streusel Topping

3 tablespoons White Sugar

3 tablespoons Dark Brown Sugar

½ cup + 3 tablespoons Flour

Pinch Coarse Kosher Salt

5 tablespoons butter, melted

Cream Cheese Filling

4 ounces cream cheese

⅓ cup white sugar

2 teaspoons beaten egg

1 tsp vanilla extract

Muffin Batter

2 cups all purpose flour

½ cup granulated sugar

2 tsp baking powder

½ tsp salt

1 egg

¼ cup canola oil

1 cup whole milk (original recipe used ¾ cup)

1 tsp vanilla extract

1½ cups strawberries, cut into small pieces

Instructions cont...

Preheat oven to 400. Line a muffin tin with cupcake liners and spray each liner with non-stick spray. Set aside.

To make the streusel topping, mix together sugars, flour and salt. Drizzle warm butter over mixture and toss with fork to form pea size pieces. Set aside.

To make cream cheese filling, beat cream cheese, sugar, egg and vanilla extract together with an electric mixer in a medium bowl until smooth. Set aside.

TO make the muffins.

Whisk flour, sugar baking powder and salt in a medium bowl.

In a separate bowl, whisk the egg, oil, milk and vanilla extract.

Add the dry ingredients into the milk mixture. Stir until just incorporated. Do not over mix or you will get a tough muffin.

Fold in the strawberries.

Scoop a heaping tablespoon of the muffin batter into each cupcake liner. Add a heaping tablespoon of the cream cheese filling. Add another heaping tablespoon on batter onto of the cream cheese filling. I was able to fill the muffin tins full. Sprinkle the streusel topping on the tops.

Bake for 25 minutes.

Allow to cool in muffin tin for 10 minutes.

Remove and chow down.

Also by Sapphire

Oath Keepers MC Series
Secrets
Exposed
Relinquish
Forsaken Control
Friction
Princess
Sweet Surrender

Russkaya Mafiya Series
Secrets
Corrupted
Unwanted Sacrifices
Russian Roulette

Standalones
Unexpected Forfeit
1ˢᵗ Time Love
Gangster

Stay up to date with Sapphire

Email

authorsapphireknight@yahoo.com

Website

www.authorsapphireknight.com

Facebook

www.facebook.com/AuthorSapphireKnight

BONUS READING
A small taste of my Russians ☺

Corrupted Revelations
By: International Bestselling Author
Sapphire Knight

Chapter 1
I Will Find You

5 Years Ago

Spartak

If another guest asks me to hold their drink, I may just tie them up. I'm security; it doesn't automatically make me a waiter or man candy. My Boss, the groom, is nowhere to be found at the moment, and that's stressful enough.

A feminine voice from my side interrupts my perusal. "Excuse me, sir." I shift, turning away from the latest cougar attempting to have me do something for them and spot Tate. He's standing next to an enormous white tent-like structure, set up behind the cabin. It's perfect weather for the outdoor, beach wedding ceremony, and guests are fluttering around like they've never been to such an event before. *Finally, someone who I can ask.*

Quickly, I make my way over to him, weaving between random people. Tate nods when he notices me approach him. "Spartak."

"Mr. Masterson." Clearing my throat, I continue, "Sir, I'm attempting to locate your brother."

Tate chuckles. "Knowing Viktor, he's probably bothering his fiancée. Those two seem glued to each other at this point."

"Right. Thank you."

He nods hurriedly, greeting the next guest approaching him.

I head toward the massive barn that's closer to the beach. The women deemed this building theirs since it has much more room to make preparations than the cabin does. This intimate wedding is turning into way more than what was originally planned.

224 | SAPPHIRE KNIGHT

Knocking on the old door, I wait and get nothing.

Rap.

Rap.

Rap.

I knock a little harder against the giant door. The wood scrapes into my knuckles and pisses me off before the door slides open about three inches.

Elaina peeks her sweet little face between the opening.

"Hi Spar, is everything okay?" She peers at me worriedly with her sapphire-colored irises.

"Yes, Miss Elaina, just checking if the Boss is in here."

"No, he's actually behaved and hasn't tried to lock me in any of the safe rooms yet." She grins, sliding the door open a little more, and I step closer, blocking the opening to keep others from seeing her.

"Wow, ma'am; he is going to be floored when he sees you."

"You like it?"

I hear women laughing behind her; they must know how silly the question is. Elaina's beyond beautiful. I nod, not sure what to say to her, without Viktor sinking me in the lake if he hears.

"This is that new Vera Wang dress he had you and Lexei go pick up."

I swallow roughly as I skate over her in the delicate white lace, formfitting gown. It's understated class and Elaina knows how to pull off every stitch of it. She touches lightly to the dainty, diamond-encrusted tiara resting in her long blonde, Cinderella hair. "This, um, this was Mishka and Vivi's; they wore it for their weddings." She gazes at me, seeking my approval.

"It's very fitting. I'm really happy for you Elaina; you and the Boss deserve this."

She leans in, clutching onto my forearm and squeezes affectionately. Elaina's eyes begin to crest with tears, full of happiness, as she whispers kindly, "Thank you, Spar. You helped keep us safe so we could have this day. I'm so happy you get to be a part of it."

I close my eyes briefly, thanking the Lord that my close friend can have this day and that she's genuinely happy.

I shoot her a sheepish grin. "I must go. Alexei is monitoring the guests on the beach and tent area. I need to find Mr. Masterson; I don't like him being alone." She smiles at me gratefully, backing up a few paces so I can slide the door closed again. At least I know Elaina's surrounded by others and is protected.

I make my way down the small grassy path, toward the shop building. It's more of the guards' building now, but it should be empty at the moment. I believe all the men are on assignment—either here or out handling business.

I don't quite make it to the shop when I hear Viktor arguing with someone. It sounds as if it's coming from behind the building, so I head straight back there.

Viktor glances up, a scowl adorning his flushed face when he sees me. I stay silent, standing in the shadow of the building in case he needs me.

The other gentleman has his back to me, but by the voice, I recognize it as his Uncle Victor. I'm curious as to why he's back here, considering he was not on the guest list.

His uncle places his placating hand on Viktor's shoulder, and Viktor glares in return as if he may head-butt the older man. "Look, Viktor, I apologize for barging in on your wedding day, but Sabrina Chestkolav was sold in a previous deal."

"She was traded to me, Uncle. I don't care which ratty family thinks they have claim to her. I've warned you about selling women. I told you to stop; you are no longer in charge, and you are forcing my hand."

"I'm not here to step on your toes, Nephew, only to collect for her betrothed."

Viktor grits angrily, "She's going nowhere. Sabrina belongs to me now. Not only that, but she was obtained for Nikoli. You are aware how close Nikoli is to my brother?" Viktor's voice turns to ice as he finishes. "You warn this interested family, that they will have every element of the Mafiya and my Bratva after them if they do not back off."

The older man huffs but keeps his words to himself.

"Now, pack up and leave. You are not going to disrupt my Printsyessa's day."

"This isn't finished, Viktor." The old man attempts to argue as Alexei appears.

Viktor glanced from me to Alexei. "Lexei, you and I shall escort my uncle off the grounds. Spartak, you may go back to the main party."

Uncle Victor stares at me angrily, unaware I was privy to the conversation, and I swallow nervously. I know my Boss is in charge of the Bratva now, but his uncle is still an extremely intimidating, powerful man.

"Yes, sir," I answer dutifully and watch as Alexei and Viktor lead his uncle to the cars.

Before I turn around myself, someone grabs onto my shoulder, startling me, since I'm still on alert from the threatening conversation I just witnessed. I grip onto the person's arm harshly, propelling them forward and bringing their back to my chest. I drop the knife resting in my jacket sleeve, sliding it carefully and swiftly down my wrist, digging it into their neck, just enough for them to stand still.

I have to stop myself from gasping when I discover long brunette hair cascading over the feminine shoulder, enveloping me in a sweet smell.

The woman stutters out in a whisper-soft voice, "Um, um."

I drop my arms, deftly stepping back and putting a few paces between us. "Forgive me," I mumble as my heart beats frantically enough to feel as if it may pop out of my chest.

She promptly spins around, and I'm met with dark, sinful eyes, wide with excitement. Her hand clutches her neck at the area my knife was just touching as she swallows nervously. Her chest is rapidly rising and falling with each labored breath.

"I didn't mean to startle you. I was following you because you ignored me at the party."

Shit. I hadn't even glanced at her face back there. *Stupid Spartak.* This woman could have stepped straight out of a fantasy, and yet she's chasing me around.

Clearing my throat, I tug on my jacket, attempting to fix the rumpled mess. "Yeah, I'm sorry about that. Did you need something?" I may as well go with being polite since I've already snubbed her once, and then almost impaled her with my blade.

She grins mischievously, her irises gleaming with intent as she approaches. She stops about four inches from my face, and I lick my lips nervously, as I feel my throat get tight. I don't do well with people in my personal space, but her, well I want to pull even closer.

"Yes, Spartak. I do need something." My eyes widen with the way her smooth voice caresses over my name, surprised that she was behind me long enough to hear Viktor mention it.

She grasps onto my suit lapels, pulling my body against hers, molding her plump breasts against my firm chest as she takes me for a kiss so powerful I've never felt anything like it in my life. With a few twists of her skilled tongue, my cock stands to attention, seeking something it hasn't had in quite a while. I clutch tightly onto her small biceps, probably bruising the lightly tanned skin as I kiss her back with everything I have. If this is some sort of attack plan, I'm screwed.

After a few minutes, I pull back, panting, heavily turned on. "Fuck," I gasp. She nods, her eyes dilated with heat.

"I want more," she orders as she deftly undoes the button on my slacks, backing me up to the shop's back wall.

"More? What's your name?" Stupid, but it's the only thing I can think of as she wraps her petite, soft hands around my throbbing member.

"Victoria," she murmurs hastily as she finishes pulling my boxer briefs down and pumping my cock a few times. I clear away the frog in my throat, twisting her body so that she's the one pressed against the wall and hike her mid-length, plum colored dress up, around her waist. Then sliding her pair of tiny lace panties over so I can get to her sweet spot, I slip my finger in her deeply, watching for any signs that I've gone too far. I've never met this woman before, yet she seems keen on getting to know me. I don't know what I've done in my previous life to deserve this sort of reward, but I'll gladly accept.

"Yessss," she lowly groans out, as her head leans against the building, exposing the smooth skin on her neck. "Mooore."

Victoria laces her fingers behind my neck, raising her breasts a little higher and causing my gut to clench tightly with need. Slipping my fingers free from her center, I hike her leg up, lining my cock up where I want to be the most.

I peer down at Victoria. "Are you sure?"

"Damn it, do it already!" Her small hands cover my scruffy jaw as she pulls my face down, vigorously taking my mouth again.

Victoria's tongue slips in my mouth at the same time I plunge into her tight heat. I groan through the fantastic sensations, pulling out slightly and then fully seating my cock inside of her.

"Perfect, Spartak!" she moans in between kisses. Her hands skate up and down my chest, further rumpling my clothes, but I can't make myself give a shit about any of that besides the delicious feeling of her wrapped snuggly around me.

"Fuck, you're amazing," I croon as I use my free hand to slip her sleeve off her shoulder, freeing her full, left breast. I hike her leg up farther around my hip, grinding into her and leaning down just enough to slip her perfect pebbled, strawberry-colored nipple into my mouth. My head is wrenched backward, my eyes meeting hers as I suck strongly. Victoria pulls my hair forcefully, gazing down at me. "Bite it," she demands.

I nip down on the morsel, treating it as if it were my favorite sweet treat, even if that would be the juncture between her thighs. She yanks on my hair again, and I wrench upwards quickly, her breast making a 'pop' as I let go. I grasp her hand, raising it above her head.

"Enough, unless you wish for me to pull your hair; you asked for it, and I'm giving it," I grit, winding my other arm around her waist to save her from hurting her back. I pump into her a few times, clenching my ass as the feelings coursed through me, begging for a quick release. Her face flushes, and she bites her lip, grinning slightly. She uses her free hand to grasp tightly onto my shoulder, helping herself climb and wrap her legs around my waist.

"Pull it."

"Excuse me?"

"Don't threaten me Spartak; pull my hair, because when you do, I'm going to cum all over your big cock."

"Fuuuck me." Groaning, I let go of her wrist and weave my hand into her thick hair, winding it around my large fist and pull.

Victoria's mouth gapes as she lets loose a near silent moan, her pussy pulling and clutching at my engorged cock. I thrust wildly through her orgasm, gritting my teeth as her cunt spasms around me. Little droplets of sweat gather on my hairline from concentrating so hard on not filling her up.

"Cum inside me, Spartak," she orders as she licks up the side of my neck. I shiver and growl low in my throat, attempting to hold myself back from slamming her into the wall like I want to. My inner beast claws inside my chest, pleading for me to rip her apart and bury my seed deep. Her tender lips pepper kisses along my neck right before she sinks her teeth into my skin, sucking intensely, no doubt leaving her mark. It doesn't faze me as I know my suit will cover it for the ceremony.

"Nooow," Victoria croons against my throat, her hot breath whispering over my skin, and my dick lets loose, painting her in my essence. My balls were so full I thought they were going to fucking explode.

I lean into her heavily against the wall as I finish throbbing through my release, resting my forehead on her shoulder and breathing in her scent. I'm startled by my Boss's voice, as I catch my breath, "Spar, time for the vows."

"Yes, sir," I reply in a gruff voice, glancing back toward him. His chest rises slightly quicker as he watches us. Viktor nods, his gaze skirting over us one last time and then turns around, giving us his back.

I draw away slowly and cover her up with her lace panties. Victoria pants, silently watching my face. I can't break eye contact as I catch myself murmuring the words I never fathomed would leave my mouth, "Come with us."

"Where are you going?" she questions softly.

"Russia, for the honeymoon. I have to work, but I'll have time off."

Victoria peers off to the side briefly, then meets my gaze again. "I'm sorry, but I can't."

"Why not?"

"Because my friend and I flew in from Italy. I leave tomorrow."

"Italy? Fuck!" Grumbling I straighten my suit, as she combs her fingers through her hair. My mind races with ways for me to see her again. Viktor grunts, drawing my attention to his stern face, nodding for me to come on.

"I have to go; are you coming, too?"

"Yes, I'll be right there; I'm going to visit the ladies room first." I bring her knuckles to my lips and kiss them softly before walking toward Viktor. Halfway to him, I turn back and glance at her, taking in her beauty once more. "How will I see you again?"

Victoria's eyes twinkle as she smiles. "If it is meant to be Spartak, then we will see each other again."

I bite my tongue and nod. I hate being unsure of things; I like simple laid out plans. Following the Boss down the short path to the lake, I can't stop picturing how her face looked while I was deep inside of her.

The beach is adorned with a wooden pergola and platform, draped in some silky white material, the little lights wrapped through it, twinkling in the evening air. The guests all sit patiently on the white wooden chairs; smiles grace their excited faces to see the other Russian leader find his happiness in love. The party isn't that large; it's overwhelming to me because of safety precautions with everything that has recently gone down.

Viktor takes his place on the platform with Tate and Alexei standing beside him. I post up a little to the side and behind them. It's the perfect spot for me to scan over everyone and keep a look out for Victoria.

Elaina glides toward us, on Nikoli's arm. They've gotten closer ever since Sabrina has come into the picture. Nikoli, decked out in his light gray suit, makes Elaina appear even more petite, dwarfing her small frame with his massive size.

A motion catches my attention off to the side, and I watch as Victoria approaches, speaking to another woman sitting toward the back of the group before she eventually takes her seat. Her irises briefly meet mine, igniting a ball of need in the center of my stomach.

Tate and Emily's daughter squeals excitedly when she sees her Aunty Elaina approach the pergola, drawing all attention to Emily. She's standing across from Tate, waiting to be beside her sister for the nuptials and proudly holding the newest addition to the

Masterson family.

Elaina lovingly kisses the baby's forehead and then takes Viktor's hands as they each say their vows, promising to love each other more than they already do. It seems impossible to me, as they are hopelessly devoted to each other.

As the wedding winds down and the honeymoon time approaches, Alexei and I follow the newlyweds to Viktor's Mercedes. I hop in the driver's seat scanning for Victoria, but I haven't seen her since she was sitting next to her friend.

Alexei climbs in beside me after the Boss and Elaina load into the back seat. Viktor leans forward between the seats. "Is she meeting you in Russia, Spar?"

"No, she's from Italy."

"You're not going to see her again?"

"I don't know. She told me if it was meant to be that we would find each other again." Elaina pipes up. I know Viktor clued her in; he tells her pretty much everything. "You got her information?"

"Nope."

"How will you find her?"

"I have the guest list," I grin cockily. All I need is some time off, and she's mine.

Chapter 2

Lasting Impressions

Now...

Rolling my eyes at Alexei, I look at my Boss, Viktor. "Mr. Masterson, I don't agree with him. I should accompany you to the fight and preliminary events. I know Alexei has been your guard for who knows how long, but you brought me along for a reason. Let me be the added security. This is obviously important, or you would've left me at home to protect your wife." He nods, glancing at me respectfully. He's taken me more serious since I've kept a good watch on his precious Elaina. I think he's learned that she's not only my Boss's prized possession but also my best friend. Being the leader of the Russian Bratva, I understand his need to have protection around all the time and bringing me along to Chicago must mean he needs an extra set of eyes to watch his back.

"I agree, this place is crawling with Italians. Alexei, use the extra help while you have it," he replies and climbs back into the waiting Mercedes. Alexei's irritated gaze meets mine as he grumbles, "Fine. Get some food and meet us at the hotel. Mr. Masterson will be having dinner with the fighter he's sponsoring, and we won't be eating, just watching."

I know the fighters Viktor sponsors are champions in their weight divisions. He knows how to pick them when it comes to business and gambling. He doesn't bet often, but he has a few horses that do extremely well when he does.

"Got it," I nod as Alexei loads into the waiting car with our boss.

Being accustomed to the warm weather nearly year-round in Tennessee has me shivering in the brisk Chicago breezes. It's obviously the windy city for a reason. There's a chill in the air crisp enough to make you feel it deep in your bones.

A bright red sign advertising hot sandwiches has my stomach growling, and my feet are quickly heading toward the shop. A sub sandwich and a warm building is pretty much the best thing on earth right now. The only thing better would be a good book and a nap along with it.

The bell above the door jingles and I'm greeted with a cheerful hello as I enter. The smells of homemade Italian food assault my senses. Even being Russian, I can still appreciate good Italian cooking. One of the things I enjoy the most about traveling with the Bosses is the opportunities

I'm presented with when it comes to tasting an array of authentic dishes from many cultures.

"Can I help you?" an older woman asks. Her hair's a short auburn cut, her face decorated with a few wrinkles, telling me she's smiled and laughed many times in her life. Kind brown eyes meet mine, waiting for me to order.

"Hi. Can I get...uh...what do you suggest?" I stammer out. Speaking to women of any age has never been a strong point for me; I prefer the quiet.

"Oh, you're cute, you!" She smiles, chuckling a little. "I have a son your age and he loves a good meatball sandwich. With extra mozzarella and parmesan to top it off and a Dr. Pepper to drink. What do ya think?"

"I think it sounds wonderful, except will you make it two orders and to go?"

"Working on putting some meat on those bones? Good boy. Of course, give me ten and it'll be ready."

"Thank you."

"My pleasure." She takes the twenty I hand her, giving me two dollars and nineteen cents in return.

I place the remainder in the tip jar next to the register and take a seat by the largest window. I love people watching. One reason why I'm good at my job; I'm always paying attention to what's going on around me.

Time escapes me as I'm sucked into watching everyone rush down the sidewalks and angry drivers blare horns at each other. I've become so comfortable in the quiet cabin Viktor lives at, that this is damn near culture shock. The cold and all the people remind me of Russia.

"Here you go, boyo. I hope you enjoy your dinner." The woman from before sets a big bag in front of me filled with more than just two sandwiches and bottles of Dr. Pepper. I kind of hope she snuck in a few of the delicious cannolis I saw in the display case as well.

"Thank you, I appreciate it." Returning her smile, I stand and push in my chair. She pats my shoulder, reaching up since I practically dwarf her. "You come back again before you leave town."

"How did you—" I'm cut off before I get the rest out.

"You're not the only one who likes to watch the world. Besides, that sweet southern voice kind of gives you away." She winks and makes her way back to the counter.

Shit. I have an accent? I sound Russian to me when I speak, but apparently not to others. It could work to my benefit if that's the case. I try to hide my accent, and if the southern one is covering it up, it'll be that much easier when we're handling business.

The door chimes on my way out, and the chill hits me again as I head back onto the sidewalk. It's not the breeze this time causing me to shiver, but a familiar feminine voice.

"Grazie!" is shouted across the street, and the beautiful sound has my eyes shooting to a woman in a long black dress coat, waving and smiling at a driver in a gray BMW seven series. He waves back, cheeks red, most likely a result of her gorgeous white smile. She turns so I can get a better glimpse of her face, and as she does, my chest tightens in excitement? Anxiety? Hope? Surprise?

"Victoria." Her name leaves my lips on an exhale.

I searched for her—for nearly five years—and never came up with a trace of her and yet she's across this very street, right in front of me.

After looking for so long, wondering, dreaming, hell even wishing for her to appear, here she is. You'd think I'd run and shout after her, but I do what any stupid man would do—I choke. Her shine has me speechless, her smile making my feet take root to stare at her, wishing I could watch her for the rest of my life.

All of those long, lonely nights, I spent scouring the internet for her, the 'what if' in the back of my mind. Nothing happened to her, though; she's here—healthy and more stunning than ever—in Chicago. The city that's full of the Italian Mafia's most notorious criminals. How did I never notice it before? She looks one hundred percent Italian. And I'm one hundred percent Russian.

Russian Bratva that is. *Fuck.*

I can't pull my eyes away from her, watching her until she disappears down a small alleyway between buildings. She's crazy to be walking down there alone. What was the driver thinking, to let her go off like that?

Horns blare loudly as my legs suddenly have me sprinting across the busy street, not paying an ounce of attention to the angry drivers being forced to screech to a halt to miss me. There's shouting, but I ignore it, heading straight for that same alleyway where Victoria disappeared.

Peeking around the corner of the building, I'm met with emptiness. There are a few dumpsters, enough space for a few vehicles to park snuggly, and nothing else. I couldn't have lost her so easily after barely finding her. Surely the universe isn't that cruel to give me a glimpse after five lengthy years just to have Victoria pull a disappearing act on me.

Striding down the asphalt, I check around the dumpsters. I want to make sure she isn't hiding or anything. You'd think I was looking for money or some other prized possession with me bending over and getting on my hands and knees to look under the garbage containers. I come back empty-handed and disappointed. Let's face it, she couldn't fit underneath the dumpster no matter how much she wiggled and squirmed. After looking around, I discover an entrance near the back corner on one of the buildings as well as what looks like a door large enough for a private garage.

What is this place anyhow? I didn't pay any attention earlier, which I should have. I get paid to notice things for shit's sake; now, here I am running off like some excited kid.

Trekking toward the busy street, I stop just shy of the sidewalk, peering up at the front of the building.

Chicago Gala de Arts.

She likes art? That would explain another reason why I couldn't shake her. I enjoy reading, and if she's the artsy type, then it could be that we both have creative minds.

Let's also not forget about the sex. *God, the sex.* It was unbelievable with her. Explosive comes to mind when I think of how I held her against the brick building at Viktor's cabin. I couldn't get enough of her body, of her smell. Her lips tasted like strawberries; I'll never forget that. Her long chocolate locks felt like silk wrapped around my fingers and her voice—*Jesus, her voice was rough with desire as I drove into her.* The back of my neck prickles with beads of sweat as I remember our one time together.

Twisting the cap off one of the Dr. Peppers, I take a large gulp. It helps with my dry throat but not with my suddenly tight pants. The wail from a passing siren brings me back to the present. Maybe I should wait in the alley for a little while and see if she comes back out anytime soon. I'd hate to leave knowing she's in there and could come back out at any time. I wonder if she'd want to see me again.

Of course, she would. I remember her parting words at Viktor's wedding:

If it's meant to be, we'll see each other again.

I was so damn cocky, thinking that since I had access to the guest info sheet that I'd easily find her after we returned from the honeymoon detail. I was wrong. The address she gave was a fake. That was the first thing that threw me off. I couldn't understand why she'd lie about it; the address info was only so the bride and groom could send thank you notes.

Her name came up as a dead-end also. Well, it did pull up a few, but one woman was eighty-eight, and the other was a twelve-year-old kid. I'd figured Victoria as twenty-nine or thirty now. Still, five years ago, she wouldn't have fit with either choice I had discovered.

Staying close to the alleyway entrance, I lean against the building to wait and pull my cell free. I should give Alexei a heads-up, so he doesn't come out with the cavalry, thinking I've been overrun by the Italian mob. He'd love that; probably laugh his ass off at me.

He doesn't pick up when I try calling so I send him a text instead.

Me: Got held up downtown, won't make it in time for dinner.

Alexei: We'll handle it.

Pretty much the response I was expecting. Neither one of us ever call off just to go shamming, so

I didn't think he'd be too pissed. Besides, I'll be there to keep watch for the fight and other errands.

While I'm texting, I should check in on Elaina. She may have other guards there to watch over her, but I've gotten used to being the one to look out for her.

Me: How are you holding up?

Elaina: Spar! I miss you guys, but Sabrina is keeping me busy. Baby planning is a lot like wedding planning.

Yuck. Maybe it's a good thing I came on this trip after all. If I were home, I'd get stuck with painting anything they find pastel and a million questions about why I don't have any kids yet.

Me: Have fun.

Elaina: OOO

Hugs. She sent me a text with three hugs. Sometimes I think she's trying to get me killed by her husband.

Smiling at her hugs message on the screen, my finger hits delete. I want to stay alive, and I can already imagine the creative ways Viktor would find to end me if he saw her message. Mine and Elaina's relationship is strictly platonic, but I'm not about to give anyone a reason to speculate differently.

Shaking my head at that thought, I stuff my phone back in my pocket and train my gaze back on the door. No way am I missing her again.

Six hours later, one hell of a temperature drop and I'm still posted up against the cold brick building keeping watch. I think it's safe to say that the building and its events are long over. About an hour ago, the oversized entry slid open to reveal a convoy of expensive cars all filled with overdressed old ladies and their drivers en route somewhere.

I'm assuming it must've been some charity event being held or an art show of some type. I wish I would've gone inside when it was still open. Judging by the women I saw, though, I'm entirely underdressed.

The ache inside has come back. It's the same feeling I had when I first realized that I couldn't find her. I could ask my Boss. He'd probably help, but I don't want him going out of his way for me.

Getting a good look at her again, I wouldn't want him discovering her Italian heritage either. He's not biased by any means, but he is Mafiya and I know there would be doubt resting in the back of his mind about my loyalty.

I can't jeopardize my own goals. Someday I hope to be right next to Alexei, next to Viktor. I want to be the Boss' right hand.

He's told me before that I have the most important job there is—protecting his wife. I'm grateful, really, but I can't help wanting to gain ranks in our organization. The right hand to the Bratva 'King' is something any real soldier in Russia would dream of. So much comes along with being a General: money, responsibility, trust, and even your own set of men directly under you. The only one you answer to is the Boss himself, a true honor.

My phone chimes. It's the alert that we're all due back at the room. Viktor must've finished with his business meetings.

Shit. I haven't seen her yet. But I have to leave. If I miss her right now, I'll regret it forever; I know it. I have to see her.

Marching over to the back door, I attempt to pull it open. Of course, it's locked.

Trekking to the main entrance up front, I try those doors as well. They're locked and the lobby's dark. The only lights on are the accent lights next to plants. Shit, how did she get by without me seeing her? I just assumed she'd exit from the back door; it didn't cross my mind that she'd leave through the front. *God, I'm such an idiot.*

The ache in my heart grows stronger knowing I've lost her again... Five years and I let her slip right through my fingers.

Chapter 3

I Must Forget

Three days have passed, yet I can't get her out of my head. Instead of doing my job, I'm busy scouring our surroundings. Every time we go somewhere, I can't help but look for her, hoping for another chance at finding her. This time I won't screw it up.

"Spartak?"

"Huh?" I'm drawn away from gazing around the restaurant. We're escorting Viktor and his brother Tate while they eat. Our priority this trip is supposed to be keeping them safe, and I've done a shit job so far. I'm not looking for potential threats, but a feisty Italian woman with a body made for sin and that could get someone injured—or worse—taken out.

"Nikoli was talking to you," Alexei grumbles and I turn toward Tate's right-hand man, Nikoli. Niko scrunches his forehead. "What is with you?" he asks in his deep Russian accent.

"Nothing, I didn't sleep well." The lie slips out before I can stop it. I don't know why I'm not truthful with him. He'd most likely understand with everything he went through with his own wife. They weren't apart as long as Victoria and me, but their relationship was much closer than mine is.

It's the Italian thing again; I know it. He may relate to me wanting to search for Victoria, but in the end, he'd be more concerned whether she posed a threat to the organization or not. Do I resent them for that?

No.

I can't. It's not fair of me to come in from the outside and then not be supportive of them being cautious. Most relationships in my line of work don't pan out anyhow. Who am I to tell them that their methods are wrong. I'm a soldier—plain and simple. They order and I follow. So why in the hell can't I just push her to the side and forget her?

One thing that's always bothered me and continues to drive a wedge in is why didn't she just come back? She knew where to find me, how to reach me. Sure, our business is secretive, but she was at Viktor's house; she could have shown up, sent a letter, something.

Maybe our one night was everything to me and yet nothing to her? I need to forget about Victoria and all of it. A quick fuck is just that—fast, satisfying, and over. They're supposed to be the best kind, but why have no others compared to the one I had with her?

"You are love-sick, not tired," Niko mutters and shakes his head, turning back to watch over the Bosses. Alexei's eyebrow rises as he glances at me skeptically. "Is it true?"

"Who would I love? There are no women around us; you know this." Besides, love-sick is taking my condition a bit too far. I'm merely distracted and that's going to stop.

"So, do you think 'The Ripper' is going to win the fight tomorrow night?" He changes the subject, as he quickly scans over the restaurant.

"I hope so; I have a few bets on it."

"Oh? Who do you bet?"

"The other men. They do a big pot each fight and those who win split the payout. They've never asked you to put in?"

"I'm a General. Viktor would never allow it."

"I didn't think of it that way. Is that why you're never at chow with us when we're all at the cabin?" He nods. "I can have a drink or a game of cards; otherwise, I usually speak to Nikoli if I require company."

"And me?"

"You're a little different; you watch the Boss' wife."

"Yeah, I always have?" I say it as a question because Alexei and I have been on a lot of details together. We may not be close by any means, but after so many years, we know each other. I still wouldn't hesitate to kill him if I had to, but I also respect him.

"It puts you above the other men. You may see yourself as one of the men, but they see you as one of us." He looks toward Nikoli, and Niko nods his agreeance.

No way.

"But I'm not one of you." It comes out absently as my mind races over my recent interactions with the other guards and if they've seemed different around me.

"No, you are not. But you're smart, Spartak; you are close to being one of us. With time, you will be. Viktor wasn't kidding when he told you that guarding his wife was the most important job. Notice he didn't give it to me."

"Why are you telling me this? Wouldn't this make you hate me?"

"I let you know because you're young and I see you distracted. If I notice it, then so does Nikoli, Viktor, and Tate. It's not a good look on you and can get you hurt—fast. And I don't hate you. I appreciate it that there's someone else who's qualified to help me do my job."

I'm in shock that he sees me like that. I always believed that he thought of me more as a nuisance than an ally. Alexei's right; if he can see it, so can others. No more, I'm a soldier first.

"Thank you."

He doesn't respond, staying alert as the Bosses and the heavy-weight champ stand up, finished with their business meal. They push their chairs in and make their way toward us.

I may not be able to forget about Victoria completely, but I'm able to tuck her away into the back of my mind long enough to do my job and get a decent night's sleep.

The next day passes by fairly quickly. After doing a sweep of the arena for the better part of a Saturday afternoon, we finally take our seats around the Bosses, ready for fight night. They've roped a small area off for our group, making things a little easier on us.

Nikoli sits to the left of Tate and Alexei to the right of Viktor. Tate's second man sits behind them, and I take the seat directly in front of them. This way they get the most protection possible, being surrounded by their guards.

Tate immediately checks his phone, grumbling. "Damn, Emily was supposed to text me and let me know how cheer practice went."

Viktor grins. "Relax moy brat; Emily can handle Angel's first cheer class. I can't believe you agreed to it in the first place."

"Em wouldn't stop going on how it was a Texas thing for little girls to be cheerleaders; I reminded her we live in Tennessee."

"And that didn't work?"

"Hell no! She threw her flip-flop at me, and I gave in."

Viktor laughs softly. "Sounds about right."

He would know all about it. Viktor was a very cold man when I first came to work for him. His wife has softened him up a bit. Well, maybe not softened, but lightened his darkness. He's learned to compromise in a world where his word is usually considered final.

The few extra seats in our section remind me that their cousin was supposed to join us. "Boss, is Beau still coming?"

"He had something come up and headed to Tennessee last night. I'm sure he'll fill us all in once we're home."

His words are code for something happened so be ready to work tonight. I better sleep on the flight; who knows how long I may end up being awake to help Beau with whatever's going on.

Tate's phone beeps and he sighs. "Finally. She sent a picture of Angel in her uniform."

"Let me see, moy brat." Viktor takes the phone, turning it so we can all see Tate's six-year-old daughter. She's dressed in a bright orange cheer uniform, blonde pigtails and holding white pom-poms. He's going to be in trouble when she gets older, and he has to start hiding bodies of teenage boys. We all grin seeing her bright smile—missing one of her front teeth—on the screen.

I don't have any children, but I know some of the guards do and they don't get to see them much. Most of their families still live in Russia, so when Tate and Nikoli's kids are around, they're very loved by us all.

Tate's daughter, Angel, loves to bring baked goods over and hand them out to everyone. She's already turning into a little Russian lady, trying to feed the guards pastries.

Still smiling about the little Printsyessa's picture, I face forward again. Hopefully, the fight starts soon. I'm going to get hungry here shortly if not. Scanning the crowd across from me, a silent gasp leaves my mouth before I can stop it.

She's here.

Of all the places to find her again, Victoria is sitting nearly straight across from me. She's in another small, roped-off area, surrounded by large Italian men. She looks like a million bucks in her white sequin dress, showcasing every curve she owns. She's thicker than when I had her at Viktor's wedding. Her thighs are slightly bigger, her waist too. She's filled out into a woman, no longer the young lady I first met, and she's absolutely ravishing.

Shit. I'd finally made myself stop thinking about her so much, and now she's here. What the hell am I supposed to do? Sit here and stare at her the entire night? Because that's what will happen, I already know it. There's no way I can watch the fight now and pay attention. Who cares who wins at this point; I just want to soak her all in, every ounce I can get away with looking at and tuck it all away to think about later.

And who are all the men with her? There are six of those mob-bish-looking goons surrounding her. Is she married? Could that old man next to her be her husband? Of course, she'd be wed by now; it's been five long years. Hell, she could've been married when we were together, and I'd have never known it. Although I didn't see a ring on her finger, but that means nothing nowadays.

Viktor taps my shoulder, nodding straight ahead at the group I've already been staring at. "Mafiya." His Russian comes out just a touch with his disgust.

"Sicilian Mafioso?" I respond, and he grunts.

"Luciano and Leopoldo Franchetti."

The names of the two famous Sicilian mobsters has my chest feeling like a ton of bricks is resting on top of it. "Old Sicily, they're brothers also?"

"Da."

Shit. Is Victoria in with the mob? And not even regular American Mafia. This is old-school, the real deal, string-you-up-in-the-streets-to-die type of gangsters. This is even worse than her just being Italian. And the Sicilians have been working against Viktor every step of the way as he's tried to shut down the sex trade outlets of the underground. This just became messy.

"Watch them."

"Yes, sir." I nod, keeping my eyes glued on the group. Well, to one person in particular. And to think I was excited when I saw her sitting over there; now it's more like dread resting in the bottom of my gut. If she's a part of their operation, I'm most likely going to be tasked with killing her. The woman I've searched so long for and there's a chance I'll be the one to send her to her deathbed. Not the kind of bed I was hoping to get her into.

"Should be starting in ten minutes or less," Nikoli announces to the group. Now I'm glad we got here early, gives me more of a chance to get familiar with our surroundings and everyone sitting in their designated seats. "Ripper is going to win the first round, and Lexei will owe me one stack."

My eyebrows shoot up, hearing his declaration. "Wait; you guys bet on the fight?" I ask him.

"Yes, he bet me last night."

Grinning, I glance at Alexei, looking for confirmation. He shrugs in return, not looking the slightest bit bothered that I know he listened to me about placing bets with the guys. I'll have to remember this for next time.

Big, brown, doe-like eyes meet mine, full of shock as Victoria notices me staring at her for the first time. After a few moments, she blinks a bunch of times, squinting, closing one eye and opening, then repeating the same with the other, until finally she must give in and realize it really is me that she sees. Her shoulders grow stiff, and by her reaction, she must remember me.

At least I hope she does.

Chapter 4

No More Games

Glancing over at the men with her, I make sure none of them are paying me any attention and then nod off to the side. Hopefully, she'll understand that I need to speak with her. I have to know if she's in with them or what's the deal.

Even if she's just sleeping with one of them, my Boss will never approve of her. Not now, after she's been seen out in public with them. I know he'll be too wary of letting her close to anyone we care about and who can blame him? I'd be the same way if I were in his position. You can't trust anyone in this lifestyle when it comes down to it. Too many people will burn you in a heartbeat if they think they can get away with it and get ahead.

It takes a few minutes of her looking around at everything but me until she stands. The older man to her left questions her and after a few words from her, he nods, slightly irritated, but resigned. You can tell he's not happy about letting her out of his sight, but he does anyway. He doesn't give in completely, though; once she's a few rows away, he sends a goon to monitor her. Hopefully, his guy's not very perceptive, or I may have to figure out a place to stuff a body.

"I'll be back," I mutter to Alexei and stand up.

I don't know where she's heading, but I figure I'll try the bathrooms and concession near their seating area. Heading for the hallway, I quickly stride down the painted concrete walkway, scanning each person with dark hair as I go.

Part of me wants to shake her, demanding she tells me why she's with someone like them. The other piece of me has missed her and wants to hold her tightly, kissing her mouth until she can no longer breathe.

I'm nearly to the hall leading to their seating section, when a metal door off to the side, opens swiftly. She peeps her head out a little, grasping my suit jacket with her petite hand and tugs until I follow her into the small janitorial closet.

The musty smell of dust and bleach hit my senses as Victoria quickly closes the door behind us.

"Is it…is it really you? Spartak?" she whispers in awe.

Her hopeful eyes swallow me up; I could drown in their sweet depths. She looks so happy and surprised to see me.

"Who are those men?" I should say something else, but I can't help myself. I need to know. I need to hear it come from her mouth so I can either strangle her or kiss her.

"Men?"

"Yes. The men you were sitting with. Is the old one your husband?"

"Gross; no, that's my father. None of them is my husband."

"So you have one then?"

"What? No! I've never been married. This wasn't what I was imagining we'd talk about when we finally saw each other again."

"You thought we'd see each other again?"

"Well, I had hoped we would. I really liked you, Spartak. Our time was short, but I had fun with you. I've thought about it many times over the years, and there have been places where I've sworn to have caught a glimpse of you. But then I'd try to find you and it would be someone else, or the person would disappear before I could catch them."

"I searched for you for years. It was hard; I didn't have much information on you. It would've helped if you hadn't used a fake last name. Is your first name even Victoria?"

"Yes, I didn't lie to you about that." Glancing at her feet, she looks ashamed that I have to question her. She shouldn't have lied; I would've found her sooner.

"Your father's Sicilian?"

"Yes." Her chin rises, proudly.

"This could be a problem. Do you realize who I am, who I'm affiliated with?"

She nods.

"And this doesn't bother you, knowing that we're enemies?"

"You're not my enemy," she replies softly and she may as well have just twisted the knife into my gut, because fuck my life I couldn't kill her now no matter how badly I needed to.

"You aren't mine either," I respond, and it's like a switch is flipped. She launches herself at me, her arms circling my neck, her thighs wrapping around my hips as I lift her, bringing her body to mine.

My mouth lands on hers—hard, wanting, craving—needing to take what it's missed so desperately. Stumbling forward, I rest her body against the cold wall, just like I did the first time we were together.

"I want you," she gasps between sloppy, rushed kisses. Her body becomes more and more turned on as my cock grows harder and rests against her center.

"How much?"

"So much, Spartak. Please!"

"Here, now?"

"Yes. It's been too long; I want to feel you inside me again."

She doesn't have to ask me twice. Hiking her dress up until the fitted material's resting at her waistline, I rip her panties to the side, pushing two of my fingers inside, priming her for me.

"Even better than I remember," I mumble moments later, slipping my hand free and pulling out my cock.

She sinks her teeth into my chin, just hard enough to make me growl. Her curves are more pronounced than I remember. My hands are full of her everywhere they roam, and I couldn't be happier about it.

"You're so sexy. Did your ass get bigger?" Through the warmness of our body heat and rush, I'm still able to make out the rosy hue on the tops of her cheeks. I don't know if she's embarrassed or angry about my observation.

"Yes, maybe a few sizes."

"I fucking love it. Your entire body is better now. You were beautiful before, but shit, you're gorgeous, Victoria."

It must be the right answer as she rewards me by squirming just enough for my cock to push inside her.

"Gorgeous and you feel fucking amazing."

"So do you, Spartak; you fit me perfectly." She moans as I thrust deeply.

I could never get my fill of this woman. It's been too long and my ideas about her have built up so much over the years that I'm at the point of wanting to kidnap her away from her family and keep her. They'd kill me if I did that, although they'd probably kill me if they found us like this too. Or I could just off them first and take care of all our problems. I don't know how Victoria would feel about that, though.

Her nails sink into my chest as she rips my button-up shirt open to reveal my muscular torso. The buttons pop off and fly in every direction, making me chuckle. She's strong and wild, just like before—just like I dreamed. I don't even know her and yet I missed her. How is that possible?

"Yes!" she gasps as I drive into her again. Victoria has my mind spinning; she feels so damn good. I can't believe that I'm holding her in my arms right now. I feel like I've waited forever for this—like it isn't real.

"Are you real?"

"Of course I am. I'm one hundred percent real and right here."

"Oh thank God," I murmur, tucking my face into her neck, breathing in her scent. "You still taste like strawberries and smell delicious," I say, staying in the same place where I can taste her skin, smell her scent, feel her soft hair, and bask in her warm body. She's exactly what I need, what I want.

I thrust deeply, driving myself in her until I'm fully seated and she's moaning so loudly that I have to cover her mouth with my palm to quiet her down.

"Shhh, moy kpacota." At my words, she begins to throb inside, her legs clenching around me tightly as her orgasm hits.

Her nails grip into my shoulder blades, as she orders me, "Suck on my nipples, now!"

I do as she tells me, pulling one pebbled nipple into my mouth, and biting down, just enough to finish pushing her over the edge. Once she's sated and her body becomes putty in my hands, I wrap my arms around her as much as possible, pulling her as close to me as I can. I want to feel all of her, surrounding me while I pour my essence deep into her. I want her to remember how I felt holding her so tightly, while I shared every piece of myself with her.

Once I'm finished, I gently set her back on her feet, pulling myself free from her blissful piece of heaven.

"It was worth the wait. But next time, I'm going to tie your hands up somewhere. Teach you to keep your claws to yourself unless I ask for them."

"Next time, hm?" She smiles. "You're already planning?"

"Once is never enough with you, Victoria. It wasn't the first time, and it isn't this time. I want every piece of you."

"Those are some strong words, Spartak."

"You promised if it were meant to be, we'd see each other again. This is twice. I saw you last week at the art gala and now here."

"Last week? You saw me?"

"Yes, you went into an alley and then I couldn't find you after that."

"But you didn't see anything else?"

"What else was there? I followed you and then waited around. The only other people I saw were some rich ladies leaving. I must've missed you leaving out of the front entrance."

"Oh yeah, the front." She nods, her eyes glancing to the side.

She's hiding something.

"What is it?"

"Huh?"

"You're not telling me something."

"I...uh...Oh, shit!" she finishes, surprised as the metal door's wrenched open. She scurries to fix her clothes behind me as two angry Sicilian faces fill the open doorway.

One is a man that was sitting next to her; not the one I thought was her husband, but another. The second man is the goon that was sent to follow her.

The one that resembles her father, orders, "Tia! Oi, get out here now. Your papa will be furious when he hears of this!"

"Please, Uncle Leo, no!" she pleads behind me to no use. He reaches past me, snatching her arm to yank her out. He starts to pull her with him as she shoves against him, begging to let her go.

"I said *now*. You're coming with me!" he responds crossly, saying something to her in their language. I try to reach for her, but the other goon's in my face. I'm pushing against him to get to Victoria when the fucker head-butts me. It's enough to daze me, and he takes full advantage of it, shoving me into the closet enough so he can shut the door.

Victoria's gone, and no matter how much I throw my body against the door, it doesn't budge.

Yelling, pounding, and kicking the door does absolutely nothing to help me out. The vent's too small for me to crawl through.

I had a cell when I came in here, but now patting my pockets, it seems to be gone. I can't pick the lock because it's not locked. I think there's something wedged in front of the door keeping it closed.

Minutes pass; how many I'm unsure. If I'd have to guess, I'd say probably twelve before the door's opened and a fresh burst of cool air pools in.

"What the hell happened to you?" Alexei's serious gaze finds mine and my head pounds, reminding me of the next asshole I plan on killing.

"One of the Sicilians head-butted me and locked me in here."

I expect yelling. What I don't expect is him breaking into a grin and chuckling. It pisses me off more than any yelling would have, and I shove past him, out into the hallway. Storming down the hall toward their seating area, Alexei follows, calling after me, "Where are you going?"

"I have to find them; they have something that belongs to me."

"Wait, Spartak," he orders, causing my feet to come to a stop.

"Yes?"

"They left already and quickly. I wondered if it had something to do with you since you'd been gone for a long time, so I came to check for you. Nikoli said you had the shits, but I knew it wasn't like you not to give us an update after fifteen minutes."

Patting my jacket pocket, I nod. "Yeah, my phone is lost."

"All that happened with a head-butt?"

"No, there was more, but that was the gist of it."

"Jesus. Let's go finish watching the fight."

"No, I need to speak with Viktor. I need his help."

"With what?"

"I need him to find someone for me."

"It was a stupid Sicilian; just let it go."

"No, I'm not talking about him. I need to find a woman."

"Who?"

"I'm not one hundred percent certain, but I think she's Victoria Franchetti, and she belongs to me."

"Shit, Spartak; he's not going to like this."

"I've lost her once, Alexei; I can't handle it happening again."

"All right then, let's see what we can do."

-I hate leaving it like this, but Spartak will return soon, and you'll find out more about his story! I hope you enjoyed *Corrupted Revelations* and you can find out more about these sexy Russians in my Russkaya Mafiya series. XO, Sapphire Knight